MW01135382

Around the Bend

Sandy Cove Series Book Four

Rosemary Hines

Copyright © 2014 Rosemary Hines

www.rosemaryhines.com

All rights reserved. No part of this book may be used or reproduced by any means, graphic, electronic, or mechanical, including photocopying, recording, taping or by any information storage retrieval system without the written permission of the publisher except in the case of brief quotations embodied in critical articles and reviews.

Because of the dynamic nature of the Internet, any web addresses or links contained in this book may have changed since publication and may no longer be valid. The views expressed in this work are solely those of the author and do not necessarily reflect the views of the publisher, and the publisher hereby disclaims any responsibility for them.

Certain stock imagery © Thinkstock.

Any people depicted in stock imagery provided by Thinkstock are models, and such images are being used for illustrative purposes only.

This novel is a work of fiction. Names, characters, places, and incidents are either the product of the author's imagination or are used fictitiously. Any resemblance to actual events, locales, organizations, or persons living or dead is coincidental and not the intent of either the author or publisher.

Formatting by 40 Day Publishing
www.40daypublishing.com

Cover photography by Benjamin Hines
www.benjaminhines.com

Printed in the United States of America

To my grandparents

Fred and Mary Hughes

Who lived life well to the very end

"I have told you these things, so that in Me you may have peace. In this world you will have trouble. But take heart! I have overcome the world."

~ Jesus (John 16:33)

CHAPTER ONE

Phil Walker glanced around the circle at the faces before him. Gray hair and softly wrinkled expressions told tales of long lives now experiencing their sunset years. Tranquil Living Residential Home had welcomed Pastor Phil as their chaplain and Bible teacher several years back when he made his retirement from full-time ministry official. Thanking God daily for this opportunity, he carried on a calling he'd felt since his youth.

Although he'd served as pastor and shepherd to far larger flocks over his nearly seventy years behind a pulpit, there was no group of people he loved any more than these seniors. Surveying their faces, he noticed several had dozed off, their heads bowed as if in prayer. Margaret, the oldest of the group, stared into space, her eyes seeing a world long passed as Alzheimer's transported her to a younger day and time. Studying her face, he wondered where she was this morning. Was she caring for her household of seven children? Or perhaps still being courted by her would-be husband?

Phil had seen the ravages of this disease as it robbed his parishioners of the present, but he'd also discovered an unexpected element of God's grace and mercy in the midst of the confusion. While a mental fog clouded occasional family visits, he knew some treasured memories were still very much alive in the hearts and minds of those who were lost to today.

He'd watched frail old women rock their baby dolls with tender love and fiercely protective maternal instincts. He'd witnessed others introduce their daughters as sisters or even mothers. And one of the much scarcer men residing here would repeatedly retell of his latest homerun on a high school all stars team. Those snapshots from the past provided meaning and purpose to their otherwise empty lives.

Perhaps the present lacked the magic of the past. Maybe they were living in a better time and place in the confines of their deteriorating minds. Might there be an element of mercy in that?

Phil turned his attention to the final prayer of their morning service. Closing the Bible resting in his lap, he nodded to the group, "Let's pray." Then he bowed his head and lovingly lifted his little flock to the Lord.

As he began walking out to the curb to await the senior transport van for his ride home, he remembered to turn his phone back on. A beep alerted him to a voice message. Sinking onto a shaded bench flanking the parking lot, he listened to his granddaughter Michelle's voice.

"Hi Gramps! You're probably at your Bible study right now. Just wanted to make sure everything's set for your trip here for Caleb's birthday party. Grandma's not picking up, so she must be running errands or out in the garden. Give me a call with your flight number when you get a chance. We're looking forward to seeing you guys. Love you!"

He smiled and sighed. Sometimes it was still hard to believe that his precious granddaughter was a mom. Where had the years gone? A wave of fatigue anchored him to the bench. Lately it seemed like he never could find his energy.

He closed his eyes for a few minutes, allowing the gentle breezes to caress his face. Feeling himself starting to drift off, he forced his eyes open and took a deep breath.

Searching the parking lot, he spotted the van pulling into the driveway.

It had been almost a year since he turned in his license at the DMV. Although he missed the convenience and independence of driving, he knew his reflexes were not as sharp as they used to be. The last thing he wanted to do was to cause injury to his precious wife or someone they encountered on the road. Besides, thanks to the baby boomers, services like Senior Rides made it easy to get from one place to another.

Pushing himself off the bench, a slight sensation of dizziness caused him to struggle for balance before heading to meet the van.

Michelle Baron stashed her students' term papers in a canvas bag and propped her feet on the coffee table. Finally! The last paper had been scored and recorded. Summer vacation was just around the corner.

Every fall, she eagerly welcomed a new batch of students to her English classes at Magnolia Middle School, and each spring she prepared herself and her students to move on to new teachers and classes the following year. Some groups were easier to send off than others. This year, she'd had an exceptional batch of students – bright and eager to learn, with very few struggles over major life issues.

What a contrast to her first year!

Sitting back in the embrace of their cozy sofa, she picked up a family photo that stood proudly on the end table. Smiling, she traced her finger over the faces of her husband, Steve, and their two kids, Madison and Caleb.

Steve still had his boyish charm and a smile that melted her heart. Madison's blonde curls and blue eyes matched her dad's as if painted with the same brush. She was tall and thin like Michelle, but lacked any other resemblance to her dark-haired, hazel-eyed mother. At eleven years of age, Maddie was almost a middle-schooler herself.

And then there was Caleb—their sweet and unexpected addition to the family.

Michelle's mind drifted back to that first year at Magnolia and her troubled student, Amber Gamble, the biological mother of their son. From the very first day of school, Amber had challenged Michelle with her attitudes and behavior. It wasn't until she perused Amber's confidential file that she'd learned about the circumstances triggering this student's hard shell and abrasive personality.

A broken home and her mom's mental collapse had left Amber and her brother Jack in the foster care system. Sadly, they'd been separated after Amber's behavior led to her removal from their initial placement, resulting in a string of foster homes for the teen girl.

Michelle had done her best to reach out to Amber, getting to know her foster mom and social worker and even volunteering to assist with supervised visits between Amber and her brother at the local park after school. Gradually, Amber had let her guard down with Michelle, confiding in her and even attending church with their family.

Unfortunately, Amber also let her guard down with her older boyfriend, Adam. A high school junior, it seemed like he really loved her. And she needed to feel loved. Eventually that need evolved into a sexual relationship that led to something no eighth grade girl should have to face— an unexpected pregnancy.

As soon as she realized how much trouble she was facing, Amber came to her trusted teacher for advice and assistance. Although Adam wanted her to abort the baby, Michelle felt Amber needed to know all her options.

An ultrasound at the doctor's appointment solidified in Amber's mind the reality of the new life beginning to develop in her womb. Her decision not to abort resulted in Adam's rejection, leaving Amber even more dependent on Michelle.

Then one morning, Amber had asked her to become the baby's adoptive mother. That moment was frozen in Michelle's memory. The gamut of emotions still surfaced each time she recalled that encounter.

Michelle glanced back down at the photo, gazing into Caleb's eyes. Although he looked a little like Amber, he'd been a part of their family from the moment of his premature birth nearly six years ago. His sandy brown hair, spiked in a long buzz cut, and his round cherub face were so indelibly imprinted on her heart that it sometimes surprised her they did not share the same DNA.

Looking away, she thought about Amber again. At this time six years ago, Amber was in her final trimester of pregnancy, and Michelle was preparing a nursery for Caleb as she tutored Amber after school to help her with her studies. Then came the late night call that Amber was in the hospital needing an emergency C-section. Michelle shuddered, remembering the dread she'd felt as she raced to the hospital, wondering if Amber would be all right and if the baby would survive.

Michelle had taken a leave of absence from the final weeks of school to be at the hospital with tiny Caleb. The days blurred together into a series of visits and preparations for a baby that hadn't been expected until later in the summer.

Closing her eyes, she relived the day Caleb was released from the NICU. She'd known Amber would be there to say her last goodbye, so she and Steve had come to the hospital without Madison, not wanting their daughter to witness whatever would unfold in the process. Although Michelle had expected it to be difficult, nothing could have prepared her for the heart-wrenching scene that unfolded in the NICU that morning.

11

Thankfully both Amber's mother and her social worker had been there. After handing Caleb to Michelle, Amber collapsed into their arms, and it had taken both of those women to nearly carry her out of the unit. *She never even looked back*, Michelle recalled with a sigh. That was the very last time she'd seen her student.

Although Caleb quickly became her focus and the attention of her maternal love, her feelings for Amber and the deep bond they had formed over that year still resided in a private place in Michelle's heart. Grateful as she was that Amber had not tried to be a part of Caleb's life, there was also a deep sorrow and yearning Michelle felt about this hurting girl who had become like one of the family.

Was she okay? How was life unfolding for her in her new home and school in Arizona? And were her parents successful in reuniting and becoming a family again? So many of her questions would probably remain unanswered.

As Michelle placed the framed photo back on the end table, she glanced at the one beside it. She smiled at her father's face sporting a lopsided grin with six-year-old Madison and one-year-old Caleb perched on his lap.

"I miss you, Daddy," she whispered, holding the photo close and gazing into her father's twinkling eyes. Her heart ached. After all they'd gone through over the past decade and a half – her father's embezzlement charges and the subsequent suicide attempt that had almost taken his life, the drawn out process of his rehabilitation and transformation from an independent, self-sufficient man to one of great compassion and faith—it was hard to believe that a stroke had taken him from them so suddenly just over a year ago.

Michelle could still remember the call from her mother. "He's gone," she'd managed to squeeze out between her tears.

"Who, Mom? Who's gone? Is it Grandpa?" she'd asked her mother frantically.

12

Then her brother Tim had come onto the line. "It's Dad, Michelle. He had a massive stroke. He was dead before they could get him to the hospital."

Michelle and Steve had packed up the kids that August afternoon and headed straight for Seal Beach from their home in Sandy Cove, Oregon. They'd driven through the night, taking turns behind the wheel and stopping for occasional coffee and food breaks. She couldn't recall how many times the kids had asked about their grandfather on that long drive.

"But why, Mommy?" Caleb wanted to know.

And his big sister's reply, "He had a stroke. That's why," followed by a question of her own, "What's a stroke, Dad?"

By the time they arrived at Michelle's childhood home, they were all exhausted and on edge. The kids were restless and had been bickering in the back seat for the last two hours of the ride.

"Caleb's throwing pretzels at me," Maddie reported.

"No, I'm not," Caleb replied with a guilty expression. "Give me my game back!" he'd exclaimed to his sister, who had picked up the electronic device out of spite.

"Both of you knock it off," Steve warned, threatening to pull the car over until they settled down.

Finally, they'd pulled into the driveway and found themselves greeted by neighbors and friends who were holding vigil with Sheila and Tim until they arrived.

Michelle vaguely recalled exchanging pleasantries with these people she'd known all her life. Soon they all dispersed, and Michelle and Steve were able to get their little family settled in. Sheila seemed to perk up a little when the kids flocked to her, and Uncle Tim tried to be his usual playful self. But Michelle knew they were both masking broken hearts for the sake of her youngsters.

Once the kids were in bed, the four adults sat around the dining room table, and Sheila explained how she had returned from errands to find John staring off into space, eyes glazed over and making garbled sounds. She'd immediately dialed 9-1-1 and called Tim, but by the time her son and the paramedics arrived, John's eyes had rolled up into his head and he was silent.

She and Tim had followed the ambulance to the hospital. After what they'd been through with John's attempted suicide, they both somehow believed he'd be okay. However, the doctor soon came out to the waiting area and explained that the stroke had overcome John, and they'd been unable to save him.

"Sometimes this happens after a severe brain trauma," he'd explained.

And so they'd reached the end. Michelle's father was gone. But now they knew he was safe in the arms of his heavenly Father, One he would never have known had he not walked the difficult path that had led him to try to take his own life a number of years back.

As Michelle reflected on all these memories and studied the photo of her father with the kids, she knew she had much for which to be thankful. He'd become a man of great faith and had found peace with God, he'd lived to see the birth of their daughter and the adoption of their son, and he'd enjoyed a family he'd often brushed aside in the past.

She also thought about the timing of his death and how it had impacted her mother. She'd watched Sheila bravely assume the role of caregiver to a man who had once been ruggedly self-sufficient – the strong provider of the family. At a time when she might have been caring for and enjoying her grandbabies, she'd found herself being a nursemaid and chauffeur to a disabled spouse.

After the memorial service for her father, Michelle asked her mom to come back with them to Sandy Cove to spend some time and think about what she wanted to do with her life. Tim announced he'd landed a new job as a sales rep for a local surf shop and would be traveling for much of the year as the company promoted its new line of boards and apparel.

So Sheila had come to Sandy Cove and decided to stay. Michelle and Steve found her an adorable cottage on the outskirts of town, close to Michelle's school. They'd helped her find a tenant for the Seal Beach house and negotiated the purchase of her new home in Oregon. Now school was about to be out for summer, and they'd be helping her move from their house into her own.

Although they'd enjoyed having her stay with them and she'd been a big help with the kids, it was a tight squeeze. Their three-bedroom house, which seemed so spacious when Steve and Michelle moved in as newlyweds, was now filled to overflowing. The kids were excited that their grandmother was moving permanently to Sandy Cove, but Madison was also eager to get Caleb out of her bedroom.

"Are you still up?" Sheila asked, interrupting Michelle's thoughts.

She looked up at her mother. "Yeah. Just finished grading the last of the term papers," she replied, placing the photo of her father and kids back on the table.

Sheila reached over and picked it up. "Your dad sure did love your kids," she said wistfully.

Michelle nodded. Standing up, she put her hand on her mom's shoulders. "I'm really glad he got the chance to know them."

"Me, too," she replied, returning the photo to its place.

"Are you feeling okay?" Michelle asked. "I thought you went to bed awhile ago."

"I'm fine, honey. I just couldn't fall asleep. I thought maybe some herbal tea would help."

"Want me to fix you some?"

Sheila smiled. "No. I can do it. You've got to get up early for school. Go on to bed. I'll be heading up in a few minutes."

15

Michelle gave her a hug. "Okay, Mom. Sleep well."

"You, too, dear." Sheila replied, walking toward the kitchen.

Michelle picked up her bag of term papers and set them by the door so she'd remember to take them with her in the morning. Then she headed upstairs, peeking in on her sleeping children before easing open her bedroom door, hoping not to awaken Steve.

As she slipped into bed, he stirred slightly and turned to face her. Drawing her into his arms, he mumbled, "Love you."

She smiled and snuggled into his embrace.

CHAPTER TWO

Michelle sat at her desk in her classroom, her lunch in an open paper bag beside her water bottle. It was the first moment of peace she'd had all day. Getting her kids off to school that morning had been a real chore. Caleb couldn't find one of his shoes, and Madison seemed to be so moody these days. Could adolescence be trying to snag her already?

By the time they'd all piled into the car with backpacks and lunches, Michelle was exhausted. She made it to school a mere ten minutes before the passing bell for first period, and her coffee mug had spilled on her white blouse as she tried to manage her mail from the office along with the term papers in her bag. *Thank God it's June,* she'd thought as she hurried into the ladies' room to try to dab off the coffee before it left a stain.

Her friend and mentor, Cassie Gibralter was washing her hands at the sink. "Are you okay?" she asked Michelle. "Here. Let me take those," she offered, reaching out and freeing Michelle's hands.

"Crazy morning," Michelle muttered. "Thanks for the hand," she added, shooting Cassie a smile.

By the time they left the bathroom, the passing bell had rung. "Have your TA get you some more coffee," Cassie suggested. "They just started a fresh pot in the lounge."

Michelle nodded and smiled. "Thanks."

A slew of students were waiting by the door when she arrived at her classroom. Loud, boisterous conversations communicated the kids' excitement that the end of the year was at hand. Several asked about the term papers, and Michelle assured them she had them with her ready to be returned.

She survived the first four classes of the day. Now she could pause for a few minutes and have some lunch. Bowing her head to say a quick prayer of thanks for her food, an image of her grandfather flashed before her mind's eye.

Wonder what that's about. Hope everything's okay with them.

She tagged on a short prayer for her grandparents health and safety, then turned her attention to her string cheese and crackers. Not exactly a nourishing lunch, but it seemed like lately that was all she had time to grab in the morning or eat at her short noon break.

With Caleb's birthday party coming up in a few weeks, she'd brought the invitations to school with her, hoping to have a chance to address them. She must have been dreaming! Ninety percent of her time now was spent keeping the kids off the ceiling as she tried to convince them they were still in school for two more weeks.

The end-of-the-year activities didn't help. Everyday seemed to hold another change of schedule for an assembly, awards ceremony, or field trip. The principal had also instituted a series of student-faculty sports challenges, requesting the teachers to select at least one event to participate in during the mid-morning nutrition break or lunch.

Thankfully, the final week would be comprised of minimum days, leaving Michelle and the other teachers with time in the afternoons to meet with their departments for annual evaluations of curriculum, to make adjustments in plans for the following year, and to begin breaking down their classrooms and packing up for summer.

Michelle managed to address three of the birthday party invitations before the phone rang. "Ms. Baron," she answered.

Silence.

"Hello?" she asked.

Still no response, but she hadn't heard a click either.

"Is someone there? This is room 107, Michelle Baron."

And then the click.

Michelle shook her head and hung up the phone. She didn't usually get prank calls at school, and there was no time to fret about it now. The bell rang again, signaling the end of her lunch break, with most of her cheese and a few crackers still uneaten. Shoving the remainder back in the paper sack, she tossed the bag into her little refrigerator and went over to prop open the door.

A couple of boys were in a heated debate in the hallway. One pushed the other, which led to a wrestling match that took them both to the floor.

"Hey!" Michelle shouted. "Knock it off!"

Both boys ignored her, cussing and pummeling each other.

Michelle turned to a girl who had been waiting to come into the classroom. "Go get Mr. Durand," she said.

The girl's eyes were as wide as saucers. Grabbing one of her friends, she took off toward the office.

"I said, knock it off!" Michelle tried again, reaching down and touching one of the boy's shoulders.

He turned to look at her, leaving himself open for another punch, this one landing on his face.

"STOP!!!" Michelle yelled to the other boy, who was now spitting curses and whose hand was bloodied.

A custodian came out of the storage closet about a hundred feet away and raced toward them. He grabbed the boy on top and pulled him to his feet. Instantly he became the target and the boy's flailing arms and kicking feet found their marks on the man's chest and shins. The other boy remained on the floor, rolling from side to side and moaning.

Before the principal could get there, the custodian managed to get his attacker in a stronghold, though the boy continued to kick and curse.

Michelle could see Daniel Durand hurrying toward them and gesturing to her classroom. She quickly ushered her students inside and closed the door.

"Take your seats, everyone," she said above the roar of the agitated students. "Come on, guys. Sit." She guided them toward their desks and finally got everyone seated.

Perfect start to the afternoon, she thought with a sigh.

Things had quieted down outside the closed classroom door, so she knew Daniel had things under control. Now she'd just need to get these kids to settle down. They all seemed to want to talk about what they'd witnessed, so she decided to give them a few minutes to debrief before starting on the warm up activity and passing back their term papers.

Several of them knew the boys involved in the fight. They claimed it was over a bike one boy had stolen from the other. Apparently the alleged thief had also been making moves on the other boy's girlfriend, and she'd subsequently broken up with him. Other contradictory allegations arose about one of the boys calling the other one a derogatory name in front of a group of girls.

"It's pretty clear to me that none of you know for certain what triggered this," Michelle began. "Why don't we change the warm up for today and rather than writing about your summer plans, you can each write about what you saw or heard. Then I'll collect the papers and pass them along to Mr. Durand. Maybe they'll give him some insights into the circumstances that were involved."

The class seemed to be in agreement, and they got to work writing their accounts. This gave all of them the chance to be heard without taking up the entire class period discussing the fight. After about five minutes, Michelle asked them to wrap it up, and she collected the papers, sending them to the office with her TA.

By the time school was over for the day, she was eager to leave. The phone rang just as she was finishing straightening up her desk. "Baron. Room 107."

Just like at lunchtime, the line was silent. *I don't have time for this*, she thought and hung up the receiver. As she walked through the office, she stopped by the reception desk and greeted her friend. "Hi, Daisy."

The blonde receptionist looked up and smiled. "You look beat."

Michelle smiled wearily. "A little. That fight in the hall didn't help."

"Yeah. Both boys got suspended. You won't see them here the rest of the week."

"What a shame to get suspended right before the end of the year. But I'm glad Daniel's sticking to his zero tolerance for fighting." She paused and then added, "Hey, I got a couple of prank calls today — one at lunch and one right after school ended. Do you remember putting them through to my classroom?"

"Yeah. Some young lady. She didn't identify herself. The first time, she said she was a family friend, and you were expecting her call. When she called back, she just said, 'Me again,' and asked for your room one more time."

"That's strange. She didn't say a word when I answered," Michelle replied.

"Hmmm. Do you want me to just take a message if she calls again?"

"Yeah. Tell her you need to take her name and number, and I'll call her back."

"You got it." Daisy jotted a note to herself and placed it by the phone. "Anything else?"

"No. Thanks, friend. See you tomorrow."

Michelle grabbed her bag and travel mug and headed toward the door.

"Hey, Michelle," the principal called from his open office. "Got a minute?"

She took a deep breath and replied, "Sure," as she walked into his room.

"I just wanted to thank you for your help in the hall at lunch today," Daniel said.

"I wasn't really much help. They were so fixated on each other, I couldn't get them to listen."

"That may be true, but just having an adult there and sending the girls to get me was all I would have expected anyway." He smiled at her and added, "So are you ready for summer?"

"Yep," she replied.

"How's that boy of yours?" he asked.

Michelle flashed back to how understanding he'd been when she and Steve had adopted Caleb at the end of another school year six years before. Caleb's mother had been a troubled student on campus that year, and Daniel knew how Michelle had poured herself into Amber's life.

"He's fine. Growing too fast. I can't believe he'll be six in a week." She reached into her bag and pulled out an envelope. "We're holding off on his birthday party until after school's out." Extending the invitation toward him, she added, "We'd love to have you drop by and join in the celebration."

He smiled and took it. "Thanks! I'll talk to my wife and let you know. She's in charge of our social calendar for summer."

Michelle nodded, gave a mock salute, and replied, "See you in the morning."

As she drove over to pick up the kids at school, she thought again about the phone calls. *Who could it be?*

Sheila was vacuuming the living room when Michelle and the kids came through the front door. She turned off the vacuum to greet them. Caleb and Madison dropped their backpacks, kicked off their shoes, and headed for the kitchen for snacks, tossing hellos over their shoulders to their grandmother.

"You're not supposed to be doing that, Mom," Michelle chided. "I told you I'd take care of it on Saturday."

"There's no way I'm going to sit around here and let you do all the housework, Michelle," her mother replied. "I've seen how tired you look lately."

Michelle shook her head. "I'm fine. Really. How about I go make us a pot of tea, and we'll sit and visit for a few minutes before I start dinner?"

Sheila smiled. "I've already got a roast in the oven."

"So that's what I smell." Michelle set her bag on the chair and pulled her mother into an embrace. "Did I ever tell you what a great mom you are?"

"Once or twice," she replied, returning the hug. "You go get changed, and I'll make us that tea."

Pulling back to look her in the eye, Michelle smiled. "Thanks, Mom." She grabbed the stack of mail from the end table and headed upstairs to slip on her jeans.

At eleven that night, Michelle found her husband, Steve, at the kitchen table still bent over his paperwork. It seemed like the work of an attorney was never finished during work hours. *Like a teacher,* she thought as she reflected on the hours she spent grading papers and planning lessons from that very same kitchen table.

"Tough case?" she asked, resting her hand on his shoulder and peering down at the yellow legal pad where he was scratching down some notes.

Steve leaned back against her, and she bent forward, wrapping her arms around him. "I didn't hear you come in," he said.

"You've been locked onto your paperwork all evening," she replied.

"You're right. Our client divulged some new information this afternoon, so I've been adjusting the presentation of the case."

Michelle stood back up and started massaging his neck and shoulders.

Tipping his head to one side, Steve moaned. "Guess I'm pretty tight."

"Yeah. Lots of knots." She worked her way up his neck to the base of his skull. Every place she touched felt like rock. "Maybe you should call it a night and stand under a hot shower to relax these muscles a little."

Steve agreed. "That sounds really good. I'll just finish this one page and come on up."

Michelle was putting her toothbrush back in the cup by the sink when he came into their bathroom. "You are a sight for sore eyes," he said with a weary smile. He plucked gently at her silky cream-colored nightie. "Is this new?"

"No," she replied. "Remember, you gave it to me for my birthday?"

"I did? Wow, smart guy," he said, wrapping his arms around her and nuzzling into her neck.

"Still going to take your hot shower?" she asked.

"Maybe later," he replied, turning her around and giving her a soft kiss.

Michelle reached up and wrapped her arms around his neck. "I've missed you," she said.

"Missed you, too." He kissed her again, this time deeper, more passionate.

Michelle's whole body responded with a hunger she hadn't felt for weeks. "I love you, Counselor," she murmured softly.

"Feelings mutual, Ma'am," he replied in a throaty voice.

Later, as they basked in the afterglow of their passion, Michelle rested her head on his chest. Tracing circles through his chest hair with her fingers, she said, "Remember when it was just the two of us?"

"Yeah. Seems like ages ago," he replied.

"Mmmm hmmm," she replied. "Now we're surrounded by people all the time. Mom, the kids, friends, work ... I know I used to get lonely living in a new town with you at work all day. Now I sometimes wish we could go back in time for just a week or two and have total quiet, our little candle lit dinners on the coffee table— you know what I mean."

He squeezed her shoulder, drawing her even closer. "Yeah, babe. I know. Maybe we should plan a getaway — just the two of us. Now that summer's coming, you'll be free, and I'm sure I can get Roger to cover the office for a week or so."

"What about the kids?"

"Couldn't your mom watch them?"

Michelle nodded. "Yeah. I'm sure she'd be fine with that. Let's just get through Caleb's birthday party and then we can make a plan. I'd love to go back to that B & B in the mountains," she added, lifting her head to look at him. "Remember?"

"I sure do. Great fishing there," he teased.

She pushed away and swatted him playfully with a pillow. "I wasn't talking about the fishing, Mr. Romantic," she said with a grin.

Pulling her back into his arms, he kissed her forehead. "A man can dream, can't he?"

"Just leave the fishing pole at home," she replied.

CHAPTER THREE

"Phil, honey, are you feeling okay?" Joan asked her husband. She'd been concerned about him for several weeks now, but he kept brushing off her queries. He looked like he was losing weight, and his appetite just wasn't normal.

Phil took a deep breath, letting it out slowly. "I guess. Seems like I can't get myself moving the way I used to. Probably just age creeping up on me." He reached across the table and squeezed her hand.

Joan studied his face. He'd never been one to let age get in his way, even now that they were well into their eighties. Always so strong and passionate about life, she couldn't recall seeing him dragging like this. "I'm calling the doctor. You're overdue for a physical, anyway. Might as well get it taken care of as soon as we get back from Sandy Cove."

Usually one to balk at the mention of doctors, Phil just nodded his head. "Whatever you say, dear." He pushed himself up from the table and carried their dinner plates to the sink.

"Why don't you go stretch out on the couch, and let me take care of the dishes tonight," she suggested.

"You must be tired, too, after all your running around today."

Joan patted him on the back. "I'm fine. Besides there's not much to do. Just a few plates and one pan. You go take a catnap, and I'll be in there in a few minutes. Maybe we can finish that mystery movie we started last night."

"Okay," he conceded. And giving her a kiss on the cheek, he shuffled into the living room.

As Joan started the soapy water for the dishes, she gazed out the window and began to pray. *What is it, Lord? What's happening with Phil?* She immersed her gloved hands in the soapy water and beseeched God for her husband's health.

It's time for you to be strong now, Joan. He's going to need you more than ever.

Her heart began pounding in her chest. Was that God speaking, or just her fears finding a voice? She quickly rinsed and dried the dishes. Untying her apron, she hung it on a hook by the pantry and went to check on her husband.

Phil was sound asleep, stretched out so that his long legs and feet hung over the arm of the sofa. She didn't have the heart to wake him. Reaching over and retrieving a soft blanket from her easy chair, she carefully spread it over him. Then she picked up her knitting project – a sweater for her granddaughter, Michelle, and went to work. Though her arthritis slowed her down considerably, she still enjoyed watching each new piece unfold. She hoped to have this one completed in time to take with them when they flew up to Oregon for Caleb's birthday.

Little Caleb. He sure was growing like a weed! As she worked each stitch, she thought about all that Michelle had gone through over the years. Moving away from her lifelong home in Seal Beach, California to begin a new marriage in Oregon, watching her father struggle to survive after an unsuccessful suicide attempt, finding herself in her own struggles when she and Steve discovered their infertility issues, a near adoption of another little Caleb that had been cancelled at the last moment leaving them both heartbroken, their miracle daughter Madison, and then the student who had gifted them with another Caleb they now called their son.

And to think almost six years had gone by since that newborn boy had joined their family! My, the time did fly!

Sometimes Joan found herself wondering what had ever become of that first little Caleb her granddaughter had almost adopted. Had his birthmother become successful as a parent? How was he making his way through life these days? Good Lord, he'd be a teenager now. Hard to imagine!

She rested her knitting in her lap and closed her eyes for a moment, saying a silent prayer for a child they'd never even met and probably never would. *Dear Lord, wherever he is, whatever's happening in his life, will You please guard and guide him? Will You draw him close and let him know how much You love him? Will You show him how very much he needs You, too?*

She heard Phil stir and glanced over to find him gazing at her. "What are you looking at?" she asked with a grin.

"My beautiful wife," he replied.

"Oh, pshaw."

"How's the sweater coming along?"

Joan glanced down at the soft blue and white yarn in her lap. "It's taking me longer than I thought. I might have to finish it while we are up there."

"You could always hold it until Christmas," he suggested, propping himself up on one elbow to face her.

"Maybe. But I'd like her to have it for those cool summer evenings they get along the coast there." She put the project off to the side and scooted forward in her chair, preparing to stand. "Want me to make some tea, and we can finish the movie?"

"Sure," he replied, throwing off the blanket and swinging himself into a sitting position. "I'll give you a hand."

Joan stood up. "You just get the show on. I'll be right back with the tea."

29

The kids were settled into bed and Steve had spread out some paperwork for the case he was presenting the following day, so Michelle decided to retreat to the family room and spend a little time with her mom. Sometimes she felt guilty being so busy with school and her family when she knew her mom was probably feeling very lonely since Michelle's father had passed away.

The family room was empty. Sheila must have gone up to her room for something. Michelle picked up a magazine and settled into the recliner. As she flipped through the pages, her mind wandered, and she found herself thinking about her grandparents. Why did they keep coming to mind? Resting her head back, she closed her eyes and thought about how great it would be to have them in Sandy Cove for Caleb's party.

It'll be good for Mom, too, she thought. And the kids were excited to see them. In addition to his sweet spirit and gentle ways, Grandpa Phil was great with riddles. Both Madison and Caleb would spend hours trying to solve them. Then there was Joan's cooking – she could almost taste her grandmother's brownies, made from scratch and frosted with dark chocolate icing. There wasn't a better brownie on earth.

"What are you thinking about, Mimi?" her mother asked as she entered the room and sat down.

Michelle looked over and smiled. "Grandma and Grandpa. I can hardly wait to see them."

"Me, too. It's been a long time." She became very quiet, and Michelle could tell she was lost in thoughts of her own.

"Anything wrong, Mom?

"No. I don't think so, honey. I'm just a little worried about your grandfather."

Michelle flashed back to her thoughts earlier and how she'd felt pressed to pray for him. "Why? What's up with Grandpa?"

"It's probably nothing. Grandma just seems a little concerned. She says he's been really tired lately—not acting like his usual self."

Michelle studied her mother to see whether or not she was telling the whole story. But Sheila just returned her gaze with a reassuring smile. "Let's not borrow trouble from tomorrow, honey. I'm sure he's fine. It's normal that he'd be slowing down at his age."

"Yeah. You're probably right," she replied, but Michelle couldn't shake the feeling that something was really wrong.

CHAPTER FOUR

Amber Gamble sat in the tiny living room of the apartment she shared with her boyfriend, Chad. He'd left for work an hour earlier, and she was supposed to be studying for a final in her sociology class at the local community college. In a couple of hours, she'd be off to her own job waiting tables at the coffee shop on campus, so there wasn't much time left to cram for the exam that night.

Focus, she told herself. Flipping to the review questions provided by their professor, she began reading through her answers scratched beneath each one and along the margins of the paper. She grabbed the highlighter on the coffee table and marked the key points to remember. Standing up, she paced the floor, reading and rereading each question, looking away to rehearse her answers.

I need some coffee, she thought. An unfinished pot of day old coffee on the kitchen counter would have to do. Chad reminded her that morning they were running short of cash this month. She'd have to make every dollar stretch, so there'd be no throwing away old coffee in favor of a fresh pot.

She filled a mug and placed it in the microwave. Setting her papers down on the counter, she opened the fridge and grabbed some creamer. As she closed the door, her eyes locked on the calendar posted with magnets. This Saturday would be Caleb's birthday.

She'd tried to keep herself so busy with school and work that she could somehow slide past it again. Every year was the same. At first she'd fought deep depression and despair when her son's birthday approached. It seemed like just yesterday she'd handed him over to be adopted by her junior high teacher.

Sinking into the chair at their kitchen table, she allowed herself a moment to travel back into time and peer down at Caleb's tiny face. He'd weighed less than five pounds and looked like a little baby doll tightly wrapped in the hospital receiving blanket. He'd gazed up at her with those big eyes, and she'd felt a connection she'd never felt to another human being.

How many times had she questioned the decision to give him up? It seemed like she'd never find a place of peace in her heart and mind about that. But how could she have been a mother at only fourteen years old? And with her parents so messed up, there really wasn't anyone to help her back then, especially not Adam, Caleb's father. What a jerk he turned out to be!

Chad was different. They'd met at school the first week of her freshman year of college. Several years older than her, he'd been a good friend when she really needed one. She remembered the day she told him she was moving out of her parents' house. He'd offered her a safe place to stay until she could get her own apartment.

But living under the same roof changed their relationship. The third week together, Amber suffered a meltdown over some family issues, and Chad's comforting embrace led to an intimacy neither had planned but neither resisted. After confiding in him about her life back in Oregon and the baby boy she'd left behind, Chad's understanding and protective responses told her he would never be like Adam—leaving her to fend for herself when she needed him most.

The beep of the microwave broke into Amber's thoughts. Carefully lifting out the hot cup, she added a generous helping of vanilla creamer, watching it swirl in the dark liquid. Then she sat back and stared at the calendar again. Twice she'd tried to call Ms. Baron, her beloved teacher and Caleb's adoptive mom. If she could just talk to her and make sure her son was okay, maybe that would help her move on.

But both times, she'd frozen and hung up.

Caleb would be six in a few days. Six years old. He was probably finishing kindergarten. It was hard to imagine that tiny baby as a schoolboy. Did he look like her? Did he even know about her? And what if something happened to him? Would she ever find out?

I've got to see him. Just one more time.

Amber nodded her head in affirmation and took her coffee and paperwork back into the living room. Maybe after class tonight, she'd talk to Chad about it and see if he'd go with her to Oregon.

"Seriously, Amber? You are really thinking of going to Oregon to see this kid?" Chad's voice was gaining volume as he locked eyes with her.

Amber looked away. "He's not just some kid, Chad. He's my son."

"*Was* your son. Remember? He belongs to another family now. He's theirs, not yours anymore."

"You don't have to remind me of that." Amber slouched back on the sofa, tears threatening to spill down her reddened cheeks.

Chad shook his head and walked over to sit beside her. His voice now lower and softer, he said, "Listen. I know this has been on your mind for a long time, Amber. But I think you've got to find some way to let it go. Do you really think showing up in Sandy Cove is going to be the best thing for Caleb? For all you know, he isn't even aware that he's adopted. And what about his parents? Don't you think it would freak them out to have you suddenly reappear in their lives?"

Amber sat silently staring ahead, unable to say a word for fear of the torrent of emotions that might be unleashed from her heart if she spoke.

Chad pulled her chin toward him, and she looked up into his eyes. "I'm here for you. You know that. I just think this could be the biggest mistake of your life."

Hardly, Amber thought to herself as she remembered her relationship with Adam and how she'd let that get out of hand. Now *that* was the biggest mistake of her life. Rallying her strength, she swallowed back her tears and replied, "I've given this a lot of thought, Chad. I just need to see that Caleb's okay—that everything turned out good for him. Then maybe I'll be able to move forward and put this behind me."

Chad shook his head again, but his eyes showed compassion. Pulling her into his chest, he murmured, "I'll go with you."

And suddenly Amber's heart experienced an emotion she hadn't felt in years—joy. She felt joy and hope, two very unfamiliar but welcome friends to a heart that had spent most of its life in pain.

The next morning she began planning their trip. Twice she picked up the phone and considered calling Magnolia Middle School again—her one point of contact with Michelle Baron. But both times she changed her mind, not wanting the excitement of seeing Caleb being doused by a potentially negative conversation with his adoptive mother. She'd just go to Sandy Cove and hope for the best.

Michelle glanced across the classroom on this final day of school. Students, who would normally have been in their seats busy with assignments, mingled around the room, sitting on desks and chatting in small clusters as they traded yearbooks and wrote notes to each other inside. She was really going to miss this group of kids. Such hard workers and most were well behaved. It had been a great year.

Next year would likely be much more like her first at Magnolia. She'd had quite a handful that year. The year of Amber Gamble. What a challenge that girl had been! But God had brought such an unexpected blessing from the fiery trials of that year—their precious son, Caleb.

This year's high achievers would be moving on to high school in the fall, and a change of policy and curriculum at Magnolia School would result in tracking the kids into various levels of language and literature for eighth grade. With Michelle being lower in seniority, she'd been appointed to teach the kids who were struggling academically, which meant they'd also be likely to have other issues such as fractured families and vulnerability to negative peer pressure.

Although she understood the seniority issue, she couldn't help but wonder why the more experienced teachers weren't ask to instruct the most challenging students. Instead they were gifted with the children whose parents were supportive and helpful, who had high expectations for the children and had instilled motivation into their lives. Sure, there were always a few exceptionally bright kids who were troubled and disruptive, but those kids were routinely removed from high achieving classes and bumped down to the other classes.

Yes, things would be different next year. Michelle just hoped at least a few good role models would find their way into her classroom to help maintain some standard of achievement for the overall student body.

One of the students who had been talking to a group of girls near Michelle's desk turned to her and asked, "What do you like most about teaching, Ms. Baron?"

Smiling, she replied, "When I can see that I really made a difference for a student."

The girl nodded. "You made a difference for me. I thought this class would be really boring, but you made it interesting and fun."

"Thanks! You just made my day," Michelle replied, her heart soaring. Sometimes the kids she least expected to be impacted by her class, the ones who seemed so quiet and detached, were actually really appreciative of the hard work and personal dedication she poured into her teaching. Kids like Amber, well it was pretty clear whether or not you were making any headway with them. But others, like this shy, sweet girl who never made waves—well those were harder to read.

"I'm coming back to visit you next year," her student promised as the bell rang, signaling the end of the final class of the day.

"I'll look forward to it," she replied.

Then Michelle straightened up the room and headed to the teachers' lounge for a catered lunch buffet to celebrate another successful year. Afterward, there'd be a department meeting where she would learn more about what would be expected of her the following year as she tackled the remedial English classes and possibly taught a reading intervention course.

Her mentor and friend, Cassie, waved Michelle over to her table. "Have a seat," she said with a warm smile. "We made it. Another year down."

Michelle nodded, returning her smile. "Yep. It's been a good one."

A moment later the principal stood from a table across the room. "I think we'll get started since most of you are here. This luncheon is the PTA's way of expressing their gratitude for all your hard work this year. We'll dismiss by tables, and you can go ahead and help yourselves to the delicious buffet spread they've provided.

"After your department meetings, be sure to turn in your year's lesson plan book. Tomorrow morning is your time to clean out your room and store your supplies in the cupboards. Please be sure to lock up all electronic devices before you leave for summer vacation. I'll be mailing information about our August start up meetings at the beginning of that month. Any questions?"

As the teachers in the room shook their heads and began to resume visiting, he dismissed the first tables to go to the buffet.

The rest of the afternoon slipped by quickly, and Michelle soon found herself in the office about to leave. Remembering the strange phone calls from earlier that week, she stopped by Daisy's desk.

"Heading out?" the perky receptionist asked.

"Yep. Off to the party store to pick up decorations for Caleb's birthday bash. Just wanted to check and see if that girl ever called back."

"Girl?"

"Yeah. The one who called twice the other day," Michelle reminded her.

"Oh. That girl. Nope. She hasn't called again."

Michelle nodded. "Okay. Thanks." She placed her lesson plan book on the stack on the corner of Daisy's desk. "Here you go."

"Until next year," Daisy replied.

"Until next year," Michelle repeated.

ROSEMARY HINES

CHAPTER FIVE

The following morning was a quiet one at school. Some teachers had stayed late the day before to pack up their rooms. Others were focused on the task of putting away another year. Occasionally one dropped by to wish Michelle a happy summer. By noon, her classroom was empty, all items locked in her cupboards.

Stretching out the kinks in her back and neck from lifting and moving electronics and boxes of supplies, she glanced around the vacant space. A sense of satisfaction swept over her. Another year successfully completed.

When she arrived home, the smell of freshly brewed coffee greeted her.

"Hi, dear. Thought you could use a little lift after your busy morning," her mom said, pouring a cup of coffee and handing it to her.

"Thanks, Mom." Michelle reached for the cup with a weary smile. "Where are the kids?"

"Kelly called and said she was taking her brood to the beach. She asked if Maddie and Caleb could come along. I figured with all the birthday preparations ahead, it would give us a chance to get more accomplished." She paused then added, "Hope that was okay."

"Sure. I'll bet they were happy to be heading to the beach."

"Maddie spent quite a bit of time getting ready," Sheila added with a wink.

"So Luke was going, too?"

"Apparently."

Michelle smiled, flashing back in her mind to the past twelve years since Madison's birth. Their pastor and friend, Ben and his wife Kelly's son, Luke, was 18 months older. Officially a teenager now, the playful friendship between him and Maddie seemed to be evolving into a new stage. Michelle and Steve assumed the kids would always see each other like brother and sister, but now they were beginning to wonder.

By the time Madison was in kindergarten, Ben and Kelly had added a daughter, Lucy (now eleven), and another son, Logan (eight) to their family. Then four years ago they'd had the twins — Liam and Lily. Caleb seemed to vacillate between hanging out with Logan or playing with the little ones, depending on his mood and the activities at hand. The beach was a perfect venue for all of them.

"Honey?" her mom's voice broke into her thoughts.

"Yeah?"

"Do you know someone with a blue Impala?"

"What?"

"There's a blue Impala that keeps driving by the house. I've noticed it several times this week. Today, it seemed to slow down as it passed."

Michelle thought for a moment and replied, "I don't think so, Mom. Could you see the person driving it?"

"It looked like a young kid, maybe in his late teens or early twenties. He had kind of long hair, but that's all I could see."

"Was there anybody else in the car?" Michelle searched her mind for any neighborhood kids it might be.

"There was someone in the passenger seat, but I really couldn't tell you any more than that. Might have been a girl or another boy with long hair."

"I'm sure it's just some kids from the area. Summer, you know. They tend to cruise around for something to do. Especially if one of them just got a license."

"You're probably right."

"If you see it again, let me know," Michelle added, glancing down at her list for the afternoon.

"Okay. So where do we start? Want me to do some cleaning around here while you finish your shopping?"

"Let's start with lunch," Michelle replied with a smile. "And no, I do not want you doing any cleaning. But if you'd like to keep me company while I finish shopping for Caleb's gifts, that would be great."

"My pleasure! Now, if you won't let me clean, at least let me whip up some lunch for my favorite daughter."

"You won't have to twist my arm on that one, Mom. I'll go change my clothes, and after we eat we'll head over to the Toy Factory."

When Michelle and her mom had finished shopping for Caleb's birthday presents, they decided to swing into the Coffee Stop for a quick latte before picking up the kids at the Johnson's house. The place was relatively quiet with only a few patrons scattered at various tables, most of them huddled over laptops or iPads.

"Michelle?" a male voice said as they passed.

Turning to look, Michelle saw her college anthropology professor. "Dr. Chambers?"

"One and the same," he said as he stood to greet her, his blue eyes sparkling and his silver hair cut short.

"Wow. I can't believe you remember my name," she said.

"I never forget a pretty face," he replied.

Michelle felt herself blush. Rick Chambers had an unnerving charm about him. A flood of memories took her back to the many class sessions where he'd made her squirm with his smooth presentation. Not to mention his very deliberate and verbal anti-Christian slant.

The last contact she'd had with him was the day of the final exam. Wanting to somehow communicate her faith to him, but having lacked the confidence to stand up to him during class discussions, she'd written him a letter explaining how she'd come to develop a relationship with God, with the hopes it might somehow impact his life.

Now he was turning to her mom, extending his hand. "Rick Chambers."

"This is my mom," Michelle said. "Mom, this is my anthropology professor from college."

"Really? Well I'm pleased to meet you," Sheila replied, accepting his handshake.

"You two look like you could be sisters," he observed, focusing his attention on Sheila.

Michelle's mother smiled. "You're very kind."

He smiled. "Please, allow me to treat you to one of the delicious concoctions here."

Michelle glanced over at her mother, who seemed to be unsure how to respond. "Thanks, but that's really not necessary," she said.

"It would be my pleasure," he said adding, "and it would give me a much needed break from this," as he gestured to his laptop.

Sheila surprised Michelle by accepting his invitation. "We can only stay for a little bit," she said. "Then we've got to pick up Michelle's kids."

"Kids?"

"Yep," Michelle replied, feeling herself regaining her footing. "A daughter who's twelve and a son who's about to turn six."

"Well, good for you! Congratulations," he said warmly. "Now what can I get you two lovely ladies?"

A few minutes later he was returning to their table with two steaming lattes in his hands. "Mocha," he said, handing one to Michelle, "and vanilla," he added, placing Sheila's in front of her.

As he took his seat, Michelle wondered if he remembered her letter and what he'd thought about it. Wow, that had been nearly thirteen years ago. Although she was confident the letter had communicated what was on her heart and mind, she couldn't help but feel a little uneasy sitting here beside him having no idea how he'd reacted to her written testimony.

"So, are you from this area?" he asked Sheila.

"Actually, I'm just relocating here from southern California," she replied.

"You and your husband must be looking forward to spending more time with your grandkids," he said.

Michelle could see her mom's face fall, and she cut into the conversation. "My dad passed away about a year ago."

Rick's face seemed to reflect genuine concern. "I'm so sorry to hear that." Turning to Sheila, he added, "Well, it must be a comfort to be moving close to your daughter and grandchildren."

She glanced over at Michelle and smiled. "Yes, it is. Do you have any grandchildren?" she asked.

"Me? No. I've never found the right woman to settle down with. One of my biggest regrets," he added, staring down into his coffee cup.

For a moment, Michelle saw something in him she'd never seen before in class. A small chink in his armor of charm.

"That's a shame," her mom piped in. "Family is so important."

He nodded. "Well, you two ladies are very blessed to have realized that and made it a priority in your lives. I'm sure I could learn a lot from the two of you," he added. Then he turned to Sheila. "Your daughter is something special."

She smiled and nodded. "Yes, she is."

"And I have a feeling you had a hand in that," he said with a wink.

Again, Sheila blushed.

Was Rick Chambers flirting with her mom? Michelle sat back and studied the two of them as they chatted on. Come to think of it, Dr. Chambers was probably about her mother's age. Perhaps a bit younger, but not by more than a handful of years. And he certainly was giving her mom his undivided attention.

"Michelle?" her mom's voice interrupted her thoughts.

"Yeah?"

"Dr. Chambers was asking you a question," Sheila said.

"Rick. Please call me Rick."

"Okay. Rick was asking you something, honey."

Michelle turned to face her professor. "Sorry. Guess I've got a lot on my mind. Come again?"

"I was wondering if you ever ended up teaching. If I recall correctly, that was your goal."

"Oh, yes. As a matter of fact, I'm an English teacher at Magnolia Middle School," Michelle replied.

Sheila smiled at her proudly. "While you two are catching up, I'm going to excuse myself to use the ladies' room."

As soon as she was out of earshot, Rick leaned forward. "I'm glad we have this moment to talk, Michelle. I want to hear more about your teaching, but first I'd like to just say that your letter meant a lot to me. I've had many Christian students pass through my classes, but none of them have taken the time to reach out to me in that way."

Michelle studied his face. Was he being sincere? Or was this another ploy to launch a conversation challenging her faith?

"I know I was pretty hard on you and your classmates," he continued. "I know the pain of losing a parent. But my loss...well, it left me cold toward the possibility of the existence of God. Instead of bolstering my faith, it was a crushing blow to it. And I didn't want my students to ever face such a disappointment themselves, when they realized their god wasn't going to be able to fix everything."

She nodded. "I see."

"At any rate, I kept your letter. And I've reread it numerous times. Especially on the days when my mother's memory resurfaces to haunt me. You need to know that the message of that letter..." He gazed off into space, then looked back into her eyes. "...it's chiseling away at the wall I'd built around my heart." Again he averted his eyes. Then clearing his throat, he picked up his coffee cup and concluded, "I thought you should know."

"Thanks for telling me that. I had no idea it would mean that much to you. In fact, I almost chickened out when it was time to hand it over."

He smiled warmly. "I'm glad you didn't." Pausing, as if trying to make a decision, he added, "And if your invitation still stands, I'd like to take you up on it."

"Invitation?" *What is he talking about?*

"Your invitation to join you at church sometime," he replied, leveling his gaze at her.

"Uh...sure. Of course. You're always welcome."

"We'd love to have you join us," Sheila added warmly as she rejoined them at the table. "Sorry. I couldn't help overhearing the last bit of your conversation. Wouldn't it be nice to have Dr. Chambers join us, honey?" she asked Michelle.

"Yes. That would be great."

"Rick. Please. I reserve Dr. Chambers for my students."

"Rick, then," Sheila replied with a smile. "This Sunday's going to be a bit busy because my folks are coming for Michelle's son's birthday party. But perhaps you could join us the following weekend?"

"I'd love to," he replied, this time completely focused on Michelle's mom.

"Michelle, give him the information, dear," Sheila instructed.

And so Michelle found herself giving Rick Chambers the location and service time they'd be attending. He carefully wrote it down on a napkin and slipped it into his shirt pocket. "It's a date then," he said. "I'll look forward to it."

"Great," Michelle replied, pushing back her chair. "We'd better get going, Mom."

"Yes. Well, it was very nice chatting with you, Rick. And thank you for the latte," Sheila added as she stood to join Michelle.

After they'd left the coffee shop, Michelle said, "Mom, Dr. Chambers was really checking you out."

Sheila blushed and shook her head as she pushed the air away with her hand. "Nonsense. He was just being a gentleman."

"Right." Michelle smiled, suddenly seeing her mother in a new way. Although Rick Chambers was *not* the man for her mother, it was wonderful to see her mom feeling attractive and young enough to still catch an eye. She noticed a new bounce in her mother's steps as they walked to the car to go pick up the kids. *Maybe God has another man in the future for Mom.*

Sheila stood in front of the full-length mirror in the bedroom and studied her image. Was it possible Michelle's professor really did find her attractive? In her youth, she'd turned a few heads. But now? In her early sixties?

Turning to the side, she examined the profile of her figure. Sucking in her stomach, she drew her shoulders back and tried to view herself objectively. Compared to the willowy thinness of her daughter, her body seemed short and somewhat rounded.

Facing forward again, she gave herself a resigned smile. *Nope. You're definitely not a youthful gal anymore,* she whispered.

Besides, she just couldn't picture herself with any other man than the one she'd married and loved for 38 years.

Sinking down onto the foot of the bed, she allowed herself a journey back in time. She was working as a salesgirl in a department store. At only nineteen years old, the temporary position during the Christmas holidays provided her with a chance to accumulate some spending money for the following semester at college.

While she'd been helping a rather impatient woman find some cologne, she'd noticed a good-looking young man waiting for assistance. Before he could wander off, she spotted the woman's fragrance and handed it to her, then turned her attention to the handsome stranger.

"Can I help you with something?" she'd asked. They'd spent the next hour trying to find just the right gift for John Ackerman's mother.

As she was ringing up his purchase, the manager came over and informed her it was time for her dinner break.

"Please let me buy you a burger," John offered. "It's the least I can do to thank you for giving me so much of your time."

She'd agreed. And the rest, as they say, was history.

Oh John. I miss you so much, she said softly.

Shaking off the past, she stood and walked out of the room. Surely Michelle could use some help in the kitchen. There was no point sitting in here reminiscing about days gone by.

Checking herself out in the mirror once again, she smoothed a loose wisp of hair and let herself hear

Michelle's claim replay in her mind one more time. *Dr. Chambers was really checking you out.*

Rick Chamber's face and his warm smile accompanied her to the kitchen.

CHAPTER SIX

It was 3:00 in the morning when Michelle awakened from a troubling dream about her grandfather. He'd been gasping for breath, gripping her arm tightly and searching her face as he said over and over again, "I tried to call you."

As she sat up in bed and shook off those images, a dozen thoughts assaulted her. What was wrong with Grandpa Phil? Was he the one who'd tried to call her classroom? No, wait. Daisy said it was a young girl. It couldn't be him. But why was her grandfather struggling to breathe? Was he sick? Was it serious?

Glancing over at Steve sleeping soundly beside her, she slipped out of bed and into her robe then headed downstairs. Experience had taught her it was better to get up and move around after a nightmare, or she'd fall asleep and be ensnared in it again.

As she settled on the couch, their old cat Max jumped up beside her, pressing against her arm and purring. "What are you doing down here, little man?" she asked. Cradling him in her arms, she scratched under his chin and behind his ears, feeling her body relax along with his.

She thought about the weekend ahead. Caleb's birthday was Sunday afternoon. Steve would be picking up her grandparents at the airport in the morning, while she ran the last few errands. Gently laying Max down on the cushion beside her, she picked up her list that she'd left on the coffee table.

Paper Goods
Balloons and Streamers
Cake and Ice Cream
Call in Pizza Order
Set up Games
Chop salad ingredients
Make sign on computer
Clean bathrooms

I'll do the errands first, she thought. If she got going early enough, she'd be home by 11:00 and would have the rest of the day to clean house, visit with her grandparents, and decorate for the party.

Better get back to bed. It was going to be a busy day and she'd need her rest. As she climbed the stairs, she flashed back to the image of her grandfather in her dream. *Please watch over him, Lord. We all love and need him so much,* she prayed silently.

Joan studied her husband across the kitchen table. "You look pale, Phil. Are you up to this trip?"

"I'm fine," he replied with a weary smile.

"When we get home from Michelle's house, I'm making appointments for our annual checkups," she said.

"You already said that, remember?"

She was stunned by his tone of voice. "Sorry, dear."

"No. I'm the one who's sorry. You're right. We should get in for our physicals when we get home." He rubbed his back and then added, "Well, I'd better get the suitcase in the car. We need to leave for the airport in half an hour." Gripping the edge of the table, he pulled himself to his feet.

"I'll just water those planters out back and then I'm ready," Joan said.

It would be so nice to be with their daughter, granddaughter, and great-grandkids again. She could hardly believe Caleb was already turning six. Seemed like less than a year ago she'd been rocking his tiny body and rejoicing with Michelle over the surprise adoption.

Thank you, Lord, for the miracles you've done for all of us. Turning her attention back to the present, she rinsed off their breakfast dishes and headed outside.

"Busy day!" Steve said, as he gave Michelle a quick hug. "What can I do to help?"

"Can you watch the kids until you pick up Grandma and Grandpa at the airport? I've got tons of errands to run."

"You've got it, babe," he replied. "What time's their flight again?"

"They're arriving at 1:30. Mom will be here with Caleb and Maddie if I'm not back from my errands." Michelle handed him a paper with the flight number. "Hey, speaking of Mom, guess who we saw yesterday at the Coffee Stop?"

"Who?"

"Rick Chambers."

"Who's that?"

"My anthropology professor. Remember? He was the one who was always picking on the Christians in class?"

"Oh yeah. That jerk. I remember. So did you talk to him?"

"Actually, he started the conversation. He recognized me before I even saw him. He was really nice. Even bought our coffee."

"Really?" Steve asked, sounding skeptical.

"Yeah. He seemed to be checking out Mom," she said with a smile.

"Whoa. That's a red flag. No way do we want your Mom ever getting involved with someone like him."

Michelle nodded. "But, you know what? He told me that my letter really made an impression on him. And he surprised me by asking if my invitation to church was still standing."

"You invited him to church?"

"Yeah. In the letter. You remember, right? I gave him a letter telling him about Dad and how I came to my faith."

Steve looked puzzled. "Not really."

"Hmmm… I thought for sure I told you."

"Maybe I just forgot," he offered.

"Yeah. Well anyway, at the end of the letter, I invited him to join us at church anytime."

"That was years ago, Michelle. I can't believe he'd still remember that."

"I know. It took me by surprise. He said he kept it and he reads it again from time to time. He also shared with me that when his mom died, he turned away from God and didn't want his students to have any false hope that their god could fix anything."

"Hmmm. Interesting. So what did you say?" he asked.

"I mostly just listened. And I told him he was welcome to join us at church anytime. Mom suggested next week, since this weekend is pretty hectic with the birthday and everything."

He nodded. "Well good for you, honey. Maybe your letter had more impact than you know."

"Or maybe he wants to make a pass at Mom," she said with a wink.

"What did you say about me?" Sheila asked, entering the room.

Michelle glanced over at her. "Just telling Steve about how Rick Chambers was checking you out yesterday at the Coffee Stop."

"I think you're imagining things, Mimi," her mother replied with a blush.

"I don't think so Mom."

"Well, I could never be interested in a man like him," Sheila said. "Especially after what you told me about his class."

Michelle nodded. "Yeah. He's a different sort of guy."

"So what can I do today to help you get ready for the party?" she asked.

"Just be here for the kids when Steve goes to get Grandma and Grandpa."

"Okay, dear. If you think of anything else, let me know." She poured a cup of coffee and left them alone in the room.

"Want me to make you some breakfast before I take off?" Michelle asked Steve.

"No. I can have cereal."

"Okay. I'll get going then."

"Just one more thing, honey," he said, catching a hold of her arm as she started toward the door.

"What?"

"This," he replied. Leaning over he kissed her gently on the lips. "I love you, Mrs. Baron."

She grinned and patted his chest. "You too, Mr. B." Then she grabbed her list and left.

Several hours and a car full of bags later, Michelle turned onto Wayburn Road. As she approached their home, she spotted a blue Impala pulling away from the curb and driving off.

An uneasy feeling settled over her. Who could that be? And why do they keep coming back? Tempted to follow the car, she glanced over and saw her grandfather coming out of the front door. He seemed to be moving more slowly and hesitantly than his normal gait.

Michelle caught his eye and waved, pulling into the driveway, eager to give him a hug. As she got out of the car and turned to greet him, she noticed the Impala had disappeared.

"Hey there, Gramps!" she said, walking into his open arms. He looked frail too, almost a little gaunt.

"Hey, yourself," he replied with a squeeze. "Can I help you with some of those bags?" he asked as he glanced into the back seat of her car.

"Sure!" She pulled out several parcels and handed them to him, and together they walked into the house.

"Mom! Caleb took my iPad," Madison said the moment they were inside.

"Did not!" Caleb argued.

Michelle set down her bags and was about to talk to them when Steve entered the room.

"Hey, you two. Knock it off," he said sternly. Then turning to Caleb, he added, "Your mother's been running all over town getting stuff for your birthday party. March into your room and get your sister's iPad right now."

Caleb looked up at him out of the corner of his eye, a look of surrender replacing the defiance that had been there moments earlier. "Okay," he mumbled.

Madison smiled. "Thanks, Daddy." She turned and followed Caleb.

"Yeah. Thanks, 'Daddy'," Michelle repeated with a smile of her own.

"Where would you like these to go?" Grandpa Phil asked as he held out the bags in his hands.

"Here, I'll take them," Steve offered.

"They can go up to our bedroom for now," Michelle replied.

"Okay. I'm on it." He headed up the stairs, juggling the packages in his arms.

Turning to her grandfather, Michelle asked, "Where's Grandma?"

"In the kitchen with your mom. They're fixing a pot of tea, I think," he replied.

"Let's go join them," she suggested.

"Good idea, pumpkin." Grandpa Phil wrapped an arm across her shoulder as they left the room.

Finally, the day was winding down. Michelle and her mother carried serving dishes into the dining room. A pot roast, some mashed potatoes, and green beans filled the air with the fragrance of a hearty meal.

"Looks delicious," Steve said. "I'll go round up the kids."

"I wish you two would let me help," Joan offered.

Michelle glanced over the table, taking inventory. "You just relax, Grandma."

As the family took their seats, Steve turned to Phil. "Would you do the honors?"

"Be happy to," he replied. Stretching out his hands, the family followed suit, and as they formed an unbroken circle, he asked a blessing on the meal and the upcoming birthday event.

"Thanks, Gramps!" Caleb said as they began passing the food around. Phil reached over and ruffled the boy's hair, and Michelle and Steve looked at each other and grinned.

The table grew quiet as the family dug into their dinner. Then Joan asked, "So Michelle, did you accomplish all your goals for the day?"

"I think so."

"You seemed a little distracted when you came in from your errands," Sheila said.

Michelle turned to her. "Yeah, that reminds me. Remember the Impala you were telling me about?"

Sheila nodded.

"I saw it. It was pulling away from the front of the house as I was approaching home."

"What Impala?" Steve asked.

"Mom's been seeing a blue Impala circling the neighborhood this week."

"Could you see the driver?" he asked Sheila.

"Some young kid. It looked like there was a passenger with him," she added.

"Maybe you should report it to the police," Joan suggested.

Grandpa reached over and placed his hand over hers in a silent gesture.

"Do you think it's someone bad, Mom?" Maddie asked, her expression clouding with concern.

"I could shoot them with my rocket blaster," Caleb offered, pretending to be holding his toy and making popping sounds to mimic the shots.

"It's nothing for you to worry about, Madison," Steve said. "Probably just some kids that live in the neighborhood." Then turning toward Michelle and her mom, he added, "Let me know if you see it again."

After dinner, Michelle insisted on doing the dishes herself. "You've been a big help, Mom. But you should take a break and visit with Grandma and Grandpa."

"I can help you, Mom," Madison offered, stacking Caleb's plate with hers and heading into the kitchen.

"She's such a sweetheart," Joan observed.

"Yep. My little helper," Michelle agreed with a smile. Stacking the rest of the plates, she noticed her grandfather's plate still had quite a bit of food remaining.

"Did you get enough to eat?" she asked him.

"Yep. Thanks, sweetheart. It was delicious. My stomach's just been a little off this week."

As she picked up Steve's plate, she asked if anyone wanted coffee.

"I'll have a cup," Steve replied.

"Not for me," Grandpa said. Turning to Caleb he added, "I think I'd like to see that rocket blaster of yours."

"Cool! Can I be excused, Dad?" Caleb asked.

"Sure. You and Gramps have fun. I've got a little work to wrap up, then maybe I'll join you."

"How about you two?" Michelle asked her mother and grandmother.

"Coffee sounds good to me," Sheila replied. "Can I help you fix it?"

"No. The coffeemaker is loaded. I'll get it started and bring you a cup as soon as it's ready. How about you, Grandma?"

"I think I will have a cup, dear. Thanks."

"You've got it."

After Michelle left the room, Sheila turned to her mom. "So how are you and Dad doing?"

Joan hesitated then said, "I think we're fine, honey."

"What do mean, you think? Is something wrong?" Worries began to flood Sheila's mind.

"It's your father. I'm just a little concerned about him."

"Why? What's going on?"

Joan glanced away and shrugged. "He just doesn't seem himself."

"How, Mom?"

"I know it sounds silly, and I can't really put my finger on it, but he just seems a little off. Like more tired than normal. A couple of times, I've noticed he's lost his balance, too. And he's as thin as a rail. I can't seem to get him to eat much."

Now Sheila was really concerned. "Has he complained of any pain?"

"No. But he definitely isn't his usual spry self."

"Well he is almost 90, Mom. Maybe he's just slowing down a little," Sheila added, trying to convince herself as well as her mother. "He might have a bug of some kind that just won't let go."

"Maybe."

"Have you talked to him about it?"

"Yes. He even agreed to go see the doctor," Joan said. "And you know how he usually is about that."

"Yep. Stubborn like John used to be."

Joan nodded.

"So when's he going?"

"As soon as we get back to town." Joan looked into her eyes. "Now don't you go getting all worried about your father. I'm sure the doctor will probably just tell him to take some vitamins and get more sleep."

"Hope so, Mom. But you call me and let me know what they say." In spite of the words of encouragement, Sheila couldn't deny the concern on her mother's face.

CHAPTER SEVEN

Ben opened the door of the family van as Kelly reminded him of Caleb's gifts in the back. "Pop open the hatch, and I'll grab them," she said.

The younger kids were playfully challenging each other. "Beat you to the bounce house!" Logan said to Liam and Lily, one on each side of him in the third row of seating.

Luke pulled out the ear buds from his iPod and glanced over at Lucy, who was adjusting a bow in her long wavy hair. "Better get out of here before the stampede," he said.

Lucy nodded, grabbed her pink backpack, and followed him out.

"Wait a second, everyone," Kelly tried to interject over the boisterous voices from the back seat.

"Hey! Listen up!" Ben commanded from the open rear door. "Logan, stop. You're mom's trying to talk."

It quieted down and Kelly said, "OK, I know you guys are excited, but remember your manners in there. It's not going to be just us at this party. Madison and Caleb's grandmother and great grandparents will be there, too."

"Plus other friends from school," Logan added with a smile.

"Right. So don't go running in there like a bunch of wild Banshees," Kelly instructed. "And take a minute to greet people before you climb into the bounce house."

"Yes, Mom," a chorus of voices replied resolutely.

"Luke, you help your dad with the gifts," Kelly added. He nodded. "Okay."

Ben looked at him and winked. They retrieved the packages from the back and turned and saluted Kelly.

"Very funny," she said, giving Ben a playful glare.

Glancing over their eager family, he smiled and said, "Let's go!"

As they approached the house, the front door flew open and Caleb ran out. "Mom! They're here!" he called back toward her as he flew out the door.

Soon everyone was ushered inside. "Look at all those gifts," Michelle exclaimed. "One would have been plenty," she added with a smile.

"They each wanted to pick something out," Kelly explained.

"Yeah!" Logan interjected. "Mine's the best!"

"No, mine is," said Liam, pushing Logan from behind.

"Hey," Ben reached out and collared Liam. "No pushing. Everyone's gifts are great."

"Why don't you take your friends out back?" Michelle suggested to Caleb. She turned to Kelly and Ben, adding, "We've pretty much set up the entire party outside since the weather's so good."

As the group headed out back, the doorbell rang with more guests arriving. This time it was some of Caleb's friends from soccer. "Come on in, guys," Michelle said. "Everyone's out back."

"What time would you like me to pick them up?" asked the chauffeuring dad.

"Around 6:00," Michelle replied. As he turned and left, she grabbed Caleb's new red baseball cap off the floor and went to join the festivities. *Always has to be red for Caleb,* she thought with a smile. Red shirts, red caps, red high-top tennis shoes.

Most of the kids were in the bounce house jumping, throwing balls, and playing loudly together. Caleb declared himself king of the castle and began ordering his subjects around. Michelle glanced at Steve, and they both grinned. *Yep, that kid's a born leader*, Michelle thought to herself.

Madison and Luke were sitting backwards on the bench of the picnic table, leaning against the table's edge and listening to a song on Luke's iPod, each wearing one of the ear buds.

"They look cozy," Michelle said to Ben and Kelly.

"Yeah. I'm keeping an eye on them," Ben replied. "I think I liked it better when they were just two preschoolers running around our house playing super heroes."

"You don't think they're actually becoming interested in each other, do you?" Steve asked. "I mean, they've been friends forever."

"I don't know, Steve," Kelly interjected. "They just act so different around each other these days. First, they were pals, then they went through that awkward stage where they pretty much avoided each other, and now they seem inseparable when they're together."

"Wouldn't it be a kick if they actually dated some day?" Sheila observed from the sidelines.

"Don't even go there, Mom," Steve said to his mother-in-law. "Madison's got a lot of years before there'll be any dating in the picture for her."

Michelle, who was sitting beside him on the loveseat, reached over and squeezed his knee. "It'll be here before you know it."

"That's what I'm afraid of," he said with a sad smile.

"Well, I think they're very cute together," Sheila added before she walked away to get more punch.

Michelle was just about to suggest that Steve call in the pizza order, when the doorbell rang. "I wonder who that could be?" she said as she headed back inside to answer it.

ROSEMARY HINES

When she pulled open the door, a familiar face stopped her in her tracks.

"Amber..." she said, feeling the blood draining from her face. *What a time for Caleb's birth mother to show up.*

"Mrs. B," were the first words out of Amber's mouth—the name she'd called Michelle when she was a student in her class.

Instinctively, the mother within Michelle took over. Opening her arms, she pulled Amber into them. It was then that she noticed the blue Impala at the curb, and a young man in the driver's seat. Pulling back, she held Amber at arms' distance. "Let me look at you—you look good. Is everything okay? Who are you with?"

"I'm with my boyfriend, Chad," she said, gesturing with her head toward the car. "Is this a bad time? Because we can come back later."

"Well, it's kind of crazy around here today. It's Caleb's birthday party." Michelle let her hands drop to her sides, noticing Amber smile when she'd mentioned their son. "Are you here to see him?"

"Yeah. Well I wanted to see both of you. But yeah. Mostly Caleb. I think about him all the time."

Michelle nodded. Her heart was still pounding, but she tried to project a calm appearance. "How long have you been in town?"

"Just about a week. I tried to call you at school, but I kept chickening out. And we drove by here a bunch of times, but I couldn't get up the nerve to come to the door." Amber clutched her locked hands to her chest looking very vulnerable.

So that's what those phone calls were about, Michelle thought. Her mind was spinning with thoughts and questions. Did Amber want Caleb back? Would she tell him who she was? How would he react if she did?

"Are you mad at me for coming?" Amber asked, interrupting her thoughts.

64

Forcing herself back to the moment, Michelle replied, "Mad? No, of course not. I'm just surprised and a little concerned." She paused and then added, "Caleb doesn't know about you, Amber. He knows he's adopted, but that's all."

Amber looked away and nodded, seeming to be deep in thoughts of her own.

"Why don't you call me tomorrow," Michelle suggested. "Let me talk to Steve, and we'll see what we can work out." She could see the disappointment on her face. "We'll work out something. I promise."

"Okay." Amber glanced out to the car, and Michelle saw her boyfriend watching them.

"Where are you two staying?" she asked.

"We're staying with a friend of my mom's. Chad said we can stay for a few more days then he's got to get back to work."

"Okay. We'll figure out some way for you to see Caleb before you leave. Today's not good. We've got lots of people over."

"I understand. I'm just glad you're not mad at me," she replied.

"Amber, you gave me one of the best gifts I could have ever imagined. I'm not mad. Promise." Michelle hugged her again. "I'll talk to you tomorrow."

"Okay. Bye." Amber gave her a smile before turning to leave. As she was about to get into the car, she looked back and waved. Then she climbed in, and Michelle watched the Impala disappear around the corner.

"Michelle! Are you still in here?" Steve's voice came from the kitchen. "The kids are ready to eat."

"I'm coming," she called back. Taking a deep breath, she checked herself in the mirror near the entryway and said softly, "It'll be okay. Everything will be okay." Then she breathed a silent prayer and went into the kitchen.

"Who was at the door?" Steve asked as they began gathering up the plates and napkins to take outside.

"I'll tell you about it later. You called in the pizza order right?"

"Yep. They'll be here any minute."

Walking out to the backyard, Michelle spotted Caleb poking his head through the bounce house window, a giant grin lighting up his face. And suddenly she saw something she'd never noticed before. He had Amber's eyes.

"Time for bed, little man," Steve said to Caleb as they gathered his new toys to take upstairs.

"You promised to read me another chapter tonight," Caleb reminded him.

"You got it, bud. One more chapter." Steve replied, following him upstairs.

Michelle turned to say something to Madison, when she noticed her daughter had iPod wires coming from both ears. "Isn't that Luke's iPod?" she asked.

Madison pulled one ear bud out of her ear. "What?"

"I said, isn't that Luke's?"

"Yeah. He let me borrow it overnight. I'll give it back at church tomorrow."

"Want to help me finish up in the kitchen?" Michelle asked.

She shrugged. "Okay." Then she placed the ear bud back in her ear and followed Michelle into the kitchen.

They found Sheila and Joan sitting at the breakfast nook. "That was a great party, honey," Sheila offered.

"Thanks, Mom."

"We never had anything like those bounce houses back in my day," Joan commented. "The kids really had fun in there. And Caleb—he was king of the castle."

Michelle smiled. "That's my boy. Large and in charge."

"Well, I think I'll head upstairs and join your grandfather. It's been a long day."

"If you don't need my help, I think I'll get ready for bed, too," Sheila added with a stretch.

I love how Mom keeps an eye on Grandma without letting her know. "Sure, Mom. Go ahead. Maddie's offered to help me." She gestured toward Madison, who was half dancing to the music in her head as she rinsed some dishes in the sink.

"That girl is so full of energy," Joan observed.

"I think Luke had something to do with that," Sheila added, winking at Michelle.

"Stop, Mom."

Turning from the dishes, Madison asked, "Did someone say something about Luke?"

"It was nothing," Michelle replied, casting a stern look at her mother, who gently led Joan out of the room.

Steve was sitting on the couch feet stretched out under the coffee table and hands clasped behind his head. When he saw Michelle come into the room, he sat up and patted the seat next to him. "Come sit with me, Mrs. B."

Immediately, Amber's greeting from earlier that day flashed before her. *Guess now's the time to tell him,* she thought.

Snuggling close and pulling her feet up under her, she leaned into his chest and sighed.

"Big day, huh?" he said.

"Yeah. Bigger than you know."

Steve pulled back a little and looked into her eyes. "What's up? You seem like something's bothering you."

"It's Amber, Steve."

"Amber?" He looked puzzled. "Amber Gamble?"

"Yeah. She's in town."

"Whoa. How do you know?" he asked.

"She came by here today during the party. Remember when you asked who was at the door?"

"That was Amber?" He sat upright and raked his fingers through his hair. "What did she want?"

"What do you think? She wanted to see Caleb."

Steve looked at her intently. "What did you say?"

"I told her I had to talk to you first," she said, and then added, "That blue Impala we've been seeing around here—it belongs to her boyfriend. He brought her out."

"Did you meet him?"

"The boyfriend? No. But he was sitting in the car watching us."

Steve sighed and slumped back into the cushions. "How did she seem to you?"

"She seemed okay. A little nervous. She was afraid I'd be mad at her for coming."

"Mad?"

"Yeah. I guess because it might cause us some trouble or something."

"What did you tell her?"

"I told her I wasn't mad and that she gave us one of the best gifts ever when she gave us Caleb." Michelle's voice started to tremble.

"Hey, come here." Steve pulled her close and caressed her hair. "I'm not going to let Amber cause any problems with our family. She has no legal right to see Caleb. You know that."

"I know. But when I saw her standing there, I felt so bad for her. It was like she was my hurting student all over again."

"It's good that you care so much about people, Michelle. That's what makes you such a great teacher." He hesitated before adding, "But Amber left Sandy Cove a total wreck. I'm not about to let her jump into our lives without first knowing her current state of mind and what her motives are for seeing our son."

Michelle nodded. "You're right." She looked up into his eyes. "So what should we do when she calls tomorrow?"

"We'll set up a time and place to meet with her without Caleb. After we see how she's doing and figure out what she wants, we'll go from there."

"Okay." Michelle replied, relaxing a little.

"Church tomorrow. Let's go to bed."

"Good idea," she agreed. Taking his hand, she trailed him up the stairs.

CHAPTER EIGHT

"Good morning, princess. You're up early," Grandpa Phil observed when Michelle came into the kitchen the next morning.

"Still calling me princess, Grandpa?" She smiled as she poured a cup of coffee her grandfather had brewed.

"You'll always be my princess, honey." He placed a hand over hers as she joined him at the table. "Why the long face?"

"I didn't sleep well last night," she offered with a sigh.

"Something I can help with?"

Michelle gazed out the window to collect her thoughts then looked back at him. "Caleb's birth mother is back in town. She came by yesterday during the party."

"I see," he replied. "I take it she wants to see him."

"Yep. She's calling later today."

"And you don't want her to?"

"To see him?"

"Yeah."

She took a deep breath. "I don't know, Grandpa. What do you think we should do?"

He sat back in his chair and studied her face. After a few moments, he leaned forward and took Michelle's hand in both of his. "I think you know my answer. Even in the hard things, God's got a plan. This is another chance to trust Him with the outcome." He paused and then added,

"You can't blame a mother's heart for wanting to see her son."

Michelle nodded.

"You don't think she's come to try to take him back, do you?"

"I doubt it. She seemed more like a nervous school girl than a mother getting ready to battle for her son."

Grandpa smiled and patted her hand. "I know this is hard for you, sweetheart, but God has a way of working these things out. You've been straight with Caleb all along. He knows he is adopted, and he knows you and Steve love him like he was your own flesh and blood. You have each other, and you always will. But Amber's been going through this alone. Maybe seeing Caleb and witnessing for herself how well he's doing will give her some closure she didn't have when she left."

Michelle flashed back in her mind to the day in the NICU when Amber handed tiny Caleb over to her. As if it were yesterday, she could see her young student crumble into her mother's arms as Stacy and the social worker practically carried her from the unit.

Grandpa's voice interrupted her thoughts. "How old is Amber now?"

Michelle calculated in her mind. "Well, she was fourteen when he was born, so she's got to be twenty."

"Does she still live with her mother? They moved to Arizona, right?"

"Yeah. I really didn't think I'd ever see her again," she admitted. "We didn't talk about her mom, except that she's staying a with friend of hers. She came with her boyfriend. They were the ones driving the blue Impala."

"Ahhh. I see. So she's been trying to get up her nerve to come to the door."

"Yeah."

"What does Steve think?" he asked.

"He said we should meet with her first, just the two of us. Then we can decide about Caleb."

"And you think she'll be calling today?"

"Uh huh. I'm guessing sometime this afternoon. She knows we go to church every Sunday."

Grandpa nodded. "Okay, let me pray with you before the rest of the gang comes downstairs. Then I've got to get back up there and finish getting ready."

As he took one of her hands in both of his, she noticed a slight tremor in his grasp. But as he prayed his voice was strong and clear. Like water on parched soil, her spirit soaked in every word.

"Father, we know you've been watching over Amber these past six years. And for whatever reason, she's found her way back here. We are so thankful for little Caleb and for all he means to us. We know he wouldn't even be here if it weren't for Amber. Please give Michelle and Steve wisdom as they meet with her. Help them listen to the intent of her heart and lean on You for guidance as they consider her request. I pray that whatever comes of this, it will be an opportunity for Amber to get a glimpse of You, and for Michelle and Steve to be reminded of Your faithfulness. Go before them, God. Don't let fear be the rudder that steers their ship. In Jesus' name, amen."

"Amen," Michelle echoed. They stood and embraced each other. "What would I do without you, Gramps?"

Phil chuckled. "You make this old man feel very loved," he replied. "Now I'd better get ready for church. I'm eager to hear that young fella, Ben, preach today."

As he walked out of the room, Michelle noticed the shuffle in his gait. He turned and gave her a wink, adding, "Everything will be fine, princess. I'm sure of it."

The phone was ringing as they walked in the door after church. "I'll get it," Madison offered.

Michelle glanced at Steve. "Let Mom get it," he instructed. "You and Caleb go get the leftover pizza out of the fridge, and we'll heat it up for lunch."

Joan and Sheila headed upstairs to change clothes as Michelle grabbed the phone. "Hello?"

"Mrs. B.?"

"Amber?" From the corner of her eye, Michelle could see her grandfather give her a reassuring smile and a nod.

"Yeah. It's me. Is this a good time to call?" she asked.

"Sure. We just got home from church," Michelle replied.

"So, can I come over sometime today? I promise I won't stay long."

"Amber, Steve and I talked last night, and we think it would be better for the two of us to meet you somewhere else first so we can talk."

"Oh." Silence. "Okay, I guess that would be alright."

"Could your boyfriend drop you off at the Coffee Stop?" Michelle asked, looking at Steve who nodded in agreement.

"Uh, yeah. Hold on a sec."

Michelle could hear muffled voices, and then Amber was back. "Okay, he said that was fine. What time should I be there?"

"How about two o'clock?" Michelle suggested. "That will give us time to have lunch and get the kids settled for the afternoon with my mom."

"Okay. See you at two," Amber agreed.

"Mom, we need to talk," Michelle said, approaching Sheila who was sitting in the backyard after lunch.

"What is it, Mimi?"

"You remember Amber Gamble, right?" Michelle asked.

Sheila's face clouded. "Yes, I do. Why?"

"She's in town, and she wants to see Caleb. She actually came to the front door during his birthday party. It was her boyfriend's Impala that's been driving by. Steve and I are going to meet with her this afternoon at the Coffee Stop to talk about her seeing him."

"Oh, honey. I'm so sorry." Sheila's expression revealed her concern for her daughter.

"Don't worry, Mom," she replied. "Grandpa and I had a good talk about it this morning. He and Steve think everything will be okay."

Her mother didn't look convinced. "Will you let her see him?"

"Most likely, yes."

"You aren't going to tell him who she is, are you?" A shadow fell across her mother's countenance.

"Probably not. He's pretty young to process that."

"Yeah. That's right."

"So anyway, we need to leave here around quarter 'til two to go meet her. Are you okay with the kids while we're gone?"

"Of course. We'll be fine. They pretty much take care of themselves these days," she replied.

Michelle smiled. "Until they get into a scuffle over something."

"Don't worry. I'll be ready to referee if need be. Before you leave, maybe you could suggest some quiet activities for them to do while you're gone. I'm sure your grandparents will end up taking a siesta about that time."

"No problem. We'll give them explicit directions to keep the noise down," Michelle promised. "And Mom," she added.

"Yes?"

"Thanks. Thanks for all your help. It's been great having you here with us. I'm really glad you decided to settle in Sandy Cove."

Sheila patted her arm. "Me, too, honey."

CHAPTER NINE

As Steve and Michelle pulled into the parking lot of the Coffee Stop, they could see the blue Impala near the entrance. Michelle glanced at the clock on the dash. 1:55. "Wonder how long she's been here," she said.

"Well, we're not late. Let's just go in and get this over with," Steve suggested.

Amber and her boyfriend were sitting at a table in the corner. When she looked up, Michelle forced a smile and waved. The two stood and approached them.

"Mrs. B, this is Chad," Amber said, gesturing to her companion.

Michelle extended her hand, and Chad rubbed his on his jeans before grasping hers in a nervous handshake. "Nice to meet you," she said.

"Likewise," the young man replied.

"Chad, I'm Steve Baron, Michelle's husband." They exchanged handshakes before Steve turned to Amber. "Amber, we'd like to talk to you alone first, if that's okay with you."

"Sure. No problem," she replied.

"I'll just wait on the bench outside," Chad offered, reaching over and picking up his coffee.

After he'd left, Michelle and Amber sat down, and Steve went to get coffee for him and Michelle, offering a cup to Amber as well, who thanked him but declined.

"So how's your mom these days?" Michelle asked while she waited for Steve.

"She's doing okay. Better than before." Amber stared down at her hands, playing with a ring she was wearing on her left hand.

"Is that an engagement ring?"

Amber looked flustered. "Oh. No. We aren't engaged."

"I figured you two must be pretty serious for Chad to drive you all the way to Oregon," Michelle offered.

"Yeah. I guess you'd say that. We've been living together for a while."

Michelle tried not to wince. She'd really hoped the time Amber had spent with them at church had given her a new perspective on how to live her life. She just hoped Chad wasn't a repeat of Caleb's biological father, Adam.

As if reading her mind, Amber chimed in, "Chad's really a great guy, Mrs. B. He takes good care of me, and we get along really well. He says maybe we'll get married in a few years. When we're older and both have good jobs."

Before Michelle could go deeper into a discussion about Amber's living situation, Steve returned with the coffee.

"So tell us, Amber—what made you decide to come out here to see Caleb?" he asked.

She glanced over at Michelle, who added, "It's okay. We're not upset or anything. We just want to understand."

"Well, I guess there are several things," the girl began. "First, of course, I think about Caleb all the time, especially this time of year…" Her voice trailed off as she looked into space.

"His birthday," Michelle added.

"Yeah."

"And?" Steve asked.

"And, well…" She hesitated and looked at Michelle again.

"What is it, Amber?"

"I just found out I might not be able to have any more kids," she replied.

Michelle sat back in her chair, uncertain how to process that information.

Steve put his hand over hers. Then, turning to Amber, he asked, "Is that because of the condition you had when you were pregnant?"

She nodded. "Yeah. Placenta previa. The doctor said because of all the blood I lost, it affected my pituitary gland. So she says she's not sure if I'll be able to have any more kids."

"I'm so sorry, Amber," Michelle said. She slipped her hand out from under Steve's and grasped Amber's with both of her own.

Amber began to cry softly. She looked up toward the ceiling and sniffed, then rubbed the back of her free hand across her cheek to wipe away the tears.

"Here," Steve said, extending a napkin to her, glancing at Michelle with raised eyebrows.

She took it and began apologizing as she tried to regain her composure. "Sorry. I just get kind of upset when I think about it."

"No need to apologize," Steve said. "We've been there, Amber. It was a miracle that we were able to have Madison."

She nodded and blew her nose. "Yeah. I remember when the social worker told me about that. That's one of the reasons I wanted you guys to have Caleb. You deserve to be parents."

They sat silently for a few moments while Amber composed herself.

"So, anyway, that's why I need to see Caleb. He might be the only kid I'll ever have. I need to know he's okay." She looked up and asked, "Does that make sense?"

"Of course it does," Michelle replied, her heart going out to Amber. "But you've got to realize that Caleb isn't the same baby you saw before you left. He's a pretty big boy now."

"Yeah. I know. He's six, right?"

"Yep," Steve answered and then added, "He's a great kid, Amber. We feel very blessed to be his parents."

"So, you'll let me see him?" she asked.

"Yes, but we need to set a few ground rules," Steve replied, leveling his gaze on her.

She looked from him to Michelle and nodded.

"First, Caleb is too young to process the whole idea that you are his birth mother, Amber. We've explained adoption in very general terms, and he knows he's adopted," Steve said. "But he's too young to be confronted with the idea that you are his biological mother."

"Okay, so who will we say I am?" she asked.

"How about if we just tell him you are one of my former students," Michelle suggested. "It's possible Madison might remember you and your brother from the park visits we had when you two were in foster care."

"Oh yeah. She might. I sure remember her and her cute blond curls," Amber said with a smile.

"Well, that little six-year-old girl is now twelve," Michelle said.

"Wow. She's only two years younger than I was when I had Caleb."

"Pretty mind-boggling, isn't it?" Michelle shuddered to think of Madison going through what Amber had experienced at fourteen.

"Yeah," Amber agreed. "She doesn't know I'm his mom, right? I mean… you know what I mean."

"His birth mom? No. We never specifically told her that. It's hard to say what she may have overheard, but she was pretty young," Michelle said.

"She probably wondered why I got so big."

"Maybe. But you did a pretty good job of hiding it," Michelle replied.

"Yeah. I tried."

"So anyway, how about if we meet at the same park where we used to go when you lived with Mrs. Harte?" Michelle suggested.

"Okay," Amber replied.

Michelle glanced at Steve, who nodded. "That sounds good. I can tell Caleb we're going to try out his new catcher's mitt, and that you happen to be meeting a former student who's in town for a visit."

"Anything else I should know?" Amber asked. "I mean like other rules."

"Yeah," Steve replied. "Just keep things casual with him. No asking a bunch of questions, just regular conversation, and no trying to make plans to see or talk with him again. It's fine to interact, just remember that he'll be thinking you are there to see Michelle."

"Got it." She turned to Michelle and asked, "Do you have any pictures of him with you?"

"As a matter of fact, I do," she said, pulling out her cell phone. She opened the photo app and scrolled to a close up of his face with a wide grin as he prepared to blow out the candles on his birthday cake.

Amber was mesmerized. She stared long and hard at the picture.

"He's got your eyes," Michelle said.

She looked closer. "Really?"

"Really."

"He's so cute," Amber added.

"Yeah. He is pretty adorable," Michelle agreed.

Amber leaned over and hugged her. "Thanks for saying 'yes' Mrs. B." Then she looked at Steve. "I promise I won't do or say anything to upset or confuse him."

"Okay, well we can go get him and meet you at the park," he said.

"Right now?" Amber seemed surprised.

"Sure. Might as well. I'll be busy at work all week, so if you're only here for a few days, today's the day to do this."

Although his words were upbeat, Michelle could see the concern on his face. "I'll call Mom and let her know, so she can have him ready."

Amber stood up. "Chad and I will head over there." She looked very nervous but happy.

"Okay, we'll see you in about twenty minutes," Steve said.

As soon as she was gone, he turned to Michelle. "I hope we're doing the right thing," he said.

Me, too, she replied in the recesses of her mind.

"So how did it go?" Chad asked as Amber got into the car.

"Good. I'm meeting them at the park in twenty minutes." She unzipped her backpack and pulled out a brush. "It's the park we passed on the way over."

"Okay." He started the car and pulled out of the lot.

Amber pulled down the visor and flipped open the mirror. She fingered her bangs and then applied some tinted lip-gloss. Turning to Chad she asked, "How do I look?"

He glanced over at her. "Fine."

"Just fine?" She could feel herself getting jumpy. "I think I need a hit," she said, wishing she had a joint with her.

"Amber, you look great, okay? And you told me you were cutting back on that stuff."

"I am. I just need a little hit to calm my nerves. Look at my hands," she said, stretching them out in front of her.

"Whatever," he replied. "I don't think it's a good idea to show up smelling like weed."

"Yeah. You're probably right." Amber reached over and turned on the radio. She slouched into her seat, tapping her hands to the beat of the music. As they pulled up to the curb by the park, a flood of memories washed over her. Memories of living in foster care, separated from her brother Jack. Memories of Mrs. B offering to supervise her and her brother at the park so they could spend more time together. Memories of her social worker, Bonnie Blackwell, who brought Jack to the park every time.

And then memories of her pregnancy, Adam's refusal to help her, and the way Mrs. B had agreed to adopt Caleb.

Now she knew he might be the only child she would ever have.

She could still feel his tiny body pressed to her chest the day she gave him up. And the way his little mouth opened like a bird's as he gazed into her eyes with such trust.

Had she made a mistake? Was it wrong to give him up? Maybe he'd think she didn't love him. That she only cared about herself and her own life.

"What's the big sigh about?" Chad asked.

"Just nervous, I guess," she replied, refusing to allow him into her secret world of doubts.

"Well, it'll be over soon," he said. "Then we can get on the road and get back home."

She nodded, but in her heart she wondered if she'd be able to pull herself away from Sandy Cove and her son ever again.

"Hey there, champ. What are you doing?" Steve asked as he sat down beside Caleb on the back step.

"Nothin'," the boy replied seeming a little let down after his big day. "Can we go to the beach?"

"Well actually, I was thinking the park. Your mom is meeting one of her old students there. She's in town for a few days."

"Okay," Caleb said with a smile.

"Why don't you go get that new catcher's mitt, and we'll throw a few balls while we're there."

"Cool! I'll be right back." Caleb stood and ran into the house.

Please let this go well, Steve prayed silently. He stood and went inside, almost bumping into Madison on her way into the kitchen.

"Where did you and Mom go?" she asked.

"Just out for coffee. We're heading out again in a few minutes. Mom's going to meet up with one of her old students. They're meeting at the park, so I thought I'd take Caleb and throw the ball with him."

"Oh. Cool."

"What are your plans for the rest of the afternoon?" he asked.

"Don't know. Luke might come over for a while," she said nonchalantly. "We might go for a walk or something."

"You should spend some time with your great grandparents. They're leaving day after tomorrow, you know."

"Yeah. I wish they could stay longer," she said, helping herself to an apple from the refrigerator.

"I think Grandpa Phil's got a doctor's appointment later this week," he said.

"Do you think he's okay, Dad? He seems a little tired to me," she observed. She leaned back against the counter and took a bite of the apple.

Something about the way she stood there, leaning back and expressing her concern for Phil — it dawned on Steve just how much she was growing up. In another six months she'd be a teenager. How could that be possible?

"Dad?"

"Yeah?"

"I said, 'Do you think Grandpa's okay?'"

He nodded and smiled. "I think he's fine, honey. He's just getting up there in age."

"Yeah." Then she added, "I miss Grandpa John." Her eyes told him just how much.

"Me, too," Steve said, pulling her into a hug. He kissed the top of her head. "We'll see him again one day."

Madison nodded, but the grieving process was still apparent.

"What are you two talking about so seriously," Michelle asked as she walked into the kitchen. Her eyes looked into Steve's with a clear question. *This isn't about Amber, is it?*

"We were just talking about Grandpa John and how much we both miss him," he replied, watching her expression change from worry to understanding.

"Your grandfather really loved you, Maddie. I think you and Caleb gave him more years than he otherwise would have had," she said.

Madison smiled through her teary eyes.

"We'd better get going," Steve said to Michelle. "Caleb went upstairs to get his mitt."

"Okay. I'll just tell Mom where we'll be," she replied. "Are you going to stick around here?" she asked their daughter.

"Yeah. I was thinking of doing something with Luke, but Dad suggested I spend some time with Gram and Gramps before they leave. So I guess I'll just read until they wake up from their nap."

"Good idea," Michelle said.

Caleb bounded into the room. "I'm ready!" He had his new baseball cap on and his mitt and ball in hand.

"We'll be in the car," Steve said to Michelle.

"Okay. Be there in a sec," she replied as she went to find Sheila.

ROSEMARY HINES

CHAPTER TEN

Amber's eyes were fixed on the road as she sat on the park bench with Chad. "They should be here."

"Want me to go wait in the car when they get here?" he asked.

"Yeah. That's probably a good idea."

They sat silently for a few minutes. Then pulling her cell phone out of her pocket, she checked the time. "It's been almost thirty minutes. I hope they didn't change their minds." She stood up and looked around.

"I'm sure they'll be here any minute," he said. "Sit down. You're making me nervous."

Just then, Amber spotted the car pulling up to the curb. Mrs. B was in the front passenger seat. "That's them," she said, starting to walk toward the street.

Chad followed her, then split off and headed for his own car. "I'll be waiting in the car," she heard him say over his shoulder.

As Amber approached the car, she spotted Caleb getting out on the other side with his dad holding the door. Michelle greeted her with a hug, looking almost as nervous as she felt herself.

"Let's go sit on the bench," Michelle said.

"Okay." As they walked from the car, Amber watched Steve and Caleb fan out on the grass to throw the ball to each other. Caleb looked so big — so old. He reminded her a lot of her little brother when he was that age. Wavy chestnut hair and a slight build. But full of energy and the cutest smile. "He looks like Jack."

Michelle nodded. "Yeah. He kind of does," she agreed with a smile.

"I'm glad he doesn't look like Adam."

They walked over to the bench and sat in the warm sun. "It's a nice day for the park," Michelle said, gazing up into the blue sky.

"Yeah. We're lucky it's not raining."

Michelle looked at her and smiled. "Guess you don't get that much rain in Arizona, do you?"

"Not like Sandy Cove. That's for sure," Amber replied.

There was an awkward silence for a few moments as they both watched Caleb and Steve. "Do you think I could throw the ball with him?" Amber asked, fixing her focus on her son.

"Yeah. I guess that would be okay," Michelle said. She stood up and called out, "Hey, guys—come over here for a minute."

Amber watched as Caleb jogged over to his dad and the two of them approached.

"Yeah, Mom?" the little boy asked.

Mom. The word pierced Amber's heart. Knowing he was her own flesh and blood, that she'd given him life—it was almost more than she could bear to hear him call someone else his mom.

Michelle's voice brought her back to the moment. "Caleb, this is a friend of mine. She used to be one of my students at Magnolia."

Caleb looked Amber in the eye. "Hey," he said with a smile.

"Hey," she replied, her heart falling in love with his grin and boyish freckles. "My name's Amber."

"I'm Caleb," he said. "I just had a birthday."

"I know," she replied.

"You do?" he looked surprised.

Amber saw Michelle's eyebrows go up and quickly replied, "Yeah, your mom was telling me."

"Oh. See my new mitt?"

"That's pretty cool. Think I could throw the ball with you for a while?" she asked.

Caleb glanced up at his father, and Steve nodded. "Okay. Sure." He handed her the ball. "Let's go over where there's more room." He pointed to the open section of the park they'd just come from.

Amber turned to Michelle and Steve for approval. Michelle's nod was all she needed.

"Come on," Caleb said grabbing her hand and leading her off.

While their son led Amber to the open space, Michelle watched Steve nervously. He was focused intently on Caleb as he showed Amber where to stand. "What do you think?" Michelle asked, tipping her head toward their son.

He put his arm over her shoulder. "I don't know. We'll keep an eye on them."

They sat together on the bench, neither talking as they took in the scene of Amber interacting with their son. At first she looked pretty awkward out there. Her throws were either too short or off to the side. Caleb moved a little closer and punched the center of his mitt, then turned it toward her as a target. Eventually she started sending him some throws he could catch. His smile indicated his delight.

Michelle started to relax a little as she realized the two of them were not really talking much. Just tossing the ball back and forth and laughing when Amber fumbled it.

"When does she leave?" Steve asked.

89

"I think in a few days," she replied. "Her boyfriend has to get back to work."

"Right. That's good."

"Watching them play reminds me of when I used to bring Maddie here and supervise Amber's visits with her brother. Before you two walked over here, she was telling me that Caleb reminds her of Jack."

"Really?" Steve asked.

"Yeah. I can see the resemblance. They have the same hair and build." She paused and took a moment to examine their son from a distance. "Of course, Jack was older than this when I met him. But I can see how she would say that. He probably looked a lot like Caleb at his age."

"Do you think she's pretty serious about this Chad guy?" Steve asked.

"Seems to be, although I don't like that they're living together when they're not married."

"Yeah. Hope she doesn't end up in the same situation as she did with that other guy."

"It sounds like it may not even be possible for her to get pregnant again," Michelle said.

"That's what she told us. But I wonder if it's true or just another way to convince us to let her see Caleb."

"I doubt she'd lie about something like that," Michelle said. But as she thought back to all the challenges she'd faced with Amber as her student, she knew it was possible. Amber had been a handful. What a year. Her first experience as a full-time teacher, Madison starting kindergarten, and then all the drama with this girl. She could still remember the day Amber told her she was pregnant. Fourteen and having a baby. Michelle shuddered.

"Are you cold?" Steve asked, pulling her close.

"No. Just thinking about when Amber told me she was pregnant. I never would have imagined things would turn out this way."

"That's for sure," he replied. "Look," he added, turning his focus to where they'd been throwing the ball.

They both sat forward a little as they noticed Amber walking over to Caleb. She put her hand on his shoulder, and the two of them started heading toward the play equipment.

"Where are they going?" Steve asked, rising to his feet.

"Looks like they're going over to the swings and climbing fort," she said, standing beside him. "Maybe we'd better go over there."

"Definitely."

When they got within earshot, they could hear Caleb say, "Really? Can I meet him?"

"Maybe someday," Amber replied. "I know he'd like that."

Their son spotted them and said, "Hey Mom, Amber says I look just like her brother. He's a baseball player, too."

"Really?" Michelle replied, trying to sound casually curious.

"Yeah. She said I could meet him."

Amber quickly interjected, "I said, maybe you could meet him someday."

"Yeah. Whatever," he responded. Then turning to Steve, he said, "Can Amber and her boyfriend come over for dinner? They could play my new baseball video game."

"That's not a good idea, Caleb," he replied. "We've still got Gram and Gramps here."

"Oh yeah. Well maybe after they leave," the boy suggested.

"I think Amber will be going back to Arizona by then," Steve said, shooting a warning glance Amber's way.

"Another time," she said. Then she looked at them and asked, "Is it okay if we go on the equipment for a few minutes?"

Michelle's heart was screaming no, but she didn't want to raise any flags in Caleb's eyes. She looked at Steve. "Maybe ten more minutes?"

He took a deep breath and gave Amber another warning glance. "Ten minutes and then we've got to get going."

Michelle backed him up. She bent down to Caleb's level and said, "We've got to get home soon, so I can fix dinner for everyone."

"Okay," the little boy replied, sounding disappointed. He grabbed Amber's hand. "Come on," he said as he led her to the ladder. Up they climbed into the fort, where Michelle could hear him giving her instructions about how to cross the suspension bridge and slide down the curvy tube at the end.

"Maybe he'll be a teacher someday," Steve observed, nudging Michelle with his elbow.

"You think?"

"He sure likes telling people what to do." He looked at her and winked.

"He likes to argue, too," she said. "Maybe he'll be an attorney."

"Touché," Steve replied.

Michelle noticed it had gotten pretty quiet over on the equipment. She saw Amber and Caleb sitting in the fort talking. "What do you think?" she asked, gesturing with her head.

"I'd better go over there."

"Good idea," she replied.

She watched Steve walk over to the equipment. Amber stood as soon as she noticed him coming. "Time to go?" she asked.

"Yep," he replied.

"Bummer," Caleb said.

Amber reached over and started tickling him, and he burst into giggles. "Got you!" she said, then headed across the bridge and down the slide with Caleb close on her heals. They both landed in a heap at the bottom of the curvy tube, Caleb laughing as Amber stood and dusted the sand off her clothes and hair.

"You're pretty fun for a girl," he said.

Amber grinned. "You're not so bad yourself."

"Are you sure you have to go back to Arizona?"

"Pretty sure. But don't worry. I'll be back. Maybe I'll bring Jack with me."

"Cool!" Caleb exclaimed. "Be sure to tell him we look alike."

"Oh, I will. Don't worry," she promised. Then she turned to Steve and Michelle. "Thanks for letting us hang out."

"Sure. I'm glad you two had a good time," Michelle said, hoping the sound of her voice matched her words.

"Well, we'd better get going, sport," Steve said to Caleb as he placed his hand on the boy's shoulder.

Caleb broke free and gave Amber a hug. She looked at Michelle with a surprised expression, and then squatted down at eye level with their son. "See you soon, kid." Then she stood back up and said to Michelle, "I'll call you."

Michelle just nodded. The three of them watched her head toward Chad's car. As she climbed in, she looked back at them and waved.

"Bye!" Caleb shouted, returning her wave enthusiastically.

As they were driving home, Caleb announced, "I really like Amber. She's nice."

Michelle turned and looked at him. "Yes, she is. She likes you, too."

"How do you know?" he asked.

"I can just tell."

"Mom?"

"Yes?"

"Did you know that Amber had a baby? She gave it up for adoption. I told her I'm adopted, too."

Michelle's heart froze in her chest.

Steve put his hand on her leg. "What else did she tell you, son?" he asked over his shoulder.

"Just that she hopes we can be friends."

"Amber lives pretty far away from here, Caleb," Michelle said, trying to steady her voice.

"I know. But she said maybe she'd move back to Sandy Cove sometime," he replied. "Wouldn't that be cool, Mom?"

Michelle took a deep breath. "Sure." She looked over at Steve. He shot her an expression that communicated his troubled thoughts.

"Okay?" Chad asked as they pulled away from the curb.

"More than okay," Amber replied, looking over her shoulder to wave one more time to her son. Turning to face Chad she asked, "Isn't he cute?"

"I guess. All kids are cute, aren't they?" he replied, eyes fixed on the road.

Amber playfully slugged him in the arm.

"Ouch! What was that for?" His tone told her he wasn't in the mood to play along.

His sharp tone surprised Amber, and her joy began to evaporate. "Can't you just be happy for me?"

"Who says I'm not happy?"

"Your tone of voice for one thing," she replied.

"Hey, I'm sorry if I'm not getting all into this with you, Amber. I've tried to be understanding, but it seems like all I've been doing is sitting around waiting for you. Caleb looks like a good kid, and I think he's doing fine with the Barons. But I'm getting a little worried about you."

"Why?"

"Because the further we take this, the more attached you seem to be getting." He turned and looked at her for a moment. "Hey, I'm ready to go home. You saw him, and he's fine. It's over. Okay?"

"Whatever." Amber turned away to look out her window her vision blurring as her eyes filled with tears.

"Don't 'whatever' me," Chad persisted, reaching over and pulling on her arm.

And in that instant, neither of them saw the car barreling through the intersection right toward his door.

CHAPTER ELEVEN

Skidding tires. A sudden jarring impact threw Amber into her door, her head banging the window. Crunching metal and the sound of breaking glass as the car spun around.

Oh God. What's happening?? Amber's hand grabbed the dash to steady herself.

Then nothing.

She looked over at Chad. His head was resting on the steering wheel, his window shattered and his door folded inward.

"Chad? CHAD?" She reached for him, but was interrupted by a pounding on her window.

"Are you okay?" a voice called through the glass.

She turned and saw a boy who looked to be about sixteen. He was peering in at her with a panicky expression.

"My boyfriend! Help my boyfriend!" she shouted. Then turning to Chad, she called his name again.

The boy had come around to Chad's side of the car and was trying to open the door, but it wouldn't budge. He came back around to her side and pulled her door open. She tried to slide across the seat toward Chad, but something was holding her. *Seat belt!* She quickly released the buckle and was instantly beside him.

Grabbing his shoulder, she shook him. "Chad? Chad, answer me!" But he didn't move. She turned to the boy, "Call 9-1-1!"

He nodded and grabbed his phone from his pocket. As he talked to the dispatcher and gave a location for the accident, Amber tried to move Chad into an upright position, but his body was like lead. "Oh God! Chad—answer me!"

His lifeless body remained draped over the steering wheel.

"The paramedics are on the way," the boy said. Gesturing to Chad, he asked, "Is he breathing?"

"I can't tell." *He has to be breathing. Oh God, what is happening?* She leaned close and put her hand on his back. She couldn't feel any movement at all.

"CHAD! BREATHE!" she screamed.

The shrill of a siren pierced her ears and then stopped. A fire truck and ambulance deposited rescuers, who rushed to both cars. As one firefighter opened her door, another tried Chad's. "Bring the jaws!" he called out.

"Are you okay?" the uniformed man asked her.

"I think so. Help my boyfriend. I can't tell if he's breathing."

"Let's get you out of here," he said, extending her his hand.

She took it and slid out the door. Immediately a paramedic took her place on the passenger seat as the other firefighters began cutting through the driver's door. Amber was shaking so hard she could barely stand.

The paramedic wrapped an arm around her and helped her to the curb. She could see the other car and a swarm of rescuers surrounding it as well. The boy stood off to the side, his bicycle lying on the grass along the sidewalk.

Amber watched the crew extract Chad from the car and place him on a gurney, quickly wheeling him to the back of the ambulance. She tried to stand up to run after him, but the paramedic stopped her. "They'll take care of him. We can get you to the hospital soon." He was taking her pulse and checking her eyes. "Anything hurt?" he asked.

"Just my head and my arm," she replied as she rubbed her right arm at the elbow.

He did a cursory exam and had her bend and flex it. "I don't think anything's broken. Probably just badly bruised. But I'm sure they'll want to x-ray it when we take you in. Do you feel lightheaded or nauseated?"

She shook her head. "Just really shaky and cold." Turning, she watched the ambulance pull away and another take it's place. Then she saw the rescuers help an elderly man out of the driver's side of the other car. They lifted him onto another gurney. But at least he was conscious, and they had him sitting up in a propped position as they rolled him to the ambulance.

Someone put a blanket over her shoulders and she pulled it tight, fighting to stop the earthquake within. Another hand extended a water bottle to her, but she refused it.

"Hang in there," the paramedic said. "We're waiting for a third ambulance to transport you to the hospital."

She nodded.

"Is there someone I can call?" he asked.

Amber thought about giving him Michelle's number, but instead she just said no.

The boy with the bike stood there watching her. "How are you doing?" he asked.

"Okay, I guess," she replied. "Hey, thanks for helping."

"No problem. Hope your boyfriend's okay," he added.

"Me, too."

"Want me to hang here with you until they take you to the hospital?"

She glanced over at the paramedic, who was now standing a little way off, talking to one of the firefighters.

"Sure," she said. "Thanks."

"You got it," he replied. "Name's Chris."

"Amber," she said.

"Nice name."

"You go to Sandy Cove High?" she asked, feeling her body beginning to relax a little.

"Yeah. One more year to go. How about you?"

"I graduated a couple of years ago from a high school in Arizona. I went to Magnolia, though."

"Really? Me, too."

"Did you have Mrs. Baron for English?" Amber asked.

"Mrs. B. Yeah. Cool class. We voted her teacher of the year," he added.

"Wow, that's great."

"You had her?"

"Her first year."

"Small world."

"Yep."

The paramedic walked back over to her. "Okay, we have a coach for you now," he said, pointing to an ambulance that was pulling up. He reached out his hand and helped her stand. "Do you think you can walk?"

"Yeah."

"Okay. Just lean on me as much as you need." He wrapped his arm around her and supported her as they started toward the ambulance.

Amber looked back at Chris. "Hey, thanks again," she said.

He nodded, hopped onto his bike, and rode away.

Michelle was just getting ready to fix dinner when her cell phone rang. She looked at the number, but it didn't look familiar. "Hello?"

"Michelle?" a frantic sounding female asked.

"This is Michelle."

"It's Amber's mom, Stacy."

"Stacy, are you okay?" Michelle asked, concern rising in her spirit.

"Amber's been in an accident. She's at the hospital."

"What? We were just with her a little while ago. What happened?"

Steve walked into the kitchen and Michelle threw him a worried look.

"She and Chad were broadsided by some guy. Amber said Chad was really badly hurt. They rushed him to the hospital and she just got there, too."

Steve caught Michelle's eye and whispered, "What?"

She covered the phone with her hand. "Amber and her boyfriend were in an accident. They're at the hospital." Turning her attention back to Stacy, she said, "We'll head over there. How did Amber sound?"

"She sounded a little shaky, but she said she's not hurt. She's really worried about Chad, though. Nobody will tell her what's going on. I tried to call Chad's mom, but she's not picking up."

"Okay. We'll go over right now. I'll call you as soon as I know anything," Michelle promised.

"Thank you so much. I'll be waiting for your call."

Michelle tucked her cell phone in her purse. "We need to go to the hospital."

"Okay," Steve replied, grabbing the keys from the counter.

Michelle hurried out to the living room where her mother and grandparents were watching the news. "Amber's been in an accident. She's okay, but we need to get over to the hospital. I'm sorry to leave you guys like this again."

Sheila stood. "Don't apologize, honey. Just go. We'll be fine. Grandma and I will wrestle up some dinner for the kids."

"Thanks, Mom." Michelle gave her a quick hug.

"We'll be praying," Grandpa Phil said. "If you need us, just call."

Michelle and Steve went up to the admitting desk of the hospital ER and were taken back to a curtained off examining room where Amber was sitting on a bed. She immediately stood and walked into Michelle's open arms protecting her right side as she held her hand to her chest. After they embraced, Michelle asked, "Have you heard anything about Chad?"

"No. They won't tell me anything. I gave them his mom's cell phone number, but they won't tell me how he is." She was clearly beside herself with worry.

"You're okay, though, right?" Michelle asked.

"Yeah. They took some x-rays of my arm just in case. But the doctor said she thinks it's just bruised. Can you see if you can find out what's taking so long with Chad? I really want to see him."

Steve nodded. "I'll go ask at the nurses' station."

Michelle and Amber sat down to wait. A moment later, a doctor pulled the curtain back and entered. She looked at Michelle and extended her hand. "I'm Dr. Crawford."

"Michelle Baron," Michelle replied, grasping the doctor's hand in hers.

Dr. Crawford flipped open the chart in her hand. "You are a very lucky young lady," she said to Amber. "Looks like there are no broken bones, but that arm's going to be pretty tender for a few days. How's your head feeling? Headache gone yet?"

Amber nodded. "It seems better."

"No dizziness or nausea?"

"No. I'm fine. Can I see Chad now?" she asked.

Dr. Crawford glanced at Michelle and then back to Amber. "Chad took the full impact of the collision. We're trying to reach his next of kin right now. I'll let you know more in a little bit." The doctor turned back to Michelle. "Good to meet you," she said.

"Thanks. You, too," Michelle replied.

Dr. Crawford's face said it all. Chad was not okay. How was Amber going to handle all this when she was so far from home? *Maybe I should offer to let her stay with us until her mother can get out here. But where will she sleep?* She tried to picture Amber sleeping on their couch. Her grandparents would be flying home in a couple of days, but until then there was really no other place for her to sleep. Unless one of the kids gave up a bed. Maybe she could have Caleb stay at Ben and Kelly's for a couple of nights.

She was about to ask Amber about going home with them, when Steve walked into the examining cubicle, another doctor on his heels. Steve's face was ashen, and Michelle knew a nightmare was about to unfold.

"My name is Dr. Spindler. I'm here to talk to you about Chad."

Amber looked up hopefully. "Is he okay? When can I see him?"

The doctor took a deep breath and sat down beside her. "I'm afraid your friend didn't make it," he said. "We did everything we could, but the trauma to his head created a massive subdural hematoma—a brain bleed."

Amber just stared at him shaking her head back and forth as if her agreement was necessary for it to be true. "No. He's going to be okay. He can't die—he's only 23. You've got to take me to him," she said as she stood up.

Dr. Spindler rose to his feet. "I'll leave you three alone for a bit," he said, directing his comment to Steve. "If it's any consolation, he didn't suffer. From what the paramedics reported, I doubt he even knew what hit him."

"Thank you, Doctor," Steve said.

Amber burst into tears, and Michelle embraced her, careful not to squeeze her right side. "Let's sit down," she said softly as she led the girl back to the bed.

Amber sunk down and rocked back and forth, cradling her right arm to her chest. "He can't be gone. He can't be," she sobbed.

Michelle's arm remained draped over Amber's shoulder. With her free hand, she gently pulled Amber's head onto her shoulder and said softly, "It's going to be okay. Everything's going to be okay." But in her heart she wondered if things would ever be okay for Amber again. Her mind searched for answers. *Why God? Hasn't she already been through enough?*

As she glanced up to Steve, he said, "I think I'll go get your grandfather."

Michelle nodded. "Good idea," she whispered in return.

CHAPTER TWELVE

By the time Steve returned with Grandpa Phil, Michelle had convinced Amber to have something to eat, and she was nibbling on a sandwich as they sat together in the cafeteria.

"Steve," Michelle called out when she spotted the two men looking around the expansive eating area.

He glanced over and nodded, then pointed them out to Phil.

Michelle watched them weave between the tables, noticing her grandfather reaching out to several tables along the way as if to keep his balance.

"Mind if I sit here?" Grandpa asked Amber, gesturing to the seat beside her.

She nodded her consent, and he eased himself down. Steve took the chair beside Michelle.

"Amber, we thought it might help if you talked to my grandfather," Michelle began. "He really helped me when my dad was in the hospital."

Amber just stared at the floor.

Phil made eye contact with Michelle and tipped his head toward the door. Michelle nodded. "Steve and I are going to find out if they've reached Chad's parents," she said, placing her hand on Amber's shoulder.

Amber looked up for a moment. "Okay," she said softly. Then she returned her gaze to the linoleum at her feet.

When they returned fifteen minutes later, Phil was sitting alone.

"Where's Amber?" Michelle asked.

"She went to the ladies' room," he replied. "That girl's got a load of hurt in her heart. It's going to take a long time for her to process this loss."

Michelle sat down beside him. "Were you able to talk to her?" she asked.

"A little. But Amber's in a frame of mind where she has to process her anger toward God first, before she can begin to understand how much He loves her. From her perspective, He's never been on her side, watching out for her needs. She blames Him for her mother's breakdown, her time in foster care, getting pregnant with Caleb and having to give him up, and now this."

"I hope she can come to see things differently," Michelle replied. "Most of what has happened in her life was the result of poor choices made by her parents and by Amber herself. It would really help if she could lean hard on God right now."

He reached out and took her hand. "In time, sweetheart. But we have to give Amber the space she needs to process everything. At this point, we need to put her into God's hands and trust Him to reach her deepest needs."

"So what do we do?" she asked.

"We pray. We listen and love her right where she is with all her anger and confusion. God will do the rest." Patting Michelle's hand as he released it, he pushed to a standing position. "I think this old fellow had better find a restroom, too."

"I'll show you the way," Steve offered. Turning to Michelle, he added, "Maybe we'd better plan on taking Amber home with us tonight."

"I agree," she replied. "I'll wait here."

When Amber returned a few minutes later, Michelle told her they wanted her to come home with them for the night. Amber nodded. She looked so forlorn and lost. Reaching out, Michelle drew her into her arms and held her close as they both cried over a life cut short far too soon.

Ben's car was in the driveway as they pulled in. "I called him to come pick up Caleb for the night," Steve explained. "Amber can sleep in his room."

"Thanks, honey," Michelle replied softly. Amber clung to her as they walked toward the house.

As Steve opened the front door, they met Ben and Caleb about to leave. Caleb had a backpack slung over his shoulder and a child's sleeping bag tucked under his arm. He looked worried when he saw Amber. "Are you okay?" he asked in a sweet voice.

She looked at him and tried to smile through her tears. "I'll be fine. Have fun at your friends' house."

"Did you get your toothbrush?" Michelle asked him.

"Yep. I got it, Mom." He patted the outer pocket of the pack.

"I'll walk out with you guys," Steve offered.

Michelle squatted down to eye level with Caleb. "Give me a hug, tiger," she said.

The little boy threw his arms around her neck and squeezed tight. Then he pulled back. "See you tomorrow!" he said with a smile. Taking his father's hand, they headed out to the car.

"Bye," Grandpa Phil called after them.

"Bye, Gramps!" Caleb replied, turning to look over his shoulder at them.

Closing the door, Michelle looked at Amber. "Are you hungry? I can fix you something."

She shrugged. "Not really."

"Why don't you try to eat something," Grandpa suggested. "There's some birthday cake left."

Michelle looked at him and caught his knowing wink.

Amber sighed. "Okay. I guess."

"I'll serve some up for both of you," Sheila suggested from the living room. She stood and walked to the kitchen, trailed by Grandpa Phil and Amber.

"Make that three, Mom," Michelle called after her.

Just then Madison's voice came from upstairs. "Mom? Is that you?"

"Down here," Michelle replied.

She could hear the sound of Madison's feet as she headed for the stairs. A moment later their daughter joined her in the living room. "I changed the sheets on Caleb's bed," she said. "It's all ready for Amber. Dad told me she's staying for the night."

"Thanks, honey. I really appreciate that."

"Is she okay, Mom? What happened to her boyfriend?"

"Dad didn't explain any of that to you?"

"No. He just said they were in an accident, and you would tell me about it when you got home. He said Caleb was going over to Ben and Kelly's, and Amber was spending the night here."

As Michelle was about to explain, Steve walked back in the door. "Ben said they can keep Caleb as long as we need them to," he told Michelle. Then turning to Madison, he asked, "Did you get the room ready for Amber?"

"Yeah. It's all set, Dad. Mom was just going to tell me about her boyfriend. Is he going to be okay?"

"Let's go up to your room and talk," Steve said. He glanced over at Michelle, and she nodded.

"Sure, Dad," Madison replied, a worried look on her face.

As the two of them walked upstairs, Michelle said a silent prayer. *Give him the words to say, God. Help him explain this to Maddie in a way she can handle.* Then she went to join Amber and her grandfather in the kitchen.

After Amber was finally settled into Caleb's bed for the night, Michelle retrieved her cell phone from her purse and sat down on the couch to call Amber's mom. The last time she'd seen Stacy was at the hospital the day they took Caleb home from the NICU.

Shrugging off the image, she punched Stacy's number into her phone.

She answered immediately. "Hello?"

"Stacy?"

"Yes. Who is this?"

"Stacy, it's Michelle Baron."

"Is Amber okay? I've been worried sick."

"We brought her home with us. She's staying here tonight."

"What about Chad?"

"He didn't make it, Stacy. They were broadsided, and he took the full impact of the blow. It caused a head trauma. Some kind of bleeding in the brain. They did everything they could to try to save him, but the bleeding was too extensive. He never regained consciousness."

"Oh my God. Should I come out?" her voice was panicky.

"It might be a good idea. We can talk more in the morning. In the meantime, you should call your friend—who they were staying with—and let her know what's happened."

"Yeah. Right. Okay, I'll do that. Can I talk to Amber?"

"She just went to bed. I can go see if she's still awake if you want. She was pretty wiped out."

"No, don't bother her. You're sure she's okay, though, right? She didn't have any injuries or anything?"

"Just some bruises to her arm. Other than that, she's fine."

"I'd better fly out there. Are Chad's parents coming tomorrow?"

"I don't know. They hadn't reached them yet when we left the hospital."

"Okay. I'll try to call them, too, as soon as we hang up. And I'll talk to you in the morning about coming out there."

"That sounds good. Try not to worry about Amber. She'll be okay. I promise we'll take good care of her."

Michelle could hear Stacy's muffled voice explaining to someone else what was going on. "Yeah, okay. Thanks so much for everything, Michelle. I'll talk to you in the morning."

Amber lay in Caleb's bed holding tight to a teddy bear she found on the shelf.

What is happening to me? Why does everything always end up so messed up? God must hate me. Maybe He just doesn't care about me at all.

Fine. I can make it on my own. I always do. So what if my life sucks. Who cares anymore? Now that Chad's gone, all I have left is Caleb. And he doesn't even know I'm his mom.

At least not yet.

She closed her eyes and tried to remember what her little boy looked like when he was a newborn. An image popped into her mind—a tiny, scrunched up face, round like the moon with puffy eyelids closed tight. And then they opened. And his blue eyes gazed up at her, searching her face and studying every feature.

"It's me. I'm your mom," she whispered in the darkness.

Holding onto that image, she drifted off to sleep, clutching his little bear against her chest.

ROSEMARY HINES

CHAPTER THIRTEEN

When Amber woke up the next morning, it took her a minute to remember where she was. Sitting up on Caleb's bed, she ran her hand over the dinosaur print comforter and then looked around at the toys scattered on the floor. A baseball mitt, a basketball, and a red remote control car seemed to have been shoved to the corner.

Reminds me of Jack's room, she thought to herself. Her younger brother always had some sport going on in his life. Soccer, baseball, and basketball—he played them all.

Not her boyfriends, though. She'd always picked guys who seemed to be on the fringe. First Adam, Caleb's dad. What a loser he turned out to be. But Chad—he was different. Not a jock, but not a jerk either.

Images of the night before rushed into her mind. The argument in the car, the screeching brakes and crunching metal. And the sights and sounds of the emergency room. She remembered the doctor telling her about Chad, and how he hadn't made it.

It seemed so surreal. Like a bad dream. She picked up the teddy bear and felt a strange numbness. *Why aren't I crying? What's the matter with me? I love Chad, and now I'll never see him again.* But all she could feel was a dead weight in her chest. Nothing but heaviness and exhaustion.

Time passed as she sat holding the bear and waiting for some kind of emotion. But none came.

She stood and walked to the window. It was a sunny day outside. Not that common for June in this seaside Oregon community. She remembered it was usually foggy or even drizzly. But not today. God didn't care that Chad was dead. Everything was sunny and fine with Him.

A soft knock on the door drew her attention back to the room. "Yeah?" she said.

The door cracked open, and Madison was standing there. "Mom said to check on you and see if you wanted some breakfast. She's making fried egg sandwiches for everyone."

"I'm not really hungry. I'll be down in a minute," Amber replied.

"She also asked me to give you this," Madison said, reaching in and handing her a duffle bag. "Your mom's friend brought it by. She thought you might need a change of clothes. You can use my bathroom to take a shower if you want."

"That's okay. Thanks," Amber said as she took the bag. "I'll just get changed and come down."

After Madison closed the door, Amber unzipped the bag and got out a pair of shorts and a shirt. She changed out of the clothes she'd slept in and made the bed. Then she forced herself downstairs. The smell of breakfast cooking made her stomach churn.

When she walked into the kitchen, Steve, Grandpa Phil, and an elderly woman she guessed was Grandpa Phil's wife were sitting at the table finishing their breakfast. Michelle was busy frying eggs, and her mother was making toast.

"Good morning, Amber," Michelle said. "Did you sleep okay?"

She nodded. "Yeah. Thanks."

"Your breakfast is about ready. Have a seat."

Steve shifted his plate and coffee cup over a little. "You can sit here," he said, gesturing to the seat beside him. "Would you like some coffee?"

"That would be great," she replied.

Scooting his chair back, Steve walked over to the coffee maker, grabbed a mug from the cupboard and poured her a cup. "Cream or sugar?"

"Black's fine," she said, reaching for it. "Thanks."

"I spoke with your mother last night," Michelle said as she handed Amber a plate with her egg sandwich on it. "She's planning to fly out today."

"Oh," Amber said. "She doesn't have to do that. I'm okay." She tried to keep her stomach in check as she glanced down at the food.

Michelle looked at her with a puzzled expression. "I think she wants to be here for you."

"Do you think I could just stay here with you guys for a few days?" Amber asked, moving the plate a little back.

Suddenly the room got very quiet, and she could feel all eyes on her. "Never mind. I shouldn't have asked," she said. "It's just hard thinking of going home without Chad." She felt like she couldn't breathe. Pushing away from the table, she left the room.

Michelle followed her out to the living room. "Amber, sit down. Let's talk," she said softly, gesturing to the couch.

As Amber sank down into the soft cushion, her stomach clenched in a tight spasm. It was hard to swallow or take a breath.

Michelle sat down beside her and gently placed her hand on Amber's shoulder. "Are you okay?"

And then the dam broke. Amber began to sob. She cried so hard that she suddenly felt like she was going to throw up. She grabbed her mouth and ran into the bathroom, barely making it to the toilet before she began heaving.

Michelle was right there with her, a hand on her back and saying, "It's okay. You're going to be okay."

Finally the waves of nausea stopped, and Amber was able to get her breath. "I'm sorry. I'm so sorry," she heard herself say.

"You have nothing to be sorry about. It's okay." Michelle brushed Amber's hair away from her face and pulled her into her arms.

"I can't go home right now. I just can't," she said. "How can I go back to that apartment without Chad? What will I do? Where will I go?"

Michelle just held her and said, "We'll figure this out. Everything will be okay. I'll talk to Steve, and maybe you can stay here for a few days. If your mom can come over the weekend, that'll give us a little time to help you figure things out."

Relief swept over Amber, and she felt exhausted to the core of her being. At least she'd be okay for the next five days. Then she'd have to figure out what to do with the rest of her life.

"I think I'd like to go back upstairs and lie down for a little while," she said to Michelle.

"That's fine. Take all the time you need. I'll call your mom and let her know you'll be staying here for a few more days."

Michelle watched Amber climb the stairs, praying silently for her as she went to lie down. Then she returned to the kitchen. Explaining Amber's request to everyone, Steve agreed to allow her to stay until the weekend.

"We should leave," Joan said to Phil.

But Michelle quickly interjected, "I wish you'd stay. I think you could be a good counselor to Amber, Grandpa."

116

"How about this, honey?" Sheila asked. "Your grandparents and I can get a room at the inn by the lighthouse for a couple of nights. I've always wanted to stay there. That way we won't be underfoot all day."

"And it'll give everyone more sleeping space," Joan added.

Michelle had to agree. "We are a little short on beds, and I hate to impose on Ben and Kelly for that many days."

"It's settled then," Sheila said. "Madison can have her room back, and Caleb can sleep on her pull out bed until Amber leaves."

"Okay, Mom. If you're sure you want to do this."

"Positive. We'll get out of your hair, but we'll be close at hand for whatever you need."

"I'll give them a call and book a couple of rooms for you," Steve offered.

"We can share a room, Steve, if they have any with two queens." Joan said, her frugal side showing.

"The rooms are on me," he replied. "If they have two vacancies, I'll grab both. If not, we'll see if they have the two queens." He picked up the phone, called the inn, and was able to secure two rooms side by side.

"I'll go pack a few things," Sheila said. "Then we'll get going."

After her mother and grandparents had left the kitchen, Michelle called Amber's mother. Stacy informed her that Chad's parents would be flying in the next day to bring his body home. "There will be a memorial service next week sometime," she added.

When Michelle explained that Amber wanted to stay for a few days, Stacy said she and her husband would come that Saturday to bring her home.

"Thank you so much for being there for her," she said. "Amber's very lucky to have you in her life. I'm not sure what she's going to do without Chad. He meant the world to her. It seemed like her future was just starting to come together."

Michelle nodded to herself. "Yeah. I'm hoping we can somehow help her sort that out. My grandfather is a pastor. He's here this week from out of town. Maybe he can help her find hope again for the future."

"You know, we've never been much for church, Michelle. But I know Amber really appreciated it when you used to let her go with your family, back when she was in your class. Maybe God can help her now."

"I hope so," Michelle replied.

CHAPTER FOURTEEN

Two days later, Amber wandered outside, her heart aching over the loss of Chad. The sun felt warm on her face, and she breathed in the fresh air.

"Pretty day," Phil commented casually from the porch swing.

"Yeah."

"Got plenty of room on this swing if you'd like to join me."

She studied him for a moment.

"I won't bite." He gave her a wink. "Promise."

Amber smiled nervously and sat down beside him.

"How are you holding up?" he asked. "Must be pretty hard to be so far from home at a time like this."

She nodded. "I'm not sure where home is now," she said. "Chad and I were sharing an apartment, and I can't picture myself living with my parents again. Sort of outgrew that a long time ago, if you know what I mean."

"Hmmm. I guess that makes it hard to think about going back. To Arizona, I mean."

"Yeah. I'm actually wondering if I should stay around here somewhere. To be close to Caleb and everything..." Then she silently chided herself. *Maybe I shouldn't have said that. What am I doing telling him this stuff?*

Phil surprised her by replying, "I could understand why you'd consider that. Caleb's a great kid." He looked over at her and smiled. "You did a wonderful thing for him, Amber. He's a huge blessing to this family."

I sure didn't expect that reaction. This guy's actually pretty cool.

The swing rocked gently back and forth as Amber gathered her thoughts. "You used to be a minister or something, right?"

Phil smiled and nodded. "Yep. I pastored a church for many years. Still do, in a way. I minister to a small group of folks at the local residential care facility near our home."

She nodded. "So maybe you can answer a question for me," she said.

"Fire away."

"If God is really so good, then why did this have to happen with Chad? Every time I think I could start to believe in Him, something really bad happens. Like to prove that He really isn't real or if He is, He just doesn't care about me. I mean, it doesn't seem like it makes any difference even when I try to do the right thing. Bad stuff just keeps happening."

Phil nodded. "Yeah. Life can throw some pretty tough curves. And it's natural to blame God. I've even done it myself once or twice," he added with a sad smile.

"Really? You?"

"Yep."

"So how come you still believe in Him and, you know, like work for Him and everything?"

He chuckled. "Well, it's because I've come to see the bigger picture over time. Many of the things I thought were really bad ended up being transformed into something good later."

"What do you mean?"

"Like take Caleb, for example."

Now Amber was really listening intently.

"When you first found out you were pregnant, how did you feel?"

She thought for a moment. "Terrified and kind of ashamed."

"And how did you feel after you told Caleb's father?"

She felt her adrenalin surge. "Mad. Really mad and scared."

"So that probably seemed like a really bad thing was happening, right?"

She nodded. "Yeah."

"But now look at how God has stepped in. Caleb is a wonderful boy, and because of you and the love God gave Michelle for you, Caleb has a great family and a promising future."

She looked him in the eye. "You think God worked that all out?"

"I do. Without question." He paused for a moment, as if to let that idea sink in. Then he asked, "How many other teachers do you think would have helped you the way Michelle did?"

"Probably none. They all thought I was a loser. They pretty much all wanted me out of their classes."

"But not Michelle."

"Yeah. She was the only cool one. The only one who cared."

"Why do you think that was, Amber?"

"I don't know. What do you think?"

Phil smiled. "I think it's because God put a special love in her heart for you. The love God Himself had for you from the very beginning. He knew you'd need someone special who could love you even when you couldn't love yourself. So He planted that seed of love in your teacher's heart, and placed you right there in her path at the time He knew you'd need her most."

Amber slumped down in the swing, feeling almost like the wind had been knocked out of her. "Really?" she asked, turning to search his face. "You really think God cared about me that much?"

"Not just cared, Amber. He loved you. And He still does. It's a supernatural, unconditional love."

"So, even though bad stuff is happening, He's got some kind of cosmic plan to make it turn out okay?"

He chuckled again. "Something like that."

"But like with murders and stuff, how can that ever turn out to be good?"

"You know, Amber, I can't give you all the answers for all the bad things that happen in this world. But I can tell you a few things about God and how He works."

She turned her body to face him.

"First, God is good. Everything He does is motivated by His pure goodness and love. Second, there are forces of darkness and evil in this world. And there is a ruler over the evil whose name is Satan."

"The devil?"

"Exactly."

She nodded.

"There's a continuous battle going on between the good of God and the evil of Satan. It's been going on since the Garden of Eden, and it's going to continue until Jesus returns."

"Okay. So when's that going to happen?"

"I wish I knew, kiddo."

"Doesn't the Bible tell that?" she asked.

"Not exactly. It gives clues, but no exact date or year."

"Bummer," she said with a sigh.

He smiled. "Yeah. I guess you could say that. But here's the good news, Amber. The Bible does promise that God is victorious in the end. So basically, even though bad things are going to keep happening in the world for a while, in the end the goodness of God wins and settles the score forever."

She nodded thoughtfully. *I like this guy. It makes sense when he explains this stuff.* "So what about the guy who was driving the car that killed Chad? Will God punish him? I mean…like…do we have to wait for Jesus to come back to settle that score? He seemed pretty old. I doubt if he's going to be around much longer."

"Yeah. It's really sad to see someone like that in a predicament like this. I'm sure he didn't mean to hurt anyone, Amber. He probably just didn't want to give up his independence. He thought he could keep driving. You know, it's a tough thing for old guys like us to realize we need to let others help us out."

"Well, now Chad's dead, and it's his fault."

"Yep. That's very true."

"So will God settle that score? How's He going to make this turn out good?"

Phil took a deep breath and let it out slowly. "I really can't tell you, Amber. God's thoughts and ways are far above mine. But I can tell you something that might be a little hard for you to hear."

"Yeah?"

"God loves that old man, honey. Just like He loves you and me. Life will not be easy for that man from now on. Did you know he didn't even have a license anymore?"

"Really?"

"The police officer told Steve that the DMV took away his license a couple of years ago because he couldn't pass a driver's test. But he just didn't want to give up his independence. Now he will be haunted by the images of that accident and the knowledge that he cut a young man's life short. And he may even spend some time in prison because of his choices. His life and the lives of his loved ones will never be the same."

She nodded.

"I've actually considered going to talk to him," Phil said.

"Really? Why?"

"Because he's probably at the lowest point of his life. I don't want the darkness he's experiencing to win the battle for his soul."

"But he's a murderer!"

"I don't think so, sweetheart. I think he's just a man who made a very big mistake. One he'll regret for the rest of his life." He paused and then added, "We all make mistakes. I know I've made my share of them."

"Yeah, but nothing like that."

"No, thankfully nothing like that."

"So what would you say to him if you go see him?"

"I'd tell him what I know about God and help him see there's still hope for him."

"You think God could forgive him?"

"I do."

"Well, I never will."

He sighed. "I understand, Amber. But there are some important things you need to know if you don't want your life to be focused on bitterness."

"Like what? I don't get how you can be so calm about everything and care about a loser like that old guy."

"It's not *me* who is the calm one, the one who cares about him. It's *God* living in this old man's heart," he said as he patted his chest. "And He's taught me three things that I try to always remember. One, love Him and let Him show me how much He loves me. Two, share His love with others, like Michelle did with you. And three, seek to live a life of no regrets."

"Too late for the third one for me," she replied.

"I know it can feel like that, but it's never to late to start a new life with God, Amber. Jesus allows 'do overs'," he added with a smile.

She shook her head in disbelief.

He looked at her intently. "Would you like me to lead you in a prayer to ask Him to help you start a new life with Him?"

Amber's heart started racing, and suddenly she felt scared. "Uh… let me think about it for a while, okay?"

"Okay. But don't wait too long. None of us is guaranteed tomorrow. Like Chad, we just don't know how long we have."

"Okay," she said. "Well, I'd better go see if Michelle needs any help fixing lunches." She stood up and started toward the door. Then she turned back and added, "Thanks for talking to me."

"Sure. Anytime," he replied with a warm smile.

As she walked into the house she thought, *Why didn't I just pray with him? I'm such a jerk.* But she was too embarrassed to turn around and go back.

CHAPTER FIFTEEN

Amber found Michelle sitting at the kitchen table drinking a cup of coffee and looking over the mail.

"I came to see if you needed any help fixing lunch," she offered.

"Actually, Steve just went out to pick up sub sandwiches for everyone," Michelle replied. "Wanna join me? There's plenty of coffee in the carafe." She pushed aside the mail to clear a spot for Amber.

"Okay, thanks." Amber helped herself to a cup of coffee and sat down. "I've been talking to your grandfather," she said. "He's a pretty cool guy."

Michelle smiled. "Yeah. I think so, too. What were you guys talking about?"

"About God and what happened to Chad and lots of stuff like that. He was saying that it's important to live life without regrets."

Michelle nodded. "Sometimes that's hard to do."

"Tell me about it," she added in agreement. "So anyway, I've been thinking about Caleb."

"And?"

"And he's really all I've got left, if you know what I mean. Now that Chad's gone." She hurried on, "And I don't want to have any regrets about him."

"Like what?"

"Like him having the wrong idea about me. About who I am and why I gave him up."

Michelle looked worried. "You know that Caleb has a good life here, right? He knows how much he is loved. He's knows he's adopted and that his birth mother let us have him so he'd have a better life than she could give him."

Amber nodded, but her mind raced. *How do I make her understand that I was a kid when I had him? I'm older now. I could give him a good life. Maybe not as much stuff as he has here, but I could give him his real mother's love. And there'd be no one else taking my attention away from him. It would be just the two of us.*

"What are you thinking about?" Michelle asked.

"Oh, I don't know. Lots of stuff."

"What would help you feel better about Caleb?"

"I guess the most important thing is for him to know who I am. That I'm not just some old student of yours. It seems like he likes me. I want him to know that I'm his other mom. The one who gave birth to him." She paused and then added, "Since I might not be able to have any other children, I just want Caleb to know that."

Michelle nodded. "And if you could tell him this, you think you'd be able to find peace in your heart about the adoption and be able to move forward with your own life?"

Amber flinched inside. *There was no way she could tell Michelle all of her thoughts and hopes for Caleb. Better to just start with this.* "Yeah. It would really help me," she said.

"I'll discuss it with Steve and let you know what we decide."

"Thanks. I really appreciate that."

"Amber?"

"Yes?"

"Have you figured out where you will live when you go home? I know it'll be tough to go back to the apartment where you and Chad were living."

"Yeah. I'm not sure where I'm going to live. Depends on a lot of things."

Just then Steve walked in carting the bags of sandwiches. "Lunch is here!" he announced.

Amber stood up. "I'll go tell everyone," she offered and disappeared.

Steve was brushing his teeth that night when Michelle came up beside him. He glanced at her in the mirror and noticed she looked really tired or worried. Spitting out the toothpaste and rinsing his mouth, he turned to face her. "What's up, honey?"

"It's Amber."

He paused and put his hands on her shoulders. "I know you're worried about her. She's been through a lot. But you can't fix everything for her. That's not your job."

She nodded, but he could tell there was more coming. Pulling her close, he whispered into her hair, "What is it?"

She was silent for a moment then pulled back. "We need to talk, Steve." She took him by the hand and led him into the bedroom where they sat side by side on the edge of the bed. "Amber had a talk with Grandpa today," she began.

"Yeah. I saw them on the porch. And?"

"And I guess they talked about living life with no regrets."

He nodded. Amber sure had plenty of regrets to overcome. Of that he was certain. They probably only knew the beginning of the bad choices she'd made over her short lifetime.

"So anyway," Michelle continued, "she came to talk to me afterward. She was saying how there were things she left unsaid with Chad, and she doesn't want that to happen with Caleb. She wants him to know that she's his birth mother, and that she didn't give him up because she didn't love him, but because she knew we could give him a better life than she could."

Steve studied her face trying to read her reaction to Amber's request. He could see the ambivalence. Michelle was a private person much of the time, but when it came to kids, she had such a soft spot. He loved how she always put the kids before herself. It was what made her such a great mom and teacher. But in addition to seeing her concern for Amber, he could also read the fear in her eyes — fear for Caleb and even for themselves.

"What did you say to her?" he asked.

"I told her I'd talk to you about it." She began twisting a strand of hair at the nape of her neck—a sure sign of her anxiety.

He reached over and guided her hand away from the twisted hair. "I guess we've always known it could come to this eventually, whether it was Caleb asking or her asserting herself into his life. But we can't have her asserting herself into our lives on an ongoing basis, Michelle."

She nodded. "She's just been through so much, Steve. It seems like maybe this would be good for both of them. Caleb really likes her, and she says this will give her a peace about going forward with her life. It's going to be pretty tough for her when she gets back to Arizona and faces her future without Chad."

"So you think we should let her tell him?" He watched her expression closely for clues. In her eyes, he saw a combination of sorrow and resignation.

"Yeah. I think we probably should." She sighed and leaned toward him, her lips meeting his. When she pulled back, she asked, "What do you think?"

"I'm not sure it's the best idea, but I'm willing to go along with whatever you want to do, honey. You know her better than I do. And at the end of the week, she'll be heading back to Arizona, so hopefully we can close this chapter of our lives and get back to some normalcy around here."

"It's not like she's asking to have Caleb back," she added. "Maybe it would be good for him to hear how much his birth mother loved him and why she gave him up. He's at an age where I think he can begin to understand this."

He raised his eyebrows, skeptically.

She looked away and stared off into space for a few moments. "You know what?"

"What?"

"I think I'll talk to Grandpa about it first and see what he says. After all, he was the one who talked to her about regrets. If he thinks it's a good idea, then we'll let her tell Caleb. Okay?"

"Okay," he replied. Reaching to pull her into an embrace, he noticed a tear escaping one of her eyes. "Hey there," he said gently, brushing it away with his thumb. "Either way, everything's going to be fine. Nothing's been decided yet. Let's just sleep on it. Tomorrow you can discuss it with your grandfather."

She leaned into him, wrapping her arms around his waist. As he pulled her close, he silently prayed for wisdom and for the young girl asleep in their son's room.

Michelle slipped out of bed early the next morning, hoping to find Grandpa Phil in his favorite early morning spot at the kitchen table with his Bible and coffee. Since Steve would be taking them to the airport after breakfast this morning, they'd come back from the inn the night before. Amber and Madison were sleeping in Caleb's room, and Caleb had returned to Ben and Kelly's house for one more night.

Wrapping her robe around her, she quietly walked past the kids' rooms and padded down the stairs.

As she peeked into the kitchen, a smile spread across her face. There he was, Bible open as he leaned over it, communing with God.

"Grandpa?" she said in a near whisper.

He turned to face her. "Well, good morning, princess," he said with a warm smile.

Smiling, she leaned down and hugged him.

"Care to join me?" he asked as he patted her hand on his shoulder.

"I'd love to!" She retrieved a mug from the cupboard and poured herself a cup of coffee, savoring the fragrant aroma as she lifted the cup to her mouth. "Yum," she murmured. "Thanks for making a fresh pot."

"You know me. Gotta have a jump start for these old bones," he replied with a wink. "So what's got you up so early on a summer day?"

"Actually, I was hoping to catch you down here before everyone else gets up," she began.

"Well have a seat honey, and let's talk," he offered, reaching over and pulling out the chair next to him.

Sitting beside him, she cupped her hands around the steaming mug and began, "So Amber told me about your talk."

He nodded. "She's got a lot to think through. She's not quite ready for the answers I could give her, but she's at least open to talking about God and asking questions."

"She said you talked about regrets and the importance of living life without them."

"That was part of the discussion. What I was trying to help her see is that God can give her a fresh start no matter how many regrets she may have about the past."

"Yeah." Michelle paused, searching for the words to say next.

"You seem troubled, honey," he said, leaning in.

"I am, Gramps. Steve and I have to make a decision about Amber."

"What kind of decision?"

"She wants to tell Caleb she's his birth mother. She says she has regrets about things she didn't tell Chad, and she doesn't want that to happen with Caleb."

"I see."

"She wants him to know that she only gave him up because she loved him so much, not because she didn't want him or didn't care about him."

"Haven't you already told him that about his birth mother, generally speaking, I mean?" he asked.

"Yes. But Amber wants him to know that she's the one who had to make that decision and how proud she is of him. That kind of thing." Michelle reached up and began twisting the frayed strand of hair that was hidden at the nape of her neck. Then she realized what she was doing and pulled her hand away.

"You seem really worried, Michelle," Grandpa replied as he reached over and gently placed his hand on hers. "What exactly is it that you are worried about?"

She sat back in her chair, careful not to pull her hand away from his. Taking a deep breath, she said. "I guess a lot of things. I'm worried that Caleb will think we lied to him since we didn't tell him from the start that she was his mom. I'm afraid that somehow after he knows who she is it will change everything for us."

"How?"

"I don't know. Maybe he'll get all excited and want to go visit her in Arizona or something. Or maybe he'll stop thinking of me as his real mom. At least until now, I'm the only mom he's ever known. He doesn't have another person or face in mind because even though he knows he's adopted, it's always just been more of an abstract concept. Nothing his little six-year-old mind really thought about."

"I can see why all those questions might spark some concern for you, sweetheart. But the bottom line is this— Who gave you Caleb? And I don't mean Amber."

She studied his face. Every line and wrinkle spelled wisdom and faith. "God. Right?"

"That's how I see it," he replied. "So if God placed him here in this family, don't you think He's already covered your concerns about all this? I mean, you intended to tell Caleb who his birth mother was eventually, right?"

"Yeah, if he ever asked or the topic came up. But he just seems so young right now. I'm afraid it's not the right time for him."

"But you're concerned about Amber, too?"

She sighed. "Yeah, I am, Grandpa. That year she was in my class and got pregnant with him, well, somehow that girl found her way into this mother's heart," she replied, holding her hand up to her chest.

"So you've got two adopted kids to consider here," he observed. "One by law and both by love."

How does he know this stuff so clearly? "I never thought of it that way, but yeah, you're right."

He nodded and offered her a gentle smile. "Tough decision."

"So what would you do?" she asked.

"Hmmm. Well, I can't know for sure since I'm not in your shoes, but here's how I see it from my perspective," he began. "Caleb is a happy, secure kid who knows he's very loved, and that he is a big part of this family. I think no matter what you decide, he will be fine. Sure, he may have some curiosity about Amber and might even want to keep in touch with her through letters and pictures. But the core of who Caleb is and the God who gave him to you will settle the truth that he is a Baron, not a Gamble. His family is here with you and Steve and Madison.

"Amber, on the other hand, has had her life rocked so deeply so many times that she struggles to even know where she belongs or who God is. She's seen her parents make some pretty bad choices, and she's lived with many regrets of her own. Now she's beginning to realize that there are literally no guarantees in life, and she wants to make things right with regard to Caleb. For her, that means making sure he knows she gave him to your family out of love for him and the desire to do what would be in his best interests."

"So, you think I should let her tell him?" Michelle asked.

"I think you should not let fear make this decision for you. I'd never advise you one way or the other on this without urging you to talk it over with God first. But after you do, if you feel He is giving the green light, I'd give Amber the chance to do this, honey."

She thought about it and nodded, trying to silence the fear that was still knocking on the door of her heart.

"I'll pray for you and Steve to have God's answer for this, but you've got to talk to Him yourself, too. Just lay it all out before Him the way you did with me. I promise He'll give you the answer you're seeking."

"Okay," she replied. Then she added, "I'm going to miss you so much when you go home, Gramps. Wish you and Grandma could stay longer."

"Me, too, honey. But I've got to get back to my little flock," he said with a wink. "And once your mother gets settled into her new place up here, we'll be back for another visit."

"I'm going to hold you to that," she said.

As she was about to stand up, he suggested, "Let's say a prayer together for your situation."

"Okay," she agreed. "Thanks." And they joined hands as Phil lifted his granddaughter's concerns to the One he knew held her answers.

CHAPTER SIXTEEN

While Steve took Michelle's grandparents to the airport, Michelle picked up Caleb and Logan and headed for the beach. Amber decided to join them at Madison's urging. The two girls walked along the shore while the boys threw the Frisbee.

Gazing out over the sea, Michelle began to pray. *Lord, I'm scared. I don't know what to do about Amber. Should I let her tell Caleb she's his mom, or should I tell her no? I understand why she wants to do it, but it scares me to think of Caleb knowing who she really is. What if it changes how he feels about me?*

She waited and listened to the sound of the pounding surf. Then a verse popped into her mind. *Romans 8:28 ~ And we know He makes all things work together for the good of those who love Him, who are called according to His purpose.*

Watching Amber and Madison walking, talking, and laughing together, she realized how very much she loved Amber and wanted to give her the peace in her heart she so desired. *I'll do it, Lord. And I'll trust You with the outcome.*

By the time they got home, Steve was pulling in the driveway from the airport. "Where've you guys been?" he asked as they piled out of Michelle's van.

"The beach!" Caleb said with a grin. "Come on, Logan, let's go get my remote control car. It's really cool. Racer red."

As the boys took off for the house, Michelle asked, "Did you drop Mom back off at the inn?"

"Yeah. She's determined to stay there until Amber leaves."

Michelle sighed. "I hate for her to feel pushed out like that."

"I don't think she feels pushed out, honey. She loves the place, and it's only for a couple of days."

"Yeah, okay. Why don't you and Maddie see what we've got in the fridge for lunch," she said. "I want to talk to Amber for a minute."

Steve looked at her with raised eyebrows, and she met his gaze with a nod. Without a word, she could tell he knew. "Sure. Come on, pumpkin," he said to their daughter. "Let's go raid the refrigerator."

"Oh, Dad!" Maddie said, rolling her eyes at his nickname. In that instant she looked so much more like the middle-schoolers Michelle taught than the little girl who'd been their first baby.

She watched as Steve draped an arm over their daughter's shoulder. "What? I can't call you pumpkin anymore?" he asked in an exaggeratedly disappointed voice.

"I'm not a little girl, Dad," she said, glancing at him with a warning look but not pulling away.

"Now you're making me feel like an old man," he replied.

They continued to banter back and forth as they walked into the house.

Once they were gone, Michelle turned to Amber. "So I've been thinking about your request to tell Caleb who you are."

"And?"

"And, after a lot of thought and prayer, I've decided it's okay for you to tell him."

Amber's face lit up, and she reached out to hug Michelle. "Thank you so much! You don't know what this means to me." She held tightly to Michelle as they embraced. Then she asked, "Can I tell him today? My parents will be coming in just a couple of days. I'd really like to tell him as soon as possible."

Her excitement was contagious, and in spite of her reservations, Michelle began feeling happy about her decision. "Okay. But Logan will be here for another hour. It'll have to wait until after he leaves."

"Of course," Amber agreed. Then she shook her head in amazement. "Thanks again. I really mean it," she said, and the two of them hugged one more time before getting out of the car.

As they joined the others in the kitchen, Michelle pulled Steve aside. "Can we talk?"

He nodded then turned to the kids. "You guys go ahead and get started with lunch. Mom and I will be back in a minute." He took Michelle's hand and led her into the other room. "So you told her?"

"Yeah. She's planning to talk to him after Logan goes home."

"Okay. But we need to be part of that conversation," he said. "Caleb needs to hear it from all of us and understand how much we wanted him to be part of this family. I don't want him getting confused about where he belongs."

Michelle could feel a wave of relief wash over her spirit. "You're right. You're absolutely right." She gave him a hug. "You know what? I'm so glad I married you," she added.

Steve looked a little surprised. "Where did that come from?" he asked, drawing her close again.

"I was really nervous about Amber talking to him, but now that you've said it needs to be the three of us, it makes perfect sense. Somehow I was picturing her telling him by herself."

"No way," he replied. "I would never go along with that."

"I'm glad. I feel so much better about all of us sitting down together. Do you think Madison should be part of the conversation?"

He paused for a moment. "I think maybe just the four of us for now. We can explain it to her later."

"Yeah. Okay. I know she's been wanting to hang out with Lucy. Maybe we can drop her off when we take Logan home."

"Good idea."

When they got back into the kitchen, the kids were all eating sandwiches and chips. "Hey, Maddie, do you want me to drop you off to hang out with Lucy when I take Logan home?" Steve asked.

"Sure! I'll text her and see if she's free."

"Can't Logan stay longer, Mom?" Caleb asked. "Please?"

"Not today, sport," Steve interjected. "Maybe tomorrow."

The boys both looked disappointed, but Michelle noticed Amber's knowing smile.

After everyone finished eating, Steve took off with Madison, Logan, and Caleb, giving Michelle a chance to talk to Amber before the big meeting with Caleb.

"Steve and I want to be present when you talk to Caleb," she told her. Immediately she noticed Amber's face drop.

"Okay," she replied, a forced smile replacing the genuine one from a moment earlier.

"We need to be there to make sure Caleb doesn't misunderstand anything. After all, we are his parents, Amber. He needs to know we are always and forever his mom and dad." She studied Amber for a reaction but couldn't read her thoughts.

"Sure. I get it."

"Are you nervous?" Michelle asked.

"Kinda."

"If you're having second thoughts, we can always put this off until a later date."

"No. No, I want to do it now."

"Alright. As soon as Steve and Caleb get back, we'll sit down together," Michelle promised.

"Good," she replied, standing up and clearing her place at the table.

A few minutes later, Caleb came bounding into the kitchen with Steve on his tail. "Wanna go throw the baseball with me?" he asked Amber.

"Hold on, there, buddy," Steve said. "Your mom and Amber and I want to talk to you about something first."

Caleb stopped in his tracks. "Are you mad at me?"

"Not at all. We just have something to tell you," Michelle replied. She could feel her own anxiety rising as she watched Caleb's puzzled expression.

"Let's go into the living room," Steve suggested. He rested his hand on Caleb's shoulder as he guided him out of the kitchen and over to the couch. Sitting on one end, Steve patted the cushion beside him. "Have a seat, sport."

Michelle sat on the other side of Caleb, and Amber took a seat in the rocking chair across from them.

Steve immediately took the lead in the discussion. "Caleb, you remember when we told you you're adopted?"

"Yeah. You guys picked me to be your kid." He looked very nervous.

"That's right," Michelle said. "We very much wanted you to be our little boy," she said, trying to keep her voice level and calm.

"We've never talked to you about the person who gave birth to you," Steve added.

"You told me she was someone you knew," the little boy said seriously.

"That's right," Steve replied.

Michelle took Caleb's hand, and he looked up at her. Then she turned to the girl in the rocker. "Amber?"

Amber smiled nervously, clasping her hands in her lap. "Caleb, I was the one they were talking about. I gave you to them to be their little boy." Tears welled up in her eyes.

"You did?" Caleb asked, amazement in his voice.

She nodded. "Yes. I did."

"So I was the baby you were talking about when you said you had to give one up for adoption?"

"Yeah." Amber cleared her throat and brushed away a stray tear. "I want you to know that I didn't give you up because I didn't love you. It's just that I was so young, and I didn't know what else to do." She took a deep breath and let it out. "Your mom was really good to me, and she cared about me, even though I had a lot of problems."

Pausing again, she glanced over at Michelle, and Michelle's heart swelled with maternal love.

"Every time I looked at your mother, I wished I had a mom like her."

Now Michelle thought she might start to cry. Glancing at Caleb, she saw him processing all this new information. Then she looked at Steve, who was watching Amber closely.

"When I found out I was going to have a baby," Amber continued, "I knew I wasn't ready to be a mom. So I decided to ask your mom if she would consider adopting you. And she said yes."

Caleb looked up at Michelle, seeming uncertain how to respond. Michelle squeezed his hand and gave him a reassuring smile.

"When you were born, you were so tiny, and you needed lots of help from the doctors," Amber said.

"Remember we told you that you were born a little bit early?" Michelle asked.

Caleb nodded.

"I was so worried about you," Amber said. "And when they finally let me hold you," her voice cracked, "well, I just want you to know that I loved you very much."

"Don't be sad, Amber," Caleb pleaded, looking very concerned.

She smiled through her tears. "I'm okay. Don't worry."

"Amber just wanted you to know how special you are to her, and that she loves you, too," Michelle added. Steve caught her eye with a warning glance. "But, of course, we are always going to be your mom and dad," she added, noticing Steve's nod in response.

"So, it's like she was my mom at first," Caleb said, gesturing to Amber. "But you are my mom now."

"Right," Michelle replied.

"But I'll always care about you, too," Amber added.

"Okay. Cool," he said, and all three of them smiled in response. "So do you want to go throw the baseball with me, now?" he asked her.

She looked at Michelle, who turned to Steve. He nodded his permission.

"Sure," she said.

Caleb scooted off the couch and went over to her. He reached out his hand. "Come on."

Michelle watched as a smile of joy spread across Amber's face. Taking Caleb's hand in hers, the two of them went outside.

Michelle and Steve scooted toward each other, filling in the gap where Caleb had been sitting. Steve took her hand in his. After a big sigh, Michelle said, "I think that went pretty well."

"Me, too," he replied, leaning over and giving her a kiss.

The feel of Caleb's little hand in hers was a soothing balm to Amber's heart. Flashing back to the feel of his tiny infant body in her arms and then looking down at his bobbing head beside her, she was so thankful that she hadn't listened to Adam when he'd try to persuade her to have an abortion. What a loser Caleb's biological dad had turned out to be. If only Chad could be here. Her throat tightened as a dark cloud covered her spirit.

"You stand there," Caleb instructed her, letting go of her hand to walk across to the other side of the yard.

Shaking off her sorrow, Amber replied, "Yes, sir," and forced a smile for him.

They threw the ball back and forth for a while, and then Caleb suggested they go inside and get some ice cream.

"Good idea," Amber replied. "And Caleb?"

"Yeah?"

"I just want you to know one more thing."

He stopped and looked at her seriously.

"If anything ever happens, and you need me, you just let me know. I'm older now than I was when you were born. I'm a grown up now, and I could be another mom to you if you ever needed that."

He looked a little worried. "What do you mean?"

"I mean, like if something really bad ever happened and you needed somewhere to go, you could always come to be with me."

Caleb just stared at her. "Like what?"

Amber realized she'd better be careful. "I'm not saying something bad will happen, Caleb. I'm just saying that if it ever does, I'm old enough to take care of you now."

He seemed to think that over for a minute. "Okay," he replied. "Let's go get our ice cream."

CHAPTER SEVENTEEN

Kelly was walking past Logan's bedroom when she heard Caleb's voice. "And she said I could come live with her anytime I want to."

"Really? Where does she live?" Logan asked.

"In Arizona. It's far away."

Kelly froze. *What is Amber up to? Is she trying to get Caleb back?* Clearing her throat, she walked into the room. "What are you boys doing?" she asked.

"Just talking," Logan replied.

"About what?"

The boys looked at each. "Nothing," he replied. Then turning to Caleb, he said, "Come on. Let's go outside."

"Okay," Caleb agreed. And the two of them walked out of the room.

I wonder if I should call Michelle. I'll talk to Ben tonight and see what he says. She pulled her cell phone out of her jeans pocket and texted her husband. Ben often did pre-marital counseling on Thursday nights, but she'd forgotten to check with him to see if he'd be home late this particular Thursday.

R U working late tonight?

Till about 8. Why?

We need to talk about something.

Everything ok? I can cancel and come home at 5 if u need me.

No. 8 is good. Will have ur dinner ready.
Thx.

She sent him a heart icon and slipped the phone back into her pocket. She'd ask Luke what his plans were for the evening. Maybe he could keep an eye on the other kids while she and Ben went for a walk after he had his dinner.

Ben looked at the young couple sitting before him, their hands clasped and their faces eager with love and anticipation of their upcoming wedding. He flashed back to his own wedding and how breathtakingly beautiful Kelly had been as she seemed to float up the aisle in her sweeping lace gown. Pulling himself back to the moment, he asked, "Did you have any questions before we wrap up tonight's session?"

The two glanced at each other and then both shook their heads. "I think we're fine," the groom replied.

"We'll go through the next chapter over the weekend," the bride promised as she patted the premarital workbook on her lap.

"Great," Ben replied. "Really take your time and talk about everything in that chapter carefully before we meet again. It's about finances, and that's an area that can cause a lot of issues in a marriage."

"We will," they chimed simultaneously and then laughed.

"Good," Ben said, a smile on his face as well. "Let's pray." The three of them bowed their heads, and Ben asked God's protection and guidance on this young couple as they launched into their lives as husband and wife. Then he stood, the two before him following suit. "See you next week."

As they left, he glanced over his desk, picked up some study material he wanted to take home, and then flipped off the lights.

When he pulled up to their house, he found Luke and Logan shooting hoops. Parking at the curb, he shut off the engine and waved at the boys. A one-sentence prayer slipped silently from his spirit as he got out of the car. *Help me focus on what's important at home now, Lord.*

"Hey, Dad," Luke called in greeting.

"Hey," he replied.

"Hi, Dad," Logan piped in.

"Who's winning?" Ben asked.

"Me!" Logan exclaimed. Then turning to Luke, he asked, "Right?"

"Right," Luke replied, sending their dad a knowing smile.

"Wanna play?" Logan asked.

"I think I'll head inside. I'm kind of hungry. But save me a game for Saturday morning, okay?"

Logan smiled and gave the thumbs up sign. "You got it, Dad," he replied.

Ben grinned. We sure do have cute kids, he thought.

He found Kelly in the kitchen serving up his dinner. "I thought I heard your car," she said as she placed a plate of spaghetti on the table. The smell of garlic bread filled the air as she pulled a small cookie sheet out of the oven and slipped two pieces onto the edge of his plate.

"Looks delicious," he observed with a smile. Leaning down and giving her a quick kiss, he walked over to the sink to wash his hands.

"How was everything at church today?" she asked.

"Good. I've got my outline ready for Sunday. I dropped by the hospital this afternoon and spent some time with Charles Trent."

"How's he doing?"

"Seems better. I think they're going to release him on Monday." Ben sat down and bowed his head in a silent prayer of thanksgiving for his meal. Then he looked over at Kelly, who'd joined him at the table, a cup of coffee in her hand. "So what did you want to talk to me about?" he asked.

Just then Liam and Lily came bursting into the room. "Tell her to give me my markers!" Liam commanded.

"Whoa there," Ben said. "Hold everything."

Both kids stopped in their tracks and looked at him seriously.

"First, that's not how you talk to your mother," he said sternly.

The twins looked at Kelly. "Sorry, Mom," they said in unison.

Ben nodded. "That's better. Now what's the deal with the markers?"

Both kids burst into talking, each adamantly disputing the ownership of the box of markers in Lily's hand.

"Okay. Time out," Ben said, making a referee's "T" out of his two hands.

"Lily, you go first," he said.

Liam scowled silently.

"These are my markers, Daddy," she said, holding them out to him. "See this?" she said as she pointed to a happy face on the bottom of the box.

Ben took the box and examined it. "Did your box have a happy face on it, Liam?"

The boy looked up out of the corner of his eye with a frown. He didn't answer.

"I think these belong to your sister. Maybe she can help you find yours," he suggested.

Liam eyed Lily suspiciously. She smiled at him. "Come on. Let's go look in the art box," she said, retrieving her markers from Ben.

"Good idea," Ben replied, watching them scamper out of the room. Then he turned to Kelly. "Where were we?"

"You asked me what I wanted to talk to you about."

"Oh yeah. So what's up?" he asked as he took a piece of the garlic bread and started scooping some spaghetti off his plate.

"I was actually thinking maybe we could go for a walk and talk about it," she replied. "Luke will be here, so he can watch the kids."

A noise from upstairs caught both of their attention. Ben started to push away from the table, but Kelly stopped him. "You eat," she said. "I'll go see what that's about."

By the time Kelly returned a few minutes later, Ben had finished dinner and was rinsing off his plate. "Everything okay up there?" he asked.

"Yeah. They knocked over the lamp by the art station in the playroom, but it didn't break or anything. Lily found Liam's markers in his backpack. So all's well," she added with a grin.

"Ready to go for that walk? I could use a little exercise," he said as he patted his stomach.

They headed out the door, stopping to alert Luke of their departure. "Liam and Lily are drawing up at the art station," Kelly said. "You might want to check on them in a few minutes."

"Got it," he replied before turning back to the basketball game.

"We've got some pretty great kids," Ben said, taking Kelly's hand in his.

"Yeah. We do," she replied, giving his hand a squeeze.

Once they were out of earshot of Luke and Logan, Ben asked, "So what's been on your mind all day?"

"It's something I heard this morning," she began. "I was walking past Logan's room, and I heard Caleb telling him that Amber said he could go live with her anytime."

"Really?" Ben asked. "She actually told him that?"

151

"Apparently. That's what Caleb said, at least."

Ben sighed. "Maybe it wasn't such a good idea for them to let Amber tell Caleb she was his birth mother. Did he say anything else?"

"Logan asked where Amber lives, and Caleb told him Arizona."

"Did you say anything to them about all this?" he asked.

"No. They didn't know I heard it."

"Did you call Michelle?"

"I thought about it, but then I decided to talk to you first. I don't want to alarm her."

He nodded. "Okay. I think I'll talk to Logan first and find out the whole conversation. Then I'll decide if I should talk to Steve."

Kelly squeezed his hand again. "Thanks, honey. It might be better coming from you anyway."

Ben slipped his hand out of hers and draped his arm over her shoulder, pulling her close. "This is nice," he said softly.

"What?"

"Just the two of us taking a walk like this. We don't get enough time alone together these days with everything going on at church and with the kids."

She leaned into him. "Yeah. It's not like the old days," she added with a light tone of voice.

Ben felt a wave of nostalgia wash over him. "Do you wish it were?" he asked.

"What? Like the old days?"

He nodded. "Yeah."

"Sometimes. I miss just being us. But I don't have any regrets, if that's what you mean. I love what you do, and the family we've built together."

"We should set aside a date night every week. The kids are older now, and with Michelle and Steve nearby, there's no reason we can't get away for an evening once a week."

"I'd love that," Kelly replied.

As they approached the house again, Ben called out, "Hey, Logan, can we talk for a minute?"

Logan glanced over at Luke, who held out his hands for the ball. "I'm ready to go inside, anyway," he said to his brother.

Logan tossed Luke the ball and walked over to where Kelly and Ben were standing. "Yeah, Dad?"

"Let's go sit on the porch," he replied. "I'll be in, in a minute," he said to Kelly, who took his cue and walked into the house.

The two of them sat down on the top step of the porch. "So I heard Caleb was over today."

"Yeah."

"What did you guys do?"

"We just messed around."

"Mom said she heard you talking in your bedroom."

Logan looked nervous. "So?"

"So what were you talking about?"

He hesitated and then answered. "Caleb was telling me some stuff about Amber."

"Like what?"

"He said she's his real mom, and that she wants him to go live with her."

Ben rested his forearms on his knees and leaned down to make eye contact with his son. "You look a little worried."

"Is she his real mom?"

"She's his birth mother, Logan. But Michelle is his real mom. She's the one who's been his mother since right after he was born."

Logan nodded. "That's what I thought."

"Did Caleb act like he wanted to go live with Amber?"

"He didn't say. He just said she told him he could live with her anytime he wanted to."

"Okay, that's a little different than what you just told me. But either way, it's still not right. Caleb can't just go live with Amber anytime."

"Really?" Logan sounded relieved.

"Really. There's this thing called custody, and it means who gets to have a child live with them."

"So do you and Mom have custody of us?"

Ben smiled. "I guess you could say that. It's really not an issue when parents are married and live together. But when a child is adopted or if a child's parents get divorced, then a court has to decide who gets custody—who gets to have that child live with him or her." As he studied Logan's face, he could see the confusion his son was experiencing.

"So it's like my friend, Blake? He lives with his dad sometimes and his mom sometimes."

"Exactly. It's like that."

"But Michelle and Steve have custody of Caleb? Not Amber?"

"Right."

"So Amber can't have him live with her?"

"No. She can't."

"Caleb thinks she can," he said.

"Maybe he misunderstood something she said to him," Ben suggested.

"I'll tell him what you said, Dad."

Ben hugged his son. "Don't worry about it, champ. I'll talk to Steve, and he can explain it to Caleb."

"Dad?"

"Yeah?"

"If you and Mom get a divorce, will we have to live with you sometimes and with her sometimes, like Blake?"

Ben felt his heart ache at the very thought of that scenario. "Logan, that will *never* happen. Not ever. I promise." And once again he pulled his son close.

CHAPTER EIGHTEEN

Steve and Michelle were sitting alone in the living room watching the news when Steve's phone began to vibrate. "Wonder who's calling this late," Michelle said.

Steve looked over at the clock. 10:30. Glancing down at the screen, he replied, "Ben."

"I hope nothing's wrong," she said.

Steve hit the 'accept call' button. "Hey Ben. Everything okay?"

"Yeah. Sorry to be calling so late," he began, "but I wanted to catch you after Caleb was in bed. Are you alone?"

Steve sat upright and leaned forward, feeling the tension begin in his shoulders. "Michelle's with me. Why?"

"Not Amber?"

"No. She's upstairs with Madison."

"Okay. Good. I need to talk to you about something Caleb said to Logan today."

Steve glanced over at Michelle. Her face looked concerned. He placed his hand over the phone and said, "It's about Caleb. Something he said to Logan."

She nodded and moved closer to him, hitting the mute button on the remote control for the television.

"Go ahead, Ben," Steve said.

"Well, Kelly overheard them talking about Amber this morning, so I questioned Logan for the details when I got home. Apparently, Amber told Caleb that he can come and live with her anytime he wants."

"You're kidding," Steve said, feeling his blood pressure rising.

"That's what he told Logan."

"I can't believe that girl," Steve said incredulously.

"I thought you should know," Ben replied.

"What's going on?" Michelle asked, placing her hand on Steve's arm.

"Hold on, Ben," he said. Then he turned to her and explained the situation. Her expression matched his emotions completely.

Turning back to the phone, he asked, "Did he say anything else about her?"

"Just that she's his real mom."

"Great!" Steve exclaimed sarcastically. "Thanks for letting me know. I'll talk to Amber tonight."

"You know, Steve, maybe it would be better if I talked to her," Ben suggested. "I can come over, if you'd like."

Steve turned to Michelle. "Ben's offering to talk to Amber. What do you think?"

She nodded. "I think it would be a good idea. She'll just get defensive if you approach her right now in your state of mind."

Steve thought for a minute and then answered Ben. "You might be right. I'm pretty worked up. Maybe you'd be able to talk more sense into her than I could right now. But I hate to pull you away from home, especially this late in the evening."

"I really don't mind. I'll be there in a few minutes."

After they hung up, Steve stood and began pacing the floor. "I can't believe she'd pull this after all we've done for her."

"She's just lonely and confused, Steve," Michelle said softly. But her eyes conveyed a fear that Steve was also trying hard to push away.

By the time Ben arrived, Michelle had made a fresh pot of coffee. While Ben and Steve talked in the kitchen, she went upstairs and knocked on Madison's door. "Come in," Maddie said.

Amber was sitting on the floor leaning up against Madison's bed where the younger girl was sprawled out. They were both looking at fashion magazines.

"Amber, we need to talk to you for a minute. Would you come down to the kitchen?"

"Sure," she replied innocently.

"Can I come?" Madison asked.

"No. We need to speak with Amber alone, honey. It won't take long."

When they walked into the kitchen, they found Ben sitting at the table and Steve standing, leaning against the counter, both with cups of coffee in their hands. "Hi, Pastor Ben," Amber said, sounding surprised and nervous.

"Hi, Amber. Have a seat," he replied, gesturing to the chair beside his.

She sat down stiffly. "Am I in some kind of trouble?" she asked.

"Well, we're going to talk about that," Ben replied. He invited Steve and Michelle to join them at the table, and they both sat down.

"Okay," she said tentatively.

"So this morning when Caleb was over at our house, he told Logan that you had said he could come and live with you," Ben began.

Amber looked down at her hands. "That's not exactly what I said."

"Okay. Why don't you explain to us what you *did* say, so Steve and Michelle can clear this up with Caleb?"

She looked over at Michelle, who nodded her head. Clearing her throat, she began, "We were out throwing the baseball, and I just wanted to make sure Caleb really understood that the reason I gave him up for adoption was because I was too young to take care of him when he was born. Then I was thinking about what happened to Chad," she paused and cleared her throat again, "and I thought that if anything ever happened to Michelle and Steve, I wanted Caleb to know that I was older now, and I could take care of him."

"So you weren't suggesting that he come and live with you now?" Michelle asked, beginning to relax a little.

"No. I mean, I would love to have him live with me. I've even been thinking about maybe moving back to Sandy Cove so I could spend more time with him, but that's not what I was talking about. I just thought about what your grandfather said about no guarantees in life, and how we should live life with no regrets and everything, and I thought that Caleb should know that I really love him and would take care of him if he ever needed me to."

"But you understand that he belongs here, right?" Steve asked. Michelle could see that he was fighting to keep his cool and let Ben run the discussion.

"Yeah. As long as you guys are both fine," she replied. "I just said that if anything really bad ever happened and he needed me, he could come live with me."

Ben cleared his throat. "You need to know that that's not going to happen, Amber. Saying things like that will only confuse Caleb."

She nodded, but Michelle wondered whether or not she really understood.

"Are you seriously considering moving back here?" Ben asked next.

"Maybe. There's nothing for me in Arizona now," she said, her voice getting a little shaky. "Don't you think it would be good for Caleb if I was close by so he could see me whenever he wanted to?" she asked, keeping her focus on Ben.

"To be honest, Amber, I think the best thing for Caleb is to put a little space between the two of you right now. It seems like he's getting confused about your role in his life and his future," he replied. "If you try to push yourself on him, I think it will cause the very regrets you are trying to avoid."

Out of the corner of her eye, Michelle could see Steve nodding his head in agreement.

Amber sat quietly, staring down at her hands. "Nothing ever works out for me," she said through tears. "I've been trying to do the right thing and get my life together. Chad and I were doing really well, and we were making plans to get married and everything."

Michelle handed her a tissue and she blew her nose.

Then Amber continued, "But no matter what I do, my life is always just a big mess. You're probably right. I should stay away from Caleb so nothing bad happens to him, too."

Michelle started to go to her, but Ben put his hand out and stopped her. He nodded toward the door to the living room, and Michelle and Steve took the cue and left.

When they got into the other room, Steve pulled her into his arms. "I'm sorry you have to go through this with her, honey. I never should have agreed to letting her tell Caleb."

Pulling back, she looked into his eyes. "I believe her, Steve. I really think she was only talking about him living with her if something ever happened to the two of us."

"Well, I sure don't like the idea of Amber moving back to Sandy Cove," he replied. "She's got too much baggage, and Caleb doesn't need that."

"I agree. Maybe we can suggest an alternative," she said, an idea suddenly popping into her mind. "What if we set something up with Amber where she can correspond with Caleb. You know—send little letters and photos back and forth every once in a while. Then she'll feel connected with him without being right here in the area. And when he gets older and can understand things better, maybe she can come up for another visit."

He hesitated as if mulling the thought over. "That makes more sense to me than a move," he replied. "But we'd definitely have to set up some parameters. Amber needs boundaries. Maybe once a month at the most."

"Yeah. I like that." Michelle began to feel better as the idea settled in. "Right now, he's not a good enough reader to be able to read her letters anyway, so we would be reading them to him and could even screen some of what she's saying if we have any concerns."

"Yeah. Good idea. We'll discuss it with her tomorrow."

After waiting about ten minutes, Steve pressed his ear to the door. Then he came back over and sat beside her on the couch. "Sounds like Ben's praying with her."

"Really?" Michelle felt a flicker of hope that the seeds she'd planted so many years ago might finally come to fruition in Amber's life. More than anything else, she knew that if Amber would reach out to God, He'd help her find a new start and give her hope for the future.

When Ben and Amber emerged from the kitchen several minutes later, Michelle could see that her prayers had been answered. Amber looked like a very heavy weight had been lifted from her shoulders. And when Ben's eyes met Michelle's, she surmised that her former student had found her way to a heavenly Father who would never leave her nor forsake her. Knowing Amber, it wouldn't mean an instant, radical change. But at least it was a start.

CHAPTER NINETEEN

"So I've been thinking a lot about my life," Amber began as she sat across from Michelle at the breakfast table the next day.

Michelle sat forward in her chair. "And?"

"I think I might want to be a teacher," she began. "It's time for me to decide what I want to do with myself, and I think I'd like to do what you do."

Michelle smiled. "That's great, Amber. With your background and life experiences, you could be a very compassionate and effective educator. What grade level do you think you'd like to teach?"

"I'm thinking maybe upper elementary or middle school." She paused.

"Sounds like a good plan to me. I've heard Arizona State has a good program."

"I was actually thinking about going to OSU if I can get in. I could start at community college first for a year and then maybe transfer." She glanced into Michelle's eyes. She looked a little unhappy with the idea. "I'd move to Corvallis, of course, so I wouldn't be too close by. But it would still give me a chance to come see Caleb sometimes."

Michelle didn't respond right away.

"I promise I wouldn't be hanging around all the time."

"It's not that we want to push you away, Amber," Michelle began. "But like we said yesterday, Steve and I think it's a good idea to put a little space between you and Caleb for a while."

Amber's heart sank. She was hoping that somehow making a commitment to God last night might have changed her position in their minds. "So you want me to go back to Arizona?"

"For now, I think that would be a good plan. You could get your general ed classes behind you and maybe volunteer in a classroom for a semester, just to see what you think."

She nodded.

"In the meantime, you and Caleb could write to each other," she suggested.

Amber felt her heart lift a little. "Really?"

"Sure. I think it would be good for both of you. It would help him practice his reading and writing. He's just learning, but we could read your letters out loud to him. And you two could exchange photos of what you are doing in your lives."

"I'd like that," Amber replied, imagining finding letters from him in her mailbox.

"We were thinking maybe once a month would be good."

"Okay," she agreed.

"Before you leave, it's important that you sit down and really clarify your relationship and what you told him. Let's make sure he understands that he belongs here with us, and you didn't mean for him to think he's going to be moving in with you."

Amber felt herself blush. "Yeah. Maybe you can help me explain it to him."

Michelle nodded. "Good plan." She reached out and squeezed Amber's hand. "And Amber, I just want you to know how proud I am of your plan to become a teacher. I hope it works out for you."

"Thanks. Me, too," she replied, feeling like a schoolgirl again.

They cleared their breakfast plates and went to look for Caleb. He was playing with his remote control car on the back patio. "Hey there, little man," Michelle said.

"Hi, Mom!" he replied with a grin, adding, "Watch out!" to Amber as the shiny red car swerved to miss her foot.

Amber pulled her foot away and gave a mock scream. "You're a pretty wild driver," she said as she smiled at him.

"Let's sit down," Michelle said, gesturing toward the picnic table.

"Okay," he replied, guiding the car to the edge of the patio and parking it.

As they sat down, Amber suddenly felt nervous. *How do I say this? I want him to know that I really care and would love to have him live with me. But I know that'll never work right now.* She cleared her throat and began. "So, remember our little talk when we were playing ball the other day?"

He looked at her and then at Michelle like he wasn't sure what to say.

"It's okay. Your mom knows what we talked about," Amber reassured him.

Looking relieved, he replied, "Yeah. I remember."

"Well, I think you might have misunderstood what I was telling you," she said.

He bit his lip as he stared at her.

"I know I said you could come live with me anytime, but I was just meaning if you ever needed a place to go if something happened to your parents."

"Like what?" he asked.

She turned to Michelle, hoping for some assistance.

"Amber was just thinking about what happened to Chad, honey. And she didn't want you to ever worry about being alone. But nothing's going to happen to us," she added firmly. "So you don't need to worry about it. Okay?"

He nodded solemnly. "So I'm not going to live with you?" he asked Amber.

"No. You get to stay here with your mom and dad and Madison," she replied, noticing the relieved expression on his face.

"Okay. Can I go play now?" he asked.

"There's just one more thing we wanted to talk to you about," Michelle said. "Daddy and Amber and I were thinking it might be fun for you and Amber to write letters to each other after she gets back to Arizona. We can help you write what you want to say in your letters and help you read the ones she sends to you."

"And we could send each other pictures," Amber added.

"Okay. Cool."

"So you'd like to do that?" Michelle asked.

"Sure. We could be pen pals," he replied casually.

"Where did you hear that term before?" Michelle asked, a surprised look on her face.

"Our Sunday School teacher said we could be pen pals with the missionary's kids in Africa."

"Really? You didn't tell me that."

"Oh. I forgot I guess."

Michelle ruffled his hair, and he playfully pulled away. *She is so good with him*, Amber thought as she watched them interact. "So we'll be pen pals," she said to Caleb.

"Deal," he replied with a grin, holding his hand up to give her a high five before trotting off to play with his car again.

After they returned to the kitchen for some coffee, Michelle asked Amber about her conversation with Ben the night before.

"He is such a great guy," Amber said. "I'm really glad he came over to talk to me."

"Yeah, we think he's pretty special," Michelle replied. "He's got a good heart and a lot of wisdom."

She nodded. "Even though I know it's going to be really hard without Chad," she began, hearing her voice begin to tremble as her heart constricted in pain, "at least I know God is going to help me through it now."

Michelle took her hand. "If you ever need someone to talk to, I hope you'll call."

"I will. Thanks." She looked at the blurry image of her teacher through the tears that had pooled in her eyes. "And thanks for being such a good mom to Caleb," she added. Then she pulled her hand away to brush off a tear that had escaped.

"It's okay to cry, Amber. Sometimes the tears can really help you heal."

She nodded, turning away as more tears fell. "I think I'll go start packing," she said as she pushed herself to her feet, careful not to make eye contact with the one person who could see into her heart like no other.

Grant and Stacy Gamble pulled into the Barons' driveway around 2:00 that afternoon. Stacy flipped down the mirror on the visor and checked her appearance, her stomach churning. Although she looked a little road weary, Grant reassured her she was fine. "Let's go get our daughter," he said.

"I still can't believe Chad is gone," she said as they got out of the car.

Grant clicked the lock on the key fob and took her hand.

"I wonder what Caleb looks like," she added. "Doesn't it seem weird that we have a six-year-old grandson?"

"I honestly don't think of him as our grandson, Stace. He belongs to their family, not ours," he added as he gestured toward the house.

"Yeah. You're right."

They approached the door and rang the bell, Stacy nervously running her free hand through her hair. "Are you sure I look okay?"

"You look fine."

The door swung open, and a girl, who looked to be about twelve or thirteen stood there. "Mom! They're here," she called back over her shoulder. Turning to them, she smiled. "Hi. I'm Madison. You're Amber's parents, right?"

Grant reached out his hand as he nodded. "Grant Gamble. And this is Amber's mom, Stacy."

Madison shook his hand and invited them in. "They'll be right down," she said, then added, "I'll go up and make sure they heard me." She left them alone in the entryway as she headed up the stairs.

Stacy had memories of Michelle Baron when she'd been Amber's teacher and during the hospital visits after Caleb had been born, but she'd never been to her house before. It seemed a little surreal to be coming into the home of this woman who had been such a godsend to their daughter and who was now the mother of their grandson.

Her immediate impression was favorable. The house felt homey and welcoming. Tidy but not stiff. A sign over the front window caught her eye. *Faith ~ Family ~ Friends.*

Before she could point it out to her husband, Amber came down the stairs, her duffle bag slung over her shoulders, followed by Michelle. Stacy reached for her daughter. "Hi, baby," she murmured into Amber's hair as they embraced. Then Amber turned and gave her father a quick hug, warming Stacy's heart as she thought about the restoration in their relationship.

"It's good to see you, Stacy," Michelle said.

"Thanks. You, too," she replied. "I don't think you've met Amber's father," she added, gesturing to her husband.

Michelle extended her hand, and Grant grasped it. "Grant," he said, adding, "You've got a nice home here."

"Thank you. Please, come in and have a seat. Can I get you something to drink? A soda or a cup of coffee?"

"Coffee sounds great," he replied.

Then she glanced at Stacy. "How about you?"

"Yeah. Coffee would be wonderful," she said.

Michelle disappeared into the kitchen and the three of them sat down in the living room. "So how was your drive?" Amber asked.

Grant replied, "Fine. Long, but fine. We had good weather, so that helped."

"Looks like you're all packed," Stacy observed.

"Yep. I'm ready to go whenever you guys want to leave."

"We thought maybe we'd grab an early dinner in town and try to make it to Sacramento tonight," Grant said. "Then we can get an early start and plow all the way through to home tomorrow."

Michelle came back into the room with a tray of coffee cups. "I brought one for you, too, Amber," she said.

Amber smiled and reached for the cup. "Thanks." Then turning to her parents she said, "I want you guys to meet Caleb before we leave."

"We were just explaining to Amber that we're hoping to make it to Sacramento tonight," Grant added to Michelle.

"A lot of driving," she said. "Amber told me you'd be needing to get back for work. I'll go see if I can find our little race car driver." She stood and left the room.

"He is so cute, Mom," Amber told her, as they sipped their coffee. "I'm really glad you guys get to meet him."

"Me, too, honey."

"I wish Chad could have known him," Amber added, her voice thick with sorrow.

"We're so sorry about what happened, honey," Grant said, moving toward Amber.

But she put up her hand to stop him. "Please, Dad. Just give me a little space. I'll be okay."

Stacy knew Amber was trying, but she still had a lot of bitterness toward her dad for all he'd put the family through when he ran off those seven years earlier. *I hope someday Amber will forgive him and put the past behind her.*

A few moments later, Michelle returned with a brown-haired boy, who looked a little nervous.

"Mom and Dad, this is Caleb," Amber said as she stood and walked over to him. "Caleb, this is my mother and father."

He sucked in his lower lip, and Stacy saw Michelle gave him a little nudge. "Hi," he replied, lifting his hand to wave. Then he leaned closer to his mom, who wrapped her arm around his shoulder.

"He's a little shy with new people," Michelle explained.

He's adorable, Stacy thought. Images of Amber's brother flashed through her mind. *He looks so much like Jack did as a boy.*

"We heard you're a race car driver," her husband said to him.

Caleb looked up at his mother.

"I was talking about your new remote control car," she explained with a reassuring smile.

"Oh," he replied, his expression relaxing a little. "Wanna see it?" he asked.

"Sure," Stacy replied as Grant nodded. They both stood and followed Caleb as he led them out to the back patio. They watched him demonstrate the car and the maneuvers he'd learned to make as he raced it around the perimeter of the concrete pad.

"Nice driving," Grant observed.

The little boy beamed. "Thanks!"

Stacy glanced at Amber, who couldn't seem to take her eyes off of him. She reached over and put her hand on Amber's shoulder. "We'd better get going, honey."

"Yep," Grant agreed. "Time to get moving." He turned to Caleb and added, "Thanks for showing us your car, kiddo," he said.

"That's what my grandpa calls me," Caleb replied seriously.

Stacy tried not to stare at him. His grandpa. Wow. Grant's his grandfather, too.

As if reading her thoughts, Michelle said, "He's actually talking about *my* grandfather. He was just in town for Caleb's birthday."

Turning to Caleb, Stacy said, "That's right. You just had a birthday, didn't you?"

"Yeah," Caleb replied with a grin. "I'm six now."

Amber looked at her and Stacy was flooded with emotions as she recalled the day Amber had handed her baby to Michelle at the hospital. She could remember Amber collapsing in her arms. *I wonder how she'll do saying goodbye to him again now?*

As if on cue, Amber walked over and squatted down to be eye level with Caleb. "It's time for me to leave," she said.

"I'll go find Maddie," Michelle interjected. "She'll want to say goodbye to you, too."

Without standing up, Amber glanced her way and nodded. As soon as Michelle was gone, she turned back to her son. "But we'll write to each other, okay?"

"Okay," he replied, suddenly surprising Stacy by throwing his arms around Amber's neck and giving her a big hug. When he released her, he said, "I'm glad you came to see me."

Stacy saw her daughter wipe away a tear.

"Me, too," Amber replied. "You be good and listen to your mom and dad."

He nodded, a serious expression on his face. "I will," he promised.

She gave him another hug and then stood up again, turning her face away so he wouldn't see her tears.

"Don't be sad," Caleb said.

Stacy felt an arrow in her heart as she watched her daughter try to smile through her tears. Glancing over at Grant, she noticed the concern on his face as well.

A moment later, Michelle and Madison came into the room. "Bye, Amber," the girl said, as she gave her a hug.

"Bye," Amber replied with a sniffle. She picked up her bag and slung it over her shoulder, and then turned to Michelle. "Thanks so much. For everything."

Michelle nodded and they embraced one last time. "We'll keep in touch," she said as she pulled back and looked Amber in the eye. "Call me anytime."

Stacy thanked Michelle again, and then the three of them walked out to their car to begin the journey home.

CHAPTER TWENTY

Phil sat across from the doctor, who was paging through a file in front of him.

A somber expression preceded the doctor's words. "I see that you've come alone," he said.

Phil nodded. "I want to hear this from you first before I tell my wife."

"All right," he replied. Looking Phil in the eye, he delivered the bad news. "According to the results of your blood work and the CT scan, it looks like we are dealing with a pretty aggressive form of pancreatic cancer."

Phil sucked in his breath. *Steady now. Hear him out.*

The doctor continued, "I'd like to do an endoscopic ultrasound to confirm this diagnosis and to determine the stage of your cancer."

"Okay, when can we do that?" Phil asked.

"Let's schedule it for Monday morning. You'll need to fast from midnight on. No food or drink that morning. You'll be asleep during the procedure, which will take about an hour. You'll need someone to drive you home afterward," he replied, flipping his file shut. "Any questions?"

"How long will it take to get the results?"

"It should only take a couple of days. We can meet again at the end of next week and go over the results as well as a treatment plan."

Phil nodded and sat forward in his chair, preparing to stand.

"I recommend you tell your wife everything we've discussed. She needs to start preparing herself for what lies ahead."

He took a deep breath. "Thank you, Doctor." *How do I tell her this, Lord?* Pressing his hands on the arms of the chair, he pushed himself to his feet, a sharp pain piercing his back.

Apparently the doctor noticed him wince. He quickly came around to the front of the desk and supported Phil at his elbow. "Do you need to sit down for a few minutes?" he asked.

Phil shook his head. "No. I'll be okay. It comes and goes." Pulling himself into an upright posture, he forced a smile and shook the doctor's hand. He could see the concern in the man's furrowed brows. "Now don't you go worrying about me," he chided. "I've been walking since before you learned how to crawl," he added with a wink. Then he turned and shuffled out of the room, his heavy heart supported tenderly in the arms of a loving God.

Thank you for the good years, Lord. And thanks for being with me today when I got this news. Maybe we'll be meeting face-to-face pretty soon.

Sheila stood in the front room of her new cottage on the outskirts of Sandy Cove. The vacant spaces and blank walls became a canvas in her mind as she imagined her furnishings and décor lovingly arranged and displayed.

"Well, Mom, everything looks good to me," her son-in-law said as he returned from his inspection of the house.

"Great! I'm glad you had the time to do the walk through with me," she replied. This was something John would have always been in charge of when he was alive.

"No problem," Steve said with a smile. "Shall we go sign the paperwork?"

She nodded and followed him into the kitchen where the realtor awaited them.

"Ready?" she asked.

"Yeah."

The woman extended a clipboard to Sheila. "You'll need to sign the highlighted places and initial these here," she instructed as she pointed to specific sections of the inspection document.

Sheila gave the clipboard to Steve, who looked it over and nodded. "Looks fine to me."

"Okay. Here goes," she said, picking up the pen and signing her name. "The beginning of a new chapter!"

"I think you'll be really happy here," the realtor said. "Sandy Cove's a great little town, and this home has so much potential."

"Thanks for all your help," Steve said to the woman.

The three of them exchanged handshakes and the realtor gave Sheila a key ring with the house key attached. "It's all yours!"

Sheila felt a rush of excitement and nervousness as she took the keys. *All mine. I can't believe I'm doing this on my own. John would be proud.* Turning to Steve, she said, "Okay. Let's go home and tell Michelle. Then I want to call the moving company and arrange for the furniture and boxes in storage to be delivered this weekend."

As they were leaving the front door, Sheila paused for a moment to look back at the empty room. Smiling, she placed the key in the bolt and locked the door before they headed to the car.

Joan was sitting on the front porch swing with her Bible on her lap as the senior transport van dropped off

Phil at the bottom of the driveway. She watched him say goodbye to the driver with a nod and a wave before he turned to approach the house.

He didn't seem to notice her, his eyes on the ground as he slowly walked in her direction. "Hi, honey," she called out.

Looking up, he gave her a nod and a smile.

As he slowly ascended the porch steps, he gripped the railing with one hand and placed the other on the small of his back.

"Still hurting?" she asked.

"Yeah." He paused and looked at her with eyes full of love.

"What? Why are you looking at me like that?" she asked, patting the swing beside her. "Have a seat, old man."

He sank down in the cushion of the swing and placed his hand over hers.

"So what did the doctor say? Did he give you a prescription for the pain?"

Her husband took a deep breath and then let it out. "Not exactly."

"You push yourself too hard, Phil," she said. "We're not kids anymore, you know. I'm sure if you'd just take a week off and rest, your back would feel much better, and you could get your energy back."

As he turned to look at her, she shifted her gaze from the yard to his face. He looked ashen and very troubled. *Oh dear God, what's going on?* Her mind began racing with possibilities, but she quickly checked herself. "What is it, Phil? Tell me."

He squeezed her hand. "It's not good, sweetheart." He seemed to be groping for the right words.

"Now you listen to me. I'm a big girl and I can take it, whatever it is," she said, trying to convince herself as much as her husband.

"I've got cancer, Joan," he replied, his voice sounding almost apologetic.

Cancer. Her heart sank. She looked away so he wouldn't see the tears that were already pooling in her eyes. She felt him release her hand and drape his arm over her shoulder, drawing her close. *I need to pull myself together. Here he is comforting me when I should be holding him.* Taking a deep breath, she turned and looked into his eyes. "Tell me everything," she said.

"I don't actually know all the details yet. The doctor wants to do another scan. Kind of an exploratory thing to determine how advanced it is and what treatment options I have. But it's in the pancreas, Joan. It's pretty serious."

"So that's why you've been feeling so tired and haven't had much of an appetite?"

"Yeah. And why I'm getting these back pains," he explained.

"Okay, so when will they do the other scan?" she asked.

"Monday."

"Should we tell Sheila?"

He shook his head. "No. Let's wait until we know more. She's got a lot going on with her move. We can tell her when we go up to see her new place." Then leaning back further in the swing, he rested his head and closed his eyes.

She nestled closer and felt the swing gently start to move as Phil nudged the ground with his feet. Closing her eyes, she let its gentle rocking motion sooth her troubled spirit as she silently prayed for her husband.

"You can put those boxes in the kitchen," Sheila said as she directed her son-in-law's unloading of the family van.

"You got it, Mom!" he replied.

Michelle smiled. Her mom looked really excited and happy to be moving into her new home, and Michelle was thrilled to know she'd be nearby from now on. With the kids settled at Ben's house for the day, they had much to accomplish in the hours ahead. A moving service had delivered the furniture early that morning, and now it was up to them to transport the boxes Sheila had been keeping in their garage, as well as her clothing and personal items.

"I want to try to sleep here tonight," she'd told them, but Michelle was skeptical that everything could be in place by that time.

"How about these?" she asked, gesturing to some boxes labeled "John's Things."

Sheila glanced over. "Those are some things of your dad's that I couldn't bear to part with. Tim didn't want them. Maybe you can look through them and see if there's anything you or Steve want. For now, just put the boxes in the extra bedroom."

Michelle nodded. "Okay." She picked up one and headed inside.

Once all the boxes had been delivered to the designated rooms, Michelle locked the car, and they all went inside to begin the unpacking process. While Steve unloaded books and albums into the bookcase and completed the assembly of Sheila's bed, Michelle and her mother attacked the kitchen. They lined the shelves and drawers with liners and put away the dishes, glasses, utensils, and pans.

At 2:00, a knock on the front door caught their attention. "I wonder who that could be," Sheila said.

"Probably one of your neighbors," Michelle replied. "I'll go see."

As she opened the door, their dear friends from church, Jim and LouEllen Morgan, greeted her. The spinster brother and sister pair lived off the highway between Portland and Sandy Cove. Michelle and Steve met them by chance shortly after they moved to Oregon. It was a fluke encounter.

Michelle's best friend, Kristin, and her fiancé had flown into the Portland airport to visit for their first Thanksgiving in Sandy Cove, and their rental car had broken down on the lonely, winding highway. Jim came to their rescue, ferrying them the remaining way. He and his sister subsequently began attending Ben's new church in Sandy Cove, and they'd been friends ever since.

"Jim! LouEllen!" Michelle exclaimed, opening her arms to embrace them.

"I was talking to Ben this morning, and he mentioned you two were helping your mom move today, so we decided to bring you some fixins," Jim explained, nudging his sister, who extended a bag of food.

Suddenly Michelle realized just how famished she was. They'd been going non-stop since 8:00 that morning, and the thought of LouEllen's home cooking made her stomach growl. "Wow. That was so sweet of you," she said as she took the bag. "Come on in! I know Mom will be happy to see you both." She moved aside and gestured for them to enter.

"Now this is a mighty fine house," Jim said with a whistle as he surveyed the front room.

Michelle smiled at his old school language and his appreciation of the simple things in life.

"Michelle?" her mom's voice called from the kitchen.

"It's Jim and LouEllen," Michelle called back. Then turning to them, she said, "Come on back and see the kitchen."

As they followed her through the dining area, Steve emerged from the bedroom. He greeted them with warm hugs. Then he said to Michelle, "I'm done in the bedroom. Anything else you'd like me to do?"

"No," she replied. "After we eat, you can go run your errands."

"Great. So what's for lunch?"

LouEllen smiled. "I made some pulled-pork sandwiches and homemade coleslaw and potato salad."

"You sure know the way into a man's heart," Steve replied with a wink.

CHAPTER TWENTY-ONE

As Sheila stood to sing the opening worship song at Ben's church the next morning, she felt the aches and pains in her shoulder and back from the hours spent unpacking the day before. She stretched her neck as she slowly moved her head from side to side.

Michelle leaned over and asked, "Feeling a little stiff, Mom?"

She nodded.

"Me, too," her daughter said.

People were still filing into the sanctuary as they finished the last chorus. After bowing their heads in prayer, the worship leader encouraged them to greet the people around them before sitting down. As they turned around to the next row back, a familiar face greeted them.

"Dr. Chambers!" Michelle said, the surprise in her voice apparent.

"Michelle," he replied with a smile. Then turning to Sheila, "and I believe your name is Sheila, right?" He extended a hand toward her.

Sheila felt herself blush as she shook his hand. *What's wrong with me?*

"This is my husband, Steve," Michelle said.

After the two shook hands, Rick said, "I thought I'd take you up on your invitation to visit. I'm looking forward to hearing your friend's message." Then he turned to

Sheila, "It's great to see you again," he added with a warm smile.

Out of the corner of her eye, she caught a glimpse of Ben up in front adjusting his microphone and looking out over the congregation. She returned Rick's smile and thanked him before turning around to sit back down.

Michelle gently nudged her in the side after they were seated, but Sheila did not acknowledge her daughter's gesture, keeping her eyes firmly fixed on Ben. She felt unexplainably nervous and self-conscious. *This is ridiculous. Why should I feel nervous around that man?*

As Ben began teaching, Sheila found herself struggling to stay focused on the message. All she could think about was Michelle's comments after they'd met Rick at the coffee shop a couple of weeks earlier. *"Mom, Dr. Chambers was really checking you out."* She felt a bit of a rush. *Focus. Listen to Ben and forget this nonsense.* She took a pen out of her purse and began taking notes to help her pay attention.

When the service was over, they filed out of the row and were side-by-side with Rick as they entered the aisle. He gestured to let Sheila go in front of him. Then he moved to her side and began talking. "Got any plans for lunch?" he asked.

"Not really. I just moved into my new house yesterday, so I'll probably just have a salad and get back to unpacking boxes."

"Could I persuade you to join me for a bite to eat? I'm free all afternoon and would enjoy the company."

She hesitated.

"I could help you unpack afterward, if you'd like," he added.

Sheila looked at Michelle, silently seeking her input. Her daughter shrugged and lifted her eyebrows. "Up to you, Mom," her words replied, but her expression communicated a protective concern.

"Just a quick bite to eat. You could bring your own car if you'd feel more comfortable," he added.

Something in her heart said '*Go*.' Looking back at Rick, Sheila replied, "I'd love to have lunch with you. But you don't need to help me unpack," she added. "No point in taking two cars." Then turning back to Michelle, she said, "I'll call you when I get home, and we can pick up where we left off."

Her daughter nodded. "Sure. Have a nice lunch."

Steve and Rick exchanged handshakes again, and then Rick gently took Sheila's elbow as they threaded their way through the departing congregation, immediately releasing his hold once they were outside in the open air. "My car's over here," he said, gesturing toward the side of the parking lot.

Sheila's stomach, which was usually ravenously hungry after church, was doing flips inside of her as she followed him to his sports car. He opened the passenger door for her, and once she was inside, gently closed it. *It's been a long time since I've had someone help me into a car*, she thought as she reflected on the last few years of John's life as an invalid, when it had been her role to help him rather than the other way around.

Rick was a perfect gentlemen, keeping the conversation going with questions about her new house and how she liked Sandy Cove, and she began to feel her nervousness dissolve. By the time they got to the restaurant, she was relaxed enough to ask him about his impressions of their church.

"It's different than I expected," he said.

"Different in a good way?" she asked.

"Yeah. I was surprised by how informative the message was. I expected something a little more…uh…preachy, I guess."

She nodded. "Ben's a good teacher."

"You know, to be honest, I've never really thought of pastors as being teachers. But that's how I felt as I listened. He didn't seem to be cramming doctrine down my throat like some I've heard from the pulpit in the past. Basically, he just read the chapter of the Bible and explained the background and culture and gave some life applications."

"Yeah. I've really learned a lot about scripture from him in the past few months," she replied. "Do you think you'll go back?"

He glanced over at her as he turned off the engine. "Definitely," he replied with a smile.

"So tell me everything," Michelle said, when she arrived at Sheila's house that afternoon.

"About what?" her mother asked.

"You know about what. I want to hear about your lunch with Dr. Chambers," Michelle replied, her curiosity demanding answers.

"Rick and I had a nice lunch at the Cliffhanger."

"The Cliffhanger? Wow, Mom, that's pretty ritzy for lunch." Noticing her mother's blush, she asked, "So what did you and 'Rick' talk about?"

"We talked about my move here, your father, things like that."

"Did he say anything about church?" Michelle was dying to know what her former professor thought about the message. It really surprised her that he still thought about the letter she gave him on the last day of class—a letter that shared her faith and challenged him to reconsider his obvious anti-Christian bias by inviting him to their new church. When he hadn't responded to her invitation at that time, she thought he'd probably just tossed her letter in the trash.

"He said he was pleasantly surprised," Sheila replied. "He liked Ben's teaching, and he wants to come back next week."

"Really?" Michelle studied her mother for a moment. "What?"

"Nothing. I'm just wondering if he's coming back for the teaching or for something else," she said with raised eyebrows.

Sheila's face turned red. "Well, I certainly hope it's for the teaching. There's no way I'm getting involved with a man who is unsure of his faith. I went through that for too many years with your father." She picked up a box of table linens and handed them to Michelle. "These can go in the drawers of the hutch."

Michelle took the box from her and rested it on her hip. "I'm glad to hear that, Mom. Dr. Chambers can be pretty critical of Christians."

"I know. I remember what you went through in his class. But at least he's coming to church," she said with a smile. "No one's beyond God's reach. I've learned that much."

Michelle nodded, her mind immediately picturing her father and the radical transformation in his life after his unsuccessful suicide attempt. Although he'd remained physically marred for the remaining years of his life, he'd grown immensely stronger in faith. "You're right. I'm glad he's coming back," she said. Glancing down at the box, she added, "I'll put these away, and then we can start working on the bathroom."

Rick sat at his dining room table, his mother's Bible spread open to the passage in Romans that Ben had been teaching that morning. He'd checked out a commentary from the religion section of the college library and was poring over the explanation of the verses.

Sitting back in his chair, he reflected on the worldview he'd embraced throughout his years in academia — a post-Christian perspective that embraced tolerance of all the things he'd been reading about in this first chapter of Romans. His first inclination was to push away and write off the scriptures as outdated the way he had for years. But something about the way Ben presented them challenged him to really give it more thought.

Was it possible he'd been wrong all these years? What if the Bible really contained timeless truth as Ben had preached?

He thought about his mother and her unfailing faith to the very end. He'd always thought she was naïve. But considering her illness, he'd never challenged the one thing that seemed to keep her going—the hope she found in the pages of this book.

He sat back and let his mind wander over the events of the day. An impressive message taught by a man much younger than himself. An encounter with his former student and her family. And a very pleasurable lunch with her mother, Sheila.

Sheila. He pictured her smile and her soft-spoken, quiet demeanor. So different than other women he'd dated or his colleagues at the university. There was a toughness about the women in his world. A need to assert their equality and independence.

Sheila didn't have that quality. Hers was a feminine approach to life. More like his mother's had been. As if she didn't need to prove herself and was comfortable in her own skin, embracing a nurturing role rather than a competitive one.

I must be getting soft in my old age, he thought with a sigh. I'm tired of wondering whether or not to open a woman's door for her or pick up the tab on a date.

He smiled at his own musings. Another image of his mom flashed before him. "I know you're up there saying 'I told you so,'" he said aloud to the ceiling. Pushing away from the table, he stood and walked over to the coffeemaker to pour another cup. He was going to make some notes from the commentary before he put away his books.

Then he'd call Sheila. Maybe she'd be willing to have lunch with him again this week. Or dinner. Yeah. Dinner would be better.

Sheila was just settling down with a cup of tea when her phone rang. "Hello?"

"Sheila? It's Rick Chambers."

Rick? I wonder why he'd be calling me. "Oh, hello, Rick."

"I just wanted to thank you for sharing lunch with me today. It was great running into you at church." His voice sounded warm and sincere.

Why does this guy make me feel so flustered? she thought. "I should be the one thanking you for treating me to such a lovely lunch."

"No problem. It was my pleasure." He paused for a moment and then added, "I've been digging into that first chapter in Romans. I checked out a commentary from the university library."

"Really?"

"Yes. I never realized there was so much academic study material for the Bible. It's got me fascinated, and I'm really looking forward to Ben's message next week."

Sheila smiled. "That's great, Rick. I know Steve's got a lot of study materials if you ever want to borrow some. He's been learning some Hebrew and Greek. It's over my head, but Michelle shares some of it with me from time to time."

"Sounds interesting. I'll have to talk to him about it sometime."

After a brief lull in the conversation, he asked, "Are you free tomorrow night? There's a new Italian restaurant up the coast about ten miles. I've been wanting to try it. My students tell me it's excellent."

Sheila glanced around at the chaos of her move. She really should concentrate on getting settled. But...a dinner out did sound nice. And she wanted to hear more about Rick's exploration of scriptures. "Okay. Yeah, that sounds nice."

"Great!" he replied. "Pick you up around six?"

"Six is good. I'll see you then." As she hung up the phone, Sheila sat back and smiled. Something inside of her stirred. A feeling she hadn't experienced in quite a while. She stood and walked over to the mirror Steve had hung over the credenza.

Gazing at her image, she looked for the young woman who had last felt this same spark so many years ago. And somewhere in the gray blue eyes that stared back, she spotted her. Smiling, she shook her head and walked away.

CHAPTER TWENTY-TWO

"Shall we finish up the pantry?" Michelle asked Sheila the next afternoon.

Glancing at the clock on the microwave, Sheila was surprised to see it was already 4:30. "Let's call it a day."

"Really? I don't mind staying awhile longer. Steve's got a meeting until seven and the kids are eating over at Ben and Kelly's."

"I'm ready to stop," Sheila replied. "We can do the pantry tomorrow."

"Okay, if you're sure. Want to go grab a bite to eat with me?"

"I can't. I have plans." Sheila replied.

"Plans? Like what?"

"Actually, I'm having dinner with Rick." She watched Michelle's face for a reaction.

"You're kidding."

"No. He called me last night and asked me to go with him to some new Italian place."

Michelle looked dumbfounded. "And you're just telling me this now?"

"It's no big deal, honey. He just wanted someone to go with him to try it out. He said his students recommended it."

"Oh really? That's what he said?" She gave her a knowing eye.

"What? What's that look for?"

"Mom, Dr. Chambers? Really? You're dating my old professor?"

"I wouldn't call it dating, Michelle. We're just having dinner."

"Right after you 'just had lunch' together at the Cliffhanger yesterday?"

Sheila could feel herself blush. This is ridiculous. Why am I feeling so self-conscious about having dinner with someone? "Should I call him and tell him I won't go?"

"Do you like him, Mom?"

"He seems like a nice enough man to me. But I know he gave you a hard time, so if you want me to call if off, I will."

Michelle paused and seemed to study her. "You like him, don't you? I mean you *like* him."

Again Sheila felt her face flush. "Let's not make a big deal out of this, Mimi. It's just dinner. And yes, I do like him, but not in the way you're implying. I don't even really know him. He just seems like a kind of lonely guy, and we enjoyed having lunch and talking about church yesterday."

She paused to watch Michelle's reaction then added, "I'll be careful. Promise."

Michelle sank into one of the kitchen chairs. "Okay, Mom. Just take it slow."

Sheila walked over and grabbed a sponge, then washed a sticky spot on the table in front of her daughter. "We're just going to dinner as friends, honey. Don't worry." But her heart had already begun to hope for more.

When Rick rang her doorbell promptly at six, Sheila quickly checked the mirror, practiced a friendly smile, and then opened the door. He looked handsome in his casual tan slacks and long sleeve navy striped pinpoint shirt. She thought about the hour she'd spent getting ready after Michelle left. *I hope he doesn't think I dressed up too much.*

"You look wonderful," he said, extending his elbow for her to take.

"Thanks. I hope this isn't too dressy," she replied.

"Not at all. It's perfect." He smiled and led her out to the car. Opening her door, he helped her in.

Sheila's heart thumped loudly in her ears. She took a deep breath and chided herself. *Get a grip. We're just friends.*

As they drove to the restaurant, he asked about her day. She filled him in on the unpacking she and Michelle had accomplished. "How about you? What was your day like?"

"Mostly just research for a new class I'm teaching in the fall. And I got some errands done. I've been looking forward to our dinner all day."

"Me, too," she replied before she could stop the words.

He glanced over at her and smiled. "I'm glad. It gets lonely eating by myself every night."

"I know the feeling. It's been pretty hard for me ever since my husband died." She suddenly felt a pang of guilt as she thought about John. Was it wrong for her to be seeing another man so soon?

"Your daughter told me quite a bit about your husband's ... situation," he said, seeming to search for the right term to use.

She nodded. "Yeah. It was the hardest thing I've ever been through. We knew he was struggling, but none of us imagined he'd try to end his own life."

Their eyes met for a moment, but Rick quickly looked back to the road. "I can't imagine how that must have impacted all of you."

"It really caused us to re-evaluate our priorities, and brought us closer to God." She thought for a moment about how her faith had been challenged and stretched. "I guess some people turn from God when their lives crumble like that, but for us it was a time to reach out and grab hold of the only source of hope we could find. I'm glad John survived long enough to find his spiritual footing."

He nodded. "My mother was like that when she had her cancer. God was her strength." Then his face became very serious. "But when the disease took her, I blamed her God."

"I'm so sorry you had to go through that," she said.

"Well, it's in the past. And, thanks to your daughter, I'm trying to look at things from a different perspective these days. I can't really explain it, Sheila, but as I'm beginning to read and study the Bible, it's like something inside is...changing. It's hard to put into words."

"That's great, Rick," she replied.

They drove into the parking lot of a quaint looking restaurant with a brick exterior decked with faux balconies and old-fashioned street lamps lit by bulbs resembling flickering candles. The large sign over the entrance read *Mama Maria's*, with a picture of a robust Italian woman's face smiling down at them.

"Here we are," he announced with a smile. "Hope you brought your appetite."

She started to open her door, but he stopped her. "Give me a second. I'll get that." In an instant he was at her side of the car, offering her his hand. When she took it, a warm tingling sensation raced up her arm. *I feel like a teenager out with the star quarterback. This is crazy.* But she gladly took his arm as he escorted her into the restaurant.

The evening flew by, filled with conversation and good food. It was clear that Rick's appetite for scripture was becoming as voracious as his appetite for Italian food.

When Sheila eventually glanced down at her watch, she was amazed. "I can't believe it's already after nine."

He smiled and nodded. "We seem to have a lot to talk about." He reached for the leather folder holding the check.

"Can I help with that?" she asked.

"Not on your life," he replied, slipping a credit card into the little pocket at the top.

She started to put her sweater on and retrieve her purse from the chair next to her.

"No hurry. Relax and enjoy your tea," he said, cupping his coffee in both hands. "We did a pretty good job on that cheesecake, but there's one bite left," he added, scooting the plate closer to her.

Sheila smiled and shook her head. "It's all yours. I haven't eaten this much in a long time."

"Okay. If you insist." He reached his fork across the table and took the last bite. "Next time we'll try the tiramisu," he said with a grin.

Next time? Sheila felt another surge of joy. *Why does this feel so right? Aren't I too old to be dating again?*

"There *will* be a next time, right?" he asked, looking her in the eye.

"If you say so," she replied, trying to sound nonchalant in her tone.

He smiled. "I do."

As they walked out to the car a few minutes later, a cool breeze caused Sheila to hug her sweater tight.

"Cold?" he asked, draping an arm over her shoulder and pulling her close.

The warmth of his body felt good, and she leaned into him. *What would Michelle say if she could see me now?* Her daughter's face appeared in her mind, guarded caution written across it. But she quickly dismissed the thought.

As soon as they were in the car, Rick turned the heater on. "Want your seat heated?" he asked, reaching to the button for the passenger side.

"The seats heat up?" she asked.

"Yep. Here, I'll show you." He punched the button and within seconds her seat was toasty warm.

"Now *that's* nice," she said approvingly. "We've never had anything like that in our cars before."

"You probably don't need them down in Southern California. But they come in handy up here."

When they pulled up in front of her house, Sheila realized she didn't want the night to end. "It's so nice and warm in here, I hate to get out."

Rick smiled. "We could sit here for a while if you'd like."

She looked at him and replied, "It's tempting, but I'd better get inside and let you go home."

"Okay, but only on the condition you promise we can do this again later in the week."

"That sounds nice."

"Okay," he said. "How's Friday?"

"Friday's good," she replied with a smile.

"It's a date, then." He opened the door and walked around to her side.

As they walked up to the house, she hoped he would put his arm around her again. But he just stayed close beside her, reaching out once to support her elbow as they climbed the steps to the door.

"I had a wonderful evening tonight," she said.

"Me, too," he replied. He leaned over and kissed her lightly on the cheek. "See you Friday."

Her heart was racing so fast she could barely reply. Nodding, she managed, "Friday." Then she opened the door and walked inside, feeling as light as air. Although she would usually be heading for bed at this time of night, she was wide awake.

"I think I'll do some unpacking," she said aloud. Standing in the middle of the living room, she looked around at all the boxes. Spotting the one marked *Albums,* she scooted it over to the foot of the couch and sat down to peel back the tape they'd used to seal its flaps. *This one should be easy to empty quickly.* She knew exactly where she planned to keep her photo albums. All she'd need to do was to place them on the built in bookshelf beside the fireplace.

Within minutes, most of the albums were standing upright in their new home. Then she lifted the last one out. Her wedding album. She stopped and sank back into the soft cushions of the couch, propping her feet on the coffee table and resting the album on her lap. She gazed at the front with its framed photo of her and John right after they'd kissed at the altar and had turned to face the congregation.

As if it had happened yesterday, she was transported back in time. Suddenly she was that twenty-two year old bride in her grandmother's antique lace gown facing an exciting new chapter of life—marriage to a man who'd swept her off her feet.

She stared into her husband's eyes and felt like he was looking right back at her from the cover of the album. Her heart ached for just one more chance to see him face-to-face, to feel his embrace, and to share the memories of a lifetime spent together.

Carefully opening the cover, she began paging through the photos of that very special day. Her parents looked so young! They'd been ten years younger than she was now. Wow. Time was slipping away.

Her eyes lit on her favorite photo of the bunch — a close up of her and John as rice was flying through the air in their direction. The camera captured the playful smile John displayed so often when courting her. *When did he lose that smile?*

She thought back over their years of marriage—the good times and the bad. And then the worst—the day he'd tried to take his own life over a false allegation of embezzlement. She could see clearly with her mind's eye his comatose body lying so still in the ICU. A shudder coursed through her body as she recalled those endless days of watching, waiting, and wondering.

Slumping down in the couch, she allowed the tears to come one more time. Tears for all the years they almost lost. Tears for the time they'd spent trying to live their lives independent of God. And tears for the day she'd finally laid him to rest last year. Was she really ready to move on and begin a new relationship at this point in her life?

Carrying the album over to the bookcase, she slid it in place beside the others. Feeling an overwhelming sense of fatigue, she turned out the lights and was heading for the bedroom when the phone rang.

I wonder who would be calling me this late. "Hello?" she said.

Rick's voice greeted her from the other end. "I'm sorry to bother you, Sheila. But I wanted to let you know you left your cell phone in my car."

"I did?" She reached over and picked up her purse and began digging through it. The phone was not there. "I guess it must have fallen out when my purse tipped over."

"Probably. I didn't want you to go crazy looking for it," he replied. "Plus, it gave me an excuse to talk to you one more time today."

She could picture his smile as he spoke. The heavy sadness that was weighing her down just a few minutes ago lifted like a mist and evaporated completely. "Thanks, Rick. I really appreciate your call."

"No problem. I'll drop it by tomorrow on my way over to the college. See you then."

Sheila smiled to herself. "See you then."

CHAPTER TWENTY-THREE

Joan studied her husband's face as they ate their breakfast. His skin looked almost yellow, and so did the whites of his eyes. He ate half his oatmeal and pushed the rest away.

"Honey, you've got to eat," she urged. It had been several days since his surgical scan, and he seemed weaker than ever. Today they'd be meeting with the doctor to go over all the test results and find out the prognosis.

"My stomach's just not right," he replied, grimacing a little as he shifted in his chair.

She glanced at the wall clock. "Okay, I'd better get myself together and get ready to go to the appointment with you." She stood and cleared the breakfast dishes, carefully rinsing them before placing them in the dishwasher.

"You don't need to go," Phil said without looking up from his morning paper.

"We've been over this a dozen times. I'm going. I want to hear what the doctor says for myself."

He shrugged. "Suit yourself."

"Suit myself? What's wrong with you, Phil?" she asked. "You never talk to me like that."

He folded the newspaper and placed it on the table. "You're right, sweetheart. I'm sorry." Pausing, he reached for her hand. "You know I don't like doctors, and I don't like not feeling well. I'm not a good patient, and I've been worried about what will happen to my ministry at the Alzheimer's facility."

"I know this is tough for you, but you need to take care of yourself first or you'll be no good to those people." She studied his face and saw the resignation in his eyes. "Let's just get this appointment over with and start whatever treatment the doctor recommends. Okay?"

"Okay." He pulled her down into his lap and wrapped his arms around her.

"What on earth are you doing?" she asked, trying to sound annoyed but feeling her spirit lift a little.

"Just hugging my bride."

"Oh, you old fool," she replied with a chuckle. She kissed the top of his head and stood up. "I'm going to make the bed and get my face on."

"Good idea," he teased, winking at her.

She grabbed the newspaper and swatted him in the arm. "You're still as ornery as ever, 'Pastor' Phil."

Sheila and Michelle were unpacking the last of the boxes at Sheila's house when the doorbell rang.

"I'll get it, Mom," Michelle said, pushing herself up from the floor where she'd been sitting sifting through some family vacation memorabilia.

Brushing her hair back from her face with her hand, she peeked out the peephole of the front door. Rick Chambers was standing on her mother's front porch, his hands in his pockets and looking almost nervous.

Michelle cleared her throat and opened the door. "Dr. Chambers. What a surprise!" She stepped aside and gestured toward the living room. "Come in."

"Hi Michelle. This is a pleasant surprise. Is your mother here?" he asked.

"Yeah. She's in the back room. Just a minute. I'll go get her." She turned and was leaving the room when she remembered her manners. "Have a seat," she offered.

He sat down on the edge of the couch. "Thanks."

"Who was it, dear?" her mother's voice called from the other room.

Michelle hurried back to where she'd left her. "It's Dr. Chambers," she said. "What's he doing here?"

Sheila was on her feet instantly, checking her image in the mirrored doors of the closet. "He's dropping off my cell phone," she replied. "I left it in his car last night."

This is too strange. What is going on with her? She didn't know if she should go out and join them or stay hidden in the guest room. Finally, her curiosity got the best of her, and she ventured out.

She found them standing at the front door saying goodbye. The both looked a little awkward and nervous.

"Well, I'll see you Friday, then," Rick said.

"Yeah. And thanks again for bringing this by," Sheila replied, holding up her cell phone.

"My pleasure."

Michelle cleared her throat so they would be aware of her presence.

Dr. Chambers looked at her and smiled. "Good to see you again, Michelle."

"You, too," she answered.

After he'd left, she turned to her mother. "What is going on here, Mom?"

"What do you mean, dear?"

"I mean, what's up with you and Dr. Chambers?"

Sheila smiled and blushed.

"Mom?" Michelle couldn't remember the last time she'd seen her mother blush about anything.

"It's nothing, honey." She gazed out the window and watched his car driving away.

Michelle took her mother's hand and led her to the couch. "Sit. I want to hear everything."

"There's really not that much to tell. At least not yet."

"Not yet?" Michelle studied her mother's face. Something had changed. The gray cloud that had been resting there since her father died was gone. Mom looked happy.

"You know, Michelle, I will always love and miss your father," she began. "But Rick and I... we... well, we seem to be kind of dating." She looked at her and grinned.

"Dating?"

"I mean, we're just friends. At least I think we are. But... well..." her mother paused, and then added, "he makes me feel special. I know this is going to sound crazy, but it's like I'm a teenager again inside." She squeezed Michelle's hand. "It's hard to explain."

"Wow. I'm speechless."

"Rick's not the same man you knew as your anthropology professor, honey. He's a gentleman who is seeking God for the first time in his life. He's lonely and so am I."

"But you have us," Michelle replied.

Sheila nodded. "And I'm very thankful for that. And for all you and Steve and the kids have done to make this new phase of my life less painful. But you have your own lives, too. And that's how it should be. Right?"

"I guess. I just never expected you to be with another man, other than Dad."

"I know. Me neither," she replied. "But let's not make a big deal of this. I'm not running off to get married or anything. Rick and I are just enjoying spending some time together."

Michelle studied her mother's face. "You know I want you to be happy, right?"

Sheila smiled. "Yes. And for now, he makes me happy. Just having a dinner date to look forward to is something I never expected at this stage of the game."

"Okay. If you're happy, I'm happy," Michelle replied. "Just be careful, Mom, okay? Like I said before, take things slowly."

Her mother gave her a hug. "I will dear. Promise."

Phil and Joan sat across from Dr. Bevins in his private office. A middle-aged man with graying hair and a few extra pounds, he had a face of compassion and a manner that evoked confidence and trust.

"I've been through all your tests and scans with my associates," he began, "and we're looking at some serious stuff ahead."

Phil squeezed Joan's hand. She looked very pale and fragile as he nodded to the doctor to continue.

"Your cancer is stage three." He paused as if to let it sink in. "That means the cancer has spread to nearby blood vessels and nerves."

Phil turned to Joan. He could see the tears swimming in her eyes. Pulling her close he held tight while she wept on his shoulder.

Dr. Bevins held a box of tissues to Phil, and he retrieved one for his wife. After a few moments she pulled herself together and used the tissue to dab her eyes and blow her nose.

"What's the prognosis?" Phil asked.

The doctor sighed. Sitting back in his chair, he replied, "At best, I'd say you have a twenty-five percent survival rate. It's not hopeless, but there are no guarantees. Most likely, we are talking about extending your life for a short time, not curing you of the disease. And I wouldn't be doing you any favors if I didn't warn you that the treatment is pretty grueling.

"At your age, your risk factors are greatly increased. We'll want to get started right away with chemotherapy and radiation treatments." He leaned forward. "I know this is a lot to process. I'd recommend you two go home and talk it over. Then call my office in the morning, and we'll get you going with a panel of doctors, including an endocrinologist and an oncologist."

"Okay, doctor," Phil replied. He stood up, helping Joan to her feet as well. "Thank you."

Dr. Bevins stood and shook his hand. "I wish I had better news for you, Phil."

He took a deep breath and nodded. "We'll be in touch," he said as he wrapped his arm around his wife and led her out of the office.

They rode home silently in the senior shuttle van that had driven them to the appointment. Once they were inside the house, Joan turned to him. "What are we going to do?" she asked, her eyes pleading for reassurance.

"We are going to pray and see what God has in store."

They sat down together at the kitchen table, their golden retriever curling up on the floor beside Phil's chair. Grasping each other's hands, they prayed for wisdom and guidance for the days, weeks, and months ahead.

As they prayed aloud, Phil added his own silent prayer for his bride and for the wisdom to know whether to fight this battle or prepare her for his journey home to Jesus.

Later that afternoon, while Phil was taking a nap, Joan walked out to her rose garden, basket in hand. All the bushes were in full bloom, a rainbow of colors against the pale blue sky. She inhaled their fragrances and carefully clipped a variety of blossoms for a bouquet. Her basket was overflowing by the time she returned to the kitchen.

Carefully cutting off the thorns and arranging them in a vase of fresh water, she admired their beauty. Vibrant reds and pinks mingled with soft yellows and whites, created a feast for the eyes. She carried the display to the kitchen counter and placed it in the center. Then she made herself a cup of tea and sat down to look over a couple of brochures they'd been given by Dr. Bevins' nurse.

As she perused the material, she tried to picture her gentle husband enduring the treatment described. Her mind journeyed back in time to her own father's battle with cancer, a battle that ended his life. He'd wasted away from a towering six-foot height and two hundred pounds to a withered shell of a man barely weighing in at 125. She'd watched him age decades in a few short months. And the side effects of the chemo had been heart wrenching to observe.

She thought about her sixty-five years with Phil. It really didn't seem possible that so many decades had passed between their early years of courting and today. She could remember how nervous he'd been when he'd asked her father for her hand in marriage. And how excited he was when they bought their first house — a tiny two-bedroom cottage that cost a grand total of $11,300.

As she sipped her tea, she was journeyed back to the small community hospital where Sheila had been born. What a happy day that was! And how proud her husband looked as he held up their tiny new babe.

Oh, Phil. I can't lose you now. How would I go on? How would I manage life without you after all these years together?

On the other hand, how could she sit by and watch him suffer through chemotherapy and radiation, knowing he had only a small chance of survival? Would he end up looking like her father with his sunken cheeks and hollow eyes, barely able to speak to those he dearly loved?

She found herself praying for something she would never have dreamed she was capable of expressing. She asked God to give her peace in her heart, whatever His plan might be, and to do whatever would spare her husband suffering, especially needless suffering that would not result in his healing.

Gradually, new strength began to course through her body and spirit. It was as if God were speaking to her saying, "It's your turn to be the strong one now." And she felt a sense of deep peace that God was in control, and would carry them through whatever lay ahead.

That night at the dinner table, she reached out and took her husband's hand in hers. "Honey, I want you to know that no matter what happens, I'll be okay. You seek God for what He has in mind for you, and don't make any decisions based on worrying about me. Alright?"

He studied her face and nodded. "Alright."

She thought she saw some relief in his teary eyes. "I mean it. I'm with you one hundred percent no matter what you decide to do."

"I sure don't know what I ever did to deserve a wife like you," he said, his voice shaking.

"Don't you go soft on me now," she warned, feeling her own tears starting to pool.

"Yes, Ma'am." He sat a little taller and gave her a warm smile.

"Do you think we should call Sheila and tell her what the doctor said?" Joan asked.

"No, I think we need to go up there. We'll just tell her we want to see her new place all unpacked and settled."

"Good idea," she replied, hoping her smile conveyed the strength she was gleaning from God. "Do you want to wait until you decide about the treatment?"

"Not necessarily. I think we should go as soon as we can."

She nodded. "Okay, I'll call up there tomorrow." She watched as he did his best to eat. *Bless his heart*, she prayed.

"It's such a nice evening," he said between meager bites. "We should take a walk after we're finished."

"I'd like that," she replied. There was something refreshingly normal about that idea after a very abnormal day.

CHAPTER TWENTY-FOUR

As soon as Steve got home from work that evening, Michelle cornered him in the kitchen. "You will not believe what is going on with my mom," she said.

He leaned over and kissed her. "Hi to you, too," he teased.

She laughed. "Okay. How was your day, honey?" she asked dutifully.

"I know you don't care about that so just tell me about your mom." His playful expression told her he wasn't really irritated at all.

"She's 'dating' my anthropology professor," she said, using her fingers to punctuate quotes around the word *dating*.

"Rick Chambers?"

"One and the same."

"I knew they had lunch together after church. But dating? How do you know?"

"She flat out told me today. Apparently they went out again last night, and she left her cell phone in his car, so he brought it by while I was helping her unpack boxes today."

Steve nodded, picking up the mail and beginning to thumb through it.

"They're seeing each other *again* on Friday," she added, turning up the volume of her voice slightly to make sure he still heard her. "She told me she feels like a teenager again."

Steve looked away from the mail and into her eyes. "Wow, honey. That's pretty amazing."

"I know. I still can't believe it."

"So what do you think?"

"I don't know. I never pictured her dating again. It's hard to imagine my mother going out on dates with someone, especially someone like Rick Chambers," she said.

"Yeah. Hope she's not wearing her heart on her sleeve."

"Me, too," she agreed, a frown furrowing her brows. "Do you think I should have a talk with her? I mean, try to discourage this before it goes too far?"

Steve looked at her intently. "I know you're concerned, honey. And I get that. But your mom's got a good head on her shoulders. She's been through a lot, with your dad and everything. Maybe this is good for her."

She nodded, trying to soak in what he was saying and battle the voice of worry that so often invaded her mind.

"There's nothing wrong with expressing your concerns. But ultimately, your mom needs to live her own life. And she does seem pretty happy about this whole thing with Rick, right?"

"Yeah."

"Then I think we should just commit it to prayer and see where God takes it. And, hey, it's pretty telling that he actually showed up at church and is open to studying the Bible now. That's a radical departure from how he was when you were in his class. Maybe God's got a hold of him."

"Yeah. Maybe," she agreed.

He pulled her into his arms. "And it's all because of you."

"Me?"

"Yep. You wrote him that letter and got him thinking. Otherwise he would never have visited our church or met your mother."

"Yeah. I just hope I don't live to regret it."

He leaned over and kissed her again, first affectionately and then more passionately. Her body responded immediately, and she hoped the kids wouldn't walk in as she dissolved in his embrace.

Sure enough, a minute later, Madison barreled into the kitchen to get a snack. "Oh, gross," she said.

Michelle pulled back, and she and Steve laughed. Then, just to tease their daughter, Steve nailed her with one more big smooch.

"You two are disgusting!" their daughter exclaimed, grabbing a couple of cookies and disappearing.

Michelle leaned back against the counter and straightened her somewhat twisted blouse. "Guess the moment's over," she said with a smile.

"We'll pick up where we left off later," he replied. "And let's not worry about your mother, honey. If she gets a second chance at love, who are we to begrudge her that?" He picked up an apple from the fruit bowl and carried it into the family room, as he headed to his usual pre-dinner news show.

Michelle retrieved the mail he'd left on the counter to finish sorting through it. A blue envelope caught her eye, and she pulled it out of the stack. It was a decorative stationery envelope with a cloudy sky design. She glanced at the address and saw Caleb's name. In the top left corner was Amber's name and address. She breathed a quick prayer before taking it into the family room to show Steve.

The television was on but he was nowhere to be seen. "Honey?" she called out.

He appeared at the top of the stairs. "Did you call me?"

"Yeah. I want to show you something."

"Okay. I'll be down in a minute. Just wanted to get out of my work clothes."

She sat in her rocking chair and fingered the envelope, tempted to open it but feeling like she should wait and give it to Caleb first. When Steve came down a few minutes later, she handed it to him.

"From Amber, huh? Caleb will be happy to see this," he said.

She sighed. "Yeah. I hope this was a good idea."

"It'll be fine, babe. He'll probably be excited for an hour and forget about it by tomorrow."

Michelle thought about their son. Steve was probably right. Caleb had settled right back into his usual routine after Amber had returned to Arizona. There was no reason to believe he'd overreact to her letter.

She went to track him down and found him playing with some superhero figures in his room. "Hey, buddy," she said.

"Watch out, Mom!" he called out as one of the heroes zoomed through the air. "We need to save the puppies!"

"What puppies?" she asked.

"The puppies that fell into the river," he replied, swooping the figure down to the corner of the room where three plastic dogs were sitting on a heaped up blue t-shirt. He pinched the arms of the superhero around one dog at a time, lifting each out of the river and carrying it to the safety of the bed.

Michelle smiled as she watched his imagination successfully rescue the drowning pups. After the emergency was over, she sat down on the bed and patted the spot beside her. "Come sit with me. I want to show you something."

Caleb scooted himself onto the bed and looked at the envelope in her hand. "Is that for me?"

"Yep. It's from Amber."

"Really?" His face lit up with a smile.

"Really," she replied, reaching over and giving him a side hug. "Shall we read it?"

"Yes!"

Michelle handed him the envelope, and he tore it open. "Take it easy, bud. You might tear the letter too."

He handed it back to her, and she slipped out the matching blue stationery. Pressing it open on her lap, she began to read aloud.

Dear Caleb,

How is your summer going? I have been busy working and taking a class at college. I miss all of you and think about you every day. I put your picture up on my refrigerator so I can see it whenever I go in the kitchen. ☺

I'll never forget all the fun we had at the park and playing ball. I told my brother and my mom what a good arm you have! You'll be a famous pitcher someday. Just wait and see.

It makes me happy to think about you and your family. You are a very lucky boy to have such great parents and such a wonderful sister. I wish I lived closer and could see you more often. But I know you are in a very good home, and I know I will see you again sometime soon.

Be good. Please write back. And tell your Mom and Dad and Maddie that I said hi.

I love you, Caleb.

~ Amber

She handed the letter to her son. "This is yours to keep, honey."

"Thanks, Mom." He took the letter and carefully tucked it back inside the torn envelope. "Can you help me write back to her?"

"Of course," she replied with a smile. "Let's get out your paper. You can tell me what to write, and I will write it first. Then you can copy it in your own printing."

He slipped off the bed and walked over to his desk, pulling out a pad of paper with school-ruled lines for first graders.

"Grab a pencil, too," Michelle said.

He took a pencil out of his pencil pouch and brought both items over to the bed. Handing them to her, he climbed back up by her side. "Tell her about my t-ball game, okay? And about Logan sleeping over tomorrow night and about the picture I drew of Noah's ark in Sunday School. Oh and tell her I'm getting a turtle."

"What? Who said you are getting a turtle?" she asked with a grin.

"Dad did. He promised if I cleaned out the closet I could get a turtle."

Michelle walked over and slid open the closet door. One side looked very neat and tidy. The other had piles of toys and clothes stashed in the corner of the floor. "This side looks great, Caleb. But what's this?" she asked as she pointed to the pile on the other side.

"Oh yeah. I still have to do that part." He shrugged and added, "I'll do it tomorrow, so we can still tell her about the turtle. Okay?"

"Promise?"

"I promise. Scout's honor." He crossed his heart with his finger.

"Okay. We'll tell her about the turtle, too."

They sat together and Michelle wrote as he dictated. She read it back to him, and he nodded approval or modified her words according to what he wanted to say. After she was finished, he took the pad over to his desk and went to work copying what she had written. "Stay here, Mom," he instructed. "In case I need help."

While he worked on his letter, she put away some clean clothes sitting on the foot of his bed. Noticing how dusty his bookshelves were getting, she made a mental note to do a thorough cleaning of the room the next day.

Peeking over his shoulder, she saw that he was almost finished. Most of the words looked fairly legible, so she figured Amber would be able to decipher it.

"Can I draw a picture for her, too?" he asked.

"I think that would be a wonderful idea, honey."

He pulled open the bottom drawer of his desk and pulled out some crayons and drawing paper. Then he set to work.

"What are you drawing?" she asked.

"A picture of Amber and me at the park."

"Wow. That looks really good! She will love it."

Caleb held up the picture and grinned. "Okay, Mom. I'm finished. Can you mail it for me?"

"Sure. I'll go get an envelope and write her address on it. Then you can go with me to put it out for the mailman."

"Cool!"

Michelle stood up. "Go get washed up for dinner and then come on downstairs."

"Okay," he replied, and then added, "Thanks, Mom."

"For what?"

"For helping me." He rushed over to her and gave her a big hug.

"I love you, kiddo." Michelle's voice caught in her throat.

"I love you, too." He turned before walking out the door and added, "Mom, when I grow up, I'm going to marry you."

She smiled to herself as he walked away.

CHAPTER TWENTY-FIVE

Joan hesitated before reaching for the phone. She closed her eyes and asked God to give her strength and a calm voice when she talked to their daughter. Since Phil did not want Sheila to know about his diagnosis until they could tell her face to face, she knew she needed to sound her usual self in spite of her emotional state.

Clearing her throat, she sat on the kitchen stool beside the phone and dialed Sheila's number. After only a couple of rings, she heard her daughter's voice on the other end.

"Hello?"

"Hi dear, it's me."

"Mom! What a pleasant surprise. How's everything with you and Dad?"

"Just fine. How about you? Are you getting settled into your new place?" *Keep the focus on her and everything will be okay.*

"I am. It's beginning to feel like home. I miss Seal Beach, of course, but it's so nice to be close to Michelle and her family. They have me over for dinner several times a week, and we see each other at church on Sundays. Overall, I think this will be a good move for me."

"You sound really happy, honey. I'm glad to hear that," Joan replied.

"How's Dad feeling these days?"

Joan took a deep breath. She hated lying to her daughter but wanted to honor Phil's wishes as well. "He's still feeling a little punk. Don't worry about him. I'm taking good care of your father," she added, steeling her voice against the emotions that threatened to overtake her.

Sheila must have been convinced because she didn't prod any further. "I sure wish you lived closer, Mom. I'd love to have you come over and see the house."

"Actually, we are thinking of coming up to do just that," she replied.

"Do you think Dad's up to traveling?"

"He's the one who suggested it," Joan said. "Do you have your guest room ready?"

"As a matter of fact, I was just making the bed in there when you called," she replied.

"Perfect! Because we've got tickets to fly up on Saturday."

"Wow, that's great! I'll tell Michelle. She'll be happy to have you guys back in town, again so soon. How long are you planning to stay?"

"We're not sure yet. Probably only a week. Your father has some appointments to attend to, and you know how he is about being away from his ministry at the Alzheimer's facility."

"A week's better than nothing," Sheila said. Her voice sounded so good. Really the happiest Joan had heard her in a long time. Sandy Cove life must agree with their daughter.

"Anything else new with you," she asked.

"Actually yes. Something good, and very unexpected, is happening in my life right now."

"Really? Do tell."

"I'm seeing someone, a man who attends Michelle's church."

"Does Michelle know him?"

"Actually, Mom, it's a former professor of hers from Pacific Northwest University. His name is Rick Chambers."

"Why does that name sound familiar?" Joan asked.

"I think she mentioned him to Dad when she was in his class. He was giving the Christian students a run for their money," she explained. "But he's changed, Mom. He's really trying to learn about the Bible and seek God now."

"Now I remember Michelle talking to your father about him." Joan thought about how Sheila had fallen for an unbeliever with her first husband and how that had impacted her life and the lives of her children. *I hope she's not getting too involved with this man. What will Phil say?*

"You know, Michelle was actually instrumental in impacting Rick's life," Sheila said.

"What?"

"I said Michelle impacted Rick's life. She actually invited him to church while she was in his class."

"Didn't she write him a letter or something?" Joan asked.

"That's right. She shared how she'd come to her own faith through John's suicide attempt. Rick didn't respond at the time, but it turns out he kept the letter. We ran into him at the Coffee Stop, and Michelle introduced me to him. We talked a little, and he asked her if her invitation to church was still standing."

"So he came after that?" Joan asked.

"Yes. We saw him the following Sunday."

"I see."

"And he took me out to lunch afterward. He really liked Ben's teaching and plans to continue attending."

"Hmmm…" Joan wondered if it was the teaching or her daughter that was motivating this man's interest in attending church. "Be careful, honey. People don't usually change that quickly."

"I will, Mom. But, from what I've seen so far, he seems like a sincere guy, and someone who throws himself fully into whatever he's pursuing."

"As long as he's pursuing God first and foremost, and not you. You lived a lot of years without God, and I'd hate to see another relationship pulling you away from Him now."

"I know. Me, too," Sheila replied. "I'll be careful. Promise."

"Okay. I'm sure your father will want to meet this man while we are up there," Joan added.

"He'll be at church. You can meet him there. Maybe we can even have a meal together, too, while you are in town," she suggested. "And, Mom, don't make a big deal of this with Dad. Rick and I are just friends right now. It's nothing serious."

"Okay," Joan agreed. *I hope she's right. No need to hurry into something with someone like that.*

"What time should I pick you up at the airport?"

"Our flight is scheduled to arrive at noon."

"Okay, I'll be there. We can have lunch in Portland before we head back to Sandy Cove. Michelle will probably want us to come to her house for dinner."

"Sounds wonderful, honey. We'll look forward to seeing you Saturday."

After they hung up, Joan went looking for Phil outside to tell him the news about their daughter. She found him on the porch swing gazing out over the garden, with Thumper sleeping peacefully at his feet. He looked up when she came near.

Patting the swing beside him, he said, "Have a seat. It's a nice afternoon to be outside."

As she took her place, she said, "I just talked to Sheila. We're all set for Saturday."

"That's good."

"She had some news for me," Joan hedged.

"Really?"

"Yes. She is 'seeing' someone." Joan watched his face for a reaction and noticed his eyebrows lift.

216

He nodded and replied, "Who is the lucky fellow?"

Joan took his hand and gave it a squeeze. "Are you ready for this?" she asked.

"For what?"

"It's that anthropology professor who gave Michelle such a rough time."

Phil turned to face her. "You're kidding."

"Nope."

"How did this happen?"

"Apparently she and Michelle ran into him at a coffee shop in town. They struck up a conversation and Rick, that's his name, asked Michelle if her invitation to visit their church was still good. You remember, she wrote him a letter and shared about her father and how she'd become a Christian as a result of what he went through."

Phil nodded.

"Well, she also invited him to church. But he never came, of course. So when they were talking at the coffee shop, he brought it up. Michelle told him the invitation was still standing, and he came to their church on Sunday. Then he took Sheila out for lunch afterward."

"Interesting," he replied. "How did Sheila sound?"

"She sounded very happy. She says the house is starting to feel like home, and she seems to be enjoying spending time with this professor."

"But you're concerned," he observed.

"I just don't want him derailing her commitment to God the way John did for so many years."

"Yeah. I feel the same way. But let's not forget that John changed and was actually instrumental in bringing our daughter back to her faith," he said, patting her hand. "We'll just have to get to know this man and give him a chance. And pray that God takes him out of her life if he's not good for her."

"You're right. We'll get to meet him this weekend. Sheila said he'll be at church on Sunday," she added.

"Good. Maybe I'll have a little man-to-man chat with him while we are up there, too," Phil added with a wink.

"Oh, Phil. I know you're teasing me," she said, "but I honestly hope that you do."

"We'll see how the week unfolds. I wish we were going up there for a different reason," he added with a sigh. "But maybe God's going to open the door for me to talk to this new suitor of our daughter, too."

She nodded, and they both sat back against the cushions of the swing, Joan resting her head on his shoulder as she savored a few moments of just sitting with her beloved husband before the onslaught of medical interventions would begin.

CHAPTER TWENTY-SIX

Sheila glanced at her watch. It was already three o'clock, and Rick was picking her up at six. "I've got to get home, Mimi," she said, as she stood up and carried her cup to the sink.

"Oh, that's right. You've got a date tonight," Michelle replied with a grin. "Where are you guys going?"

"I'm not sure. Rick said he wants to surprise me."

"Sounds interesting. Well, I'll be eager to hear all about it tomorrow. Call me in the morning."

Sheila nodded. "I will, honey. And thanks for the coffee."

"Anytime." Michelle poked her head out of the kitchen and called the kids. "Maddie, Caleb—Grandma's going home."

Madison appeared from the family room, and Caleb bounded down the stairs. They gave Sheila hugs and said goodbye. Then Michelle walked her to the front door.

"I'll talk to you tomorrow, Mimi," Sheila said, giving her daughter a hug.

"Okay. Have fun tonight. And don't stay out too late," she added, teasingly.

Sheila just laughed and waved as she walked out the door.

When she got home, she opened her closet and stared at its contents. Rifling through the hangers, she tried to decide what to wear. "I wish I knew where we were going," she said aloud.

She pulled out a pair of black pants and a black and white striped boat-necked cotton sweater. "I could dress this up with a necklace and some earrings." Carrying the outfit over to the bed, she laid it out and pulled a silver chain and some matching dangling earrings out of the jewelry drawer, placing them on the sweater to complete the look.

She studied the outfit, cocking her head to the side. Then a smile spread across her face as she got an idea. Heading back into the closet, she reached up on the top shelf and pulled out a shoebox. The pair of shoes inside it had only been worn once. Michelle had talked her into buying them, but who had use for red shoes? Certainly not someone her age.

Lifting the lid, she took them out and set them on the bed beside the slacks. Normally, she would just wear black flats. But when she'd bought these, Michelle said they would be great with black. And they were very comfortable in spite of their bright shine. What was the word, Michelle had used? Oh, yeah. *Sassy.* She'd said they would look sassy with black.

Sheila took a deep breath. *What would John say if he could see me now?* Shaking off the thought, she made her decision. "Tonight, I'm going sassy," she said to the mirror over her dresser.

Leaving the outfit displayed on the bed, she went out to the living room to straighten things up before Rick arrived. She folded the throw on the couch, carried her coffee cup from that morning into the kitchen, and put away some magazines she'd been looking through.

"Maybe I'd better dust," she said, noticing a film on the coffee table. She quickly cleaned the various furniture pieces and finished by wiping down the kitchen counter and putting a few stray dishes in the dishwasher.

"There," she said. "Now I can get ready."

At exactly six o'clock, the doorbell rang. Sheila quickly checked the full-length mirror one last time. "Coming!" she called out, as she slipped on the red shoes and hurried to the door.

Rick looked handsome in his sports coat and tie. She caught a slight whiff of aftershave as she welcomed him into her home. "I hope I'm dressed okay for wherever we're going," she said.

"You look perfect," he replied, taking her in with his eyes. "We're actually headed to the university."

"We are?"

"Yep. The students' summer theater group is performing *Father of the Bride* tonight. Although they're students, the performances are always entertaining and well done. I like to support them when I can."

"Sounds fun," she replied. "Are we going somewhere for dinner first?"

"We are. There's a cozy little Greek restaurant near school. We have a reservation in twenty minutes, so we should probably get going," he added.

"Great. I'll grab my purse." As they walked out the door, Sheila noticed the clouds forming and asked him to wait while she got her umbrella from the car.

"Good idea," he said. "You never know."

She nodded. "I'm still getting used to it. I'm just a sunny Southern California gal, I guess."

"A beautiful one at that," he replied, opening her door.

Fifteen minutes later, they were pulling up in front of the restaurant. The fragrance of Greek food wafted out to greet them as Rick opened the front door.

"Dr. Chambers! So nice to see you," the host said with a warm smile. "And who is the lovely lady?"

"Alex, this is Sheila. Sheila, Alex," Rick gestured as he introduced them.

"Lucky man," Alex said with a wink. Turning to Sheila, he said in a mock whisper, "He's never brought a date here before."

She blushed and looked around the room, avoiding eye contact with either man.

"Did you save my favorite table?" Rick asked.

"Of course," the host replied. Again he turned to Sheila. "This way, please." Weaving between the tables, he led them to a back corner with a small, semi-private booth.

As they slid into their seats, he held out the menus. "Our specialties tonight are the Moussaka and our Swordfish Santorini." He went on to describe both dishes and take their drink order. When the server returned with their wine, Rick ordered for them both.

Turning his attention back to Sheila, he said, "So tell me more about Seal Beach."

"It's a quaint little beach town in Orange County. Similar to Sandy Cove, but more crowded and with warmer weather, of course."

"This will be your first summer here, won't it?"

She nodded.

"We'll just have to make the most of the good weather, then," he said. "Summers are beautiful here. I can't promise no rain, but there's less than during the rest of the year. Of course, we do have some fog, too, especially early in the day."

Sheila nodded. "Will you be off all summer?" she asked.

"Other than my writing and plans for the fall classes, I'm pretty free. By mid-August, I'll be spending most of each week in my office on campus. But there will be lots of time to show you around until then," he said. "If you want me to, that is."

She smiled. "Sounds like fun."

They continued to enjoy discussing possible summer plans throughout their meal. Then it was time to head to the theater on campus.

When they entered the auditorium, Sheila was surprised by its size, expecting something much smaller. Seating around a thousand people, it had a sloped floor and tastefully elegant interior. "This is really nice," she remarked.

Rick looked pleased. "I'm glad you like it."

A student usher checked their tickets and led them to seats in the center section about midway from the stage. "Enjoy the show," he said as they took their seats.

Soon the performance began. Both the sets and the acting impressed Sheila. Rick leaned over and spoke softly into her ear a few times, telling her that the art department created all the backdrops and the play was not only student acted but also directed by members of the drama department.

As she watched the familiar tale of a father trying to adjust to his firstborn daughter's engagement and wedding, she flashed back to Michelle's wedding. Sentiment swept over her, and she reached out and took Rick's hand, forgetting for a moment that she was not with John.

He glanced at her, and she felt her face flush. *What must he think of me?* She wanted to pull back, but it seemed just as awkward to take her hand away as it was to leave it in his. Thankfully, a particularly funny scene unfolded on stage, and as they both laughed, she was able to pull her hand away to retrieve a tissue from her purse.

Dabbing her eyes from the tears of laughter, she rested her hands on her lap. Rick leaned over and murmured something in her ear, but she didn't catch it. Then he put his arm over the back of her seat, resting his hand on her shoulder. Once again she felt her heart race like a teen on a first date.

On the way home afterward, they discussed the play. "This was a great idea," Sheila said as they arrived at her house. "Thanks for thinking of it. I'll have to remember to keep up with their performances."

"I'll get us tickets for their fall play," he replied. "They usually have something related to the holidays that comes out in November."

"Sounds wonderful. And thanks for dinner, Rick. The swordfish was excellent."

He escorted her to the door and when he leaned over, she expected a kiss on the cheek like the last time. But tonight, his lips met hers. It was brief and sweet.

She slipped inside and closed the door, then leaned back against it, trying to calm her pounding heart. *Did that just happen?* she asked herself.

Slipping off the red shoes, she put her purse up and sank into the rocker, replaying the evening in her mind.

CHAPTER TWENTY-SEVEN

Sheila called Michelle the next morning.

"Hi, Mom! How was your date?"

Nothing like getting right to the point, Sheila thought. "It was very nice, honey. We went to a Greek restaurant by the university and then attended the drama department's performance of *Father of the Bride.*

"Sounds fun."

"Guess what?" Sheila asked.

"What?"

"I wore the red shoes."

"Really? Good for you, Mom. I told you they'd come in handy someday," Michelle replied. Sheila could picture her daughter's grin. "So how are you feeling about Dr. Chambers now that you've had a few dates?"

"I like him. He's a good conversationalist, and he's very thoughtful." She paused and then added, "How do you feel about me seeing him?"

"If *you're* happy, *I'm* happy. It's just hard for me to imagine him being so kind and considerate when I think back to how he was when I was in his class."

"I know. But that was a long time ago. People change," Sheila said. "Look at your father and what a different man he became."

"Um hmm," Michelle replied. "So are you two getting, you know, serious?"

"What do you mean?"

"I mean like beyond friends?" Michelle seemed to be searching for the right words.

"Well, he did kiss me last night when we were saying goodbye."

"Okay. That tells me what I wanted to know."

Sheila laughed. "Is it hard to imagine your mother being kissed on a date?"

"Kind of. Just be careful, like you always told me."

"I will, honey. For now, I'm just trying to enjoy the newness of my life up here in Oregon. And Rick is a fun companion to show me around. I do like him, but I'm not in any hurry to settle into a long term relationship."

"That's good," she replied. "So when do you leave to pick up Grandma and Grandpa?"

"Pretty soon. In fact, I'd better get off the phone and get ready."

"Okay. You're bringing them here for dinner tonight, right? Steve's planning to barbeque some chicken."

"We'll be there. What time do you want us?"

"Anytime after five is good," she said. "Hey, do you want to invite Dr. Chambers so Grandma and Grandpa can get to know him?"

Sheila couldn't tell if she was kidding or serious. "No. Thanks for asking, though. They can meet him at church tomorrow, and maybe we'll have dinner with him later in the week. They'll probably be pretty tired tonight, so I'm thinking an early family dinner and then back here for bed is best."

"Okay. See you tonight."

As Sheila drove to the airport to pick up her parents, she allowed her mind to wander back to the night before. Rick's aftershave and the feel of his lips caressing hers, the warm conversation over dinner, and the laughter that brought tears to her eyes during the play—it had been a wonderful evening.

Part of what made her time with Rick so special was the way he took care of her. Opening every door, making all the arrangements for the dinner reservations and tickets for the performance, picking up all the checks. It was such a contrast from all the care giving she'd had to do with John after he'd become disabled.

It hadn't always been that way. John was so determinedly independent for most of their marriage. An excellent provider and a man of great intellectual prowess, she'd been in awe of him and at times intimidated by his strength. But the last years of his life, it had been like living with a different person.

On the one hand, he was much sweeter. And his newfound faith in God was a radical turnaround from his adamant atheism of the past. She could talk to him in ways she'd never been able to before. And he appreciated her so much more, too.

But the flip side was the reality of how draining it was to meet all of his physical needs on a daily basis. So many trips to rehab, helping him learn to do even the most basic tasks of feeding himself, changing his clothes, brushing his teeth. The list went on and on.

She could see him sitting in his wheelchair; a mere shadow of the man he'd been before he tried to take his own life. Although she still missed him, it was God's mercy that He took him home to heaven last year.

In contrast, Rick, who was a few years younger than her, was very much alive and well. His attractive features and vigorous health made Sheila feel more alive and youthful, too. She hoped her parents would understand and accept her blossoming relationship with him.

After finding a parking place at the airport, she worked her way through the terminal to baggage claim and found her father trying to wrestle a suitcase off the conveyor belt. "Here, let me help you with that," a man standing nearby offered as he reached over and lifted the canvas bag, placing it upright on its wheels.

"Thanks, young man," her father replied with a smile.

A moment later, her mother spotted her. "Sheila!"

"Hi Mom! Dad!" she said as she moved quickly through the crowd and embraced them both. "Can I get that for you?" she asked, reaching for the handle of the suitcase.

"I've got it now, sweetheart," her father answered as he began pulling it toward the exit. After wrestling their luggage into the trunk of Sheila's car, they started for the restaurant where they'd be eating lunch.

Although nearly every table was taken, the hostess found an empty booth near the kitchen, and they enjoyed a casual meal as Phil and Joan talked about the flight and how distressed Thumper had been to be left behind. "Poor fellow," Phil said. "The neighbors are great, but he seems to have a harder and harder time without us as he gets older."

Sheila nodded. She could see the fatigue in her father's eyes, and she worried that he hadn't gained any weight. "How are you feeling these days, Dad?"

"A little tuckered out. Not to worry, honey."

Joan's eyes told a different story, warning her not to take the conversation any further.

As Sheila drove them back to her house, both of her parents nodded off, sleeping for most of the trip.

"Did you two get your rooms picked up?" Michelle asked her kids while she pulled out the ingredients to make a salad. "Your grandmother and great grandparents should be here any minute," she reminded them.

"Come on, Caleb," Madison said, pushing away from their game of Battleship.

"Can't we finish?" he whined.

"Later," Michelle said. "Now scoot upstairs and get those rooms in order."

Caleb sighed loudly and pushed his chair back a little too forcefully, rocking the table and nearly toppling their game pieces.

"What's going on in here?" Steve asked, entering the room just in time to see their son's actions.

"Mom told us to go clean our rooms," Madison explained, "but Caleb's being a baby."

Steve put his hand on Caleb's shoulder. "Do what your mother told you, sport." He guided the boy toward the stairs.

"Thanks, honey," Michelle said, giving Steve a warm smile.

"You bet. Anything I need to do for the dinner?" he asked.

"You can fire up the barbecue."

"Okay, I'm on it," he replied. "What time will your mom and grandparents be here?"

"They said around six." She glanced at the clock. 5:30. Better get the table set and make the salad.

"Are we having your famous potato salad?" Steve asked.

"Yes, we are. And this time Madison helped me make it."

"Great. She's becoming quite the cook these days. Just like her mother," he added, wrapping his arms around her and giving her a kiss. "Maybe I should have Caleb help me with the chicken."

She laughed. "Next time. I'm sure he'll be tethered to that bedroom until everyone gets here."

"Probably right." He grabbed a lighter from the junk drawer and headed out to the backyard.

As Michelle got to work on the salad, the phone rang. Expecting it to be her mother telling her they were on the way, she answered, "Hi Mom!"

After a pause, she heard a familiar voice on the other end. "It's Amber."

"Amber," Michelle turned and leaned against the counter. "How are you doing?"

"Okay, I guess." The line was silent for a moment and then she continued, "It's harder than I thought—without Chad, I mean."

Michelle felt her heart squeeze tight. "I'll bet." She grasped for words to show her understanding. "You two really loved each other."

"Yeah, we did."

Silence.

"So how's Caleb?" Amber asked, her voice picking up some.

"He's fine. He's upstairs right now picking up his room."

"Do you think I could talk to him?" she asked.

Michelle took a deep breath. *What should I do here?* She shot up a quick prayer, and believed that God was nudging her to say yes. "Okay. Sure. Hold on a minute, and I'll get him."

Walking to the bottom of the steps, she called, "Caleb! Phone call for you!"

A moment later, he appeared from his bedroom, an airplane in his hand. He made engine noises as he "flew" the plane down the stairs toward her.

"Have you been cleaning up there or playing?" Michelle asked.

He smiled at her with a telling grin. "Who's on the phone?"

"Amber."

"Amber?? Really?" he raced down the stairs and grabbed the receiver from the phone in the family room. "Hello?"

Michelle watched as he held the receiver tightly to his ear, the airplane cast aside on the sofa.

Caleb nodded in response to something that was said. "Me, too," he replied. "Okay, I guess." Pause. "I know." His expression looked eager. "Yeah. You should come out here again. I'm sure it would be fine."

Michelle cleared her throat to get his attention, and he looked her way. She shook her head.

"Hold on, Amber," Caleb said into the phone. He placed the receiver against his chest. "What, Mom?"

"Honey, we need to talk to Daddy before we invite Amber to come back out this soon. Just tell her what you've been doing lately and ask her how she is, okay? But don't make any plans."

His face dropped. "Okay," he said dejectedly. Putting the phone to his ear again, he said, "You can't come over until we talk to my dad."

Michelle winced. She put her hand on his shoulder, and he looked up. Without seeming angry, she tried to give him her most serious warning face.

"I'd better go," he said, handing the phone back to Michelle. He picked up his airplane and trudged back up the stairs.

Turning her attention back to Amber, Michelle said, "He really misses you. We'll have to plan a time when you can come back out. Maybe later in a few months."

"Yeah," Amber replied. "Okay. Well, I won't keep you guys. I just wanted to hear his voice." She hesitated and then asked, "It's alright for me to call sometimes, right?"

"Let me talk to Steve about it."

Silence.

"Your letters really mean a lot to Caleb," she added.

"Okay, good. I love his, too," Amber replied.

Just then the doorbell rang. "Amber, I've got to go now. My mom and grandparents are here for a barbecue."

"Oh. Well, I guess I'll talk to you later, then." She sounded so lost and alone, and Michelle wished she had some timely word of encouragement to give her.

"Can I call you tomorrow?" she asked. *Maybe that will give me some time to collect my thoughts.*

"Sure. Yeah, that would be great." Amber's voiced brightened. "I'll be home all morning, then I have to be at work by twelve."

"Okay. I'll call you in the morning," she promised.

A knock on the door hastened their goodbyes, and Michelle hurried over to greet her mother and grandparents. "Sorry about that," she said as she welcomed them into her home and embraced her loved ones. "I was stuck on the phone with Amber."

"Amber?" her mother asked.

"How's that poor girl doing?" Grandma Joan wanted to know.

Her grandfather also seemed eager to hear more about Amber. "I've been meaning to write a letter to that young lady," he said. "God's put some things on my heart to share with her."

"I know she'd love to hear from you, Grandpa. You really helped her while she was here. It's still pretty rough for her. Losing Chad and all," Michelle replied.

"I'll try to work on that while I'm here and get it in the mail," he said.

Michelle nodded, and then asked, "How was your flight?" She couldn't help noticing he looked rather drawn and tired in spite of his warm smile.

"Uneventful," he replied. "So where's that lawyer of yours?" he asked with a wink.

"Steve's out working the barbecue. I'm sure he'd love your company."

"Go," Grandma said.

He nodded. "I'll go keep an eye on him."

The three ladies retreated to the kitchen, where Michelle poured them some iced tea and then busied herself getting the salad ready.

"Where are the children?" Sheila asked, as she helped her chop some vegetables.

"Upstairs. They're supposed to be cleaning their rooms."

"Supposed to be?" Joan asked.

"Well, you know how that goes. Caleb's probably playing with his superheroes, and Madison—my guess is she's busy working on her friendship bracelets," Michelle explained.

"Mind if I go up there and say hi?" her grandmother asked.

"Not at all. In fact, you can also tell them to wash up and come down for dinner."

Joan smiled and nodded. "I'll go round them up."

As soon as she was out of earshot, Michelle turned to Sheila. "Mom, do you think Grandpa's okay? He really looks tired."

Her mother's serious expression matched Michelle's unshakable feelings of concern. "I know what you mean. I've been worried about him. We haven't really had a chance to talk yet. They both dozed on the way home from the airport and then spent the rest of the afternoon checking out my new place and getting settled into the guest room before we came over here."

"Let me know what Grandma says when you talk to her."

"I will, honey. Don't worry. Your grandfather's a hardy fellow. Hopefully it's just his age creeping up on him."

Michelle knew her mother was trying to reassure her, but the expression on her mother's face said much more than her words. *Dear Lord, don't let anything happen to Grandpa. We all need him so very much.*

CHAPTER TWENTY-EIGHT

After Michelle's mother had taken Grandpa Phil and Grandma Joan back to her place, and the kids were tucked into bed, Michelle joined Steve on the couch, propping her feet up next to his on the coffee table.

"Great job tonight, honey," Steve said as he draped his arm over her shoulders.

"Thanks, but you did half the work," she replied, leaning her head against his arm. "What did you think of Grandpa?"

"What do you mean?"

"I mean how he looked."

Steve squeezed her shoulder. "He's looking a little tired, but that's probably to be expected at his age."

"Hmmm," she murmured. "I just get this feeling something's not right. That there's more to this visit than seeing Mom's place."

"Have you asked your mother what she thinks?"

"Yes, but we didn't really get a chance to talk about him. She seemed to think it was just age, too."

They sat quietly for a few minutes, then Michelle spoke again. "I forgot to tell you that Amber called today."

"She did?" His voice tensed. "What did she say?"

"She sounded pretty lonely. She just wanted to talk to Caleb."

He pulled back and looked at her. "What did you say?"

"What could I say? I let them talk for a couple of minutes." She could see his jaw clenching. "I felt sorry for her, honey. It's tough trying to rebuild her life without Chad."

Although she could still see the concern on his face, he nodded. "What did they talk about?"

"I only heard Caleb's side of the conversation. Seemed like it was pretty basic at first. Then they talked about her coming out again. I gave Caleb a warning look, and he cut off the conversation at that point."

"I'll talk to him about it," Steve said. "It's fine for them to write to each other, but I don't want to encourage the phone thing. And we're definitely not going to establish ongoing visits."

Michelle nodded. She knew where he was coming from, and his desire to protect the family. But she couldn't help feeling a little sad for Amber. "I told her I'd call her back tomorrow morning. But I forgot tomorrow's Sunday. She's working all afternoon and into the evening, and we'll be at church in the morning."

"Just call her another time. She'll understand." He took her hand and added, "You can't rescue everyone, honey."

She smiled. "I'll text her and tell her we can talk later in the week. It'll probably be pretty busy around here with Grandma and Grandpa in town."

"Yep. And they need to be your priority now. Amber will find her way."

I hope he's right, she thought. "Guess I'll go finish up in the kitchen." She stood but Steve's grasp on her hand didn't loosen.

"Let's go to bed. The kitchen will be there in the morning. I promise I'll help before church."

"Yeah, I've heard that before," she replied with a weary smile. But bed sounded inviting, so she let him lead her up the stairs.

Sheila could hear her parents talking in the other room, as she quickly got ready for church the next morning. Her hands shook nervously as she applied her mascara. *This is ridiculous! Why am I so nervous?* The thought of her mother and father meeting Rick had her stomach doing somersaults. *I feel like a teenager needing my parents' approval.* She shook her head as if to shake off the notion.

Other than her husband, she'd really never had a serious relationship with a man. John Ackerman swept her off her feet at a young, impressionable age, and she'd spent most of her life as his wife. Dating meant pioneering an uncharted land of opportunities for both blessings and disappointment. Somehow getting her parents' nod of approval seemed to be the thumbs up she needed to pursue this new relationship.

Better go fix breakfast, she thought. She found her parents sipping coffee in the kitchen. Her father looked up and smiled, but his eyes held a sorrow she rarely saw. "Good morning," she said in her cheeriest voice. "Everything okay in here?"

Joan stood and busied herself at the sink. "We were just discussing breakfast," she said, with her back turned to Sheila.

"I've got cereal and English muffins, if you'd like that. Or I can whip up some eggs," Sheila offered.

"English muffin sounds good to me," Phil said, and Joan agreed.

Soon breakfast was behind them and they were on their way to church, Sheila praying silently for their meeting with Rick.

As they entered the sanctuary, Sheila spotted Rick standing near the front talking to Ben.

"There's that young pastor of yours," Phil said, tipping his head toward them.

"Yeah, and that's Rick standing beside him," she replied.

"So this is your new beau?" Joan asked, eyeing him from across the room.

"He's not my beau, Mom. We're just starting our friendship."

"Well, let's go meet the fellow," Phil suggested.

As they approached, Rick looked up and gave Sheila a warm smile. He turned to Ben and excused himself, turning to greet all of them.

"Rick, I'd like you to meet my parents, Phil and Joan Walker. Mom, Dad, this is Rick Chambers."

"It's so very nice to meet you," Rick said, extending his hand to her mother first and then her father. "Sheila tells me you used to be a pastor."

"Yes. Well, actually I still am. To a handful of people at an Alzheimer's home."

They chatted for a few minutes, and then the worship team began to play. After they'd been seated with Rick on one side of Sheila and her parents on the other, Michelle and Steve slipped in and sat beside Phil. Sheila leaned forward and waved, happy to see her daughter and son-in-law join them.

As Ben began to teach, Sheila struggled to focus on the message. Usually she was immediately drawn into his teaching, but the smell of Rick's aftershave and the feel of his arm slightly touching hers were an ongoing distraction. She glanced over to see him riveted to the message, breaking his focus momentarily to give her a smile, which only caused her heart to race a little more than it had been.

Pay attention, she chided herself, pulling out a pen and beginning to make notes in the journal that she'd brought along for just such a purpose. She knew her father would likely bring up some points of the sermon over their lunch with Rick, and she didn't want to sound clueless.

After what seemed like hours, Ben wrapped up his message with a prayer, and the worship team returned to the front to lead them in one final song. As they stood together praising God, Rick reached over and took her hand. She held on throughout the song, but quickly pulled her hand away afterward, hoping her parents had not noticed.

She invited Michelle and Steve to join the four of them for lunch, but Steve had some work to do, and Michelle wanted to take the kids down to the beach. Rick offered to drive to the restaurant, suggesting they pick up her car afterward.

Soon the four of them were seated at a table at the Cliffhanger, overlooking the ocean. Sheila noticed her mother carefully eyeing Rick throughout the meal, listening intently to his input about the sermon they'd just heard as well as his answers to questions about his position at the university. She seemed guardedly encouraged by Rick's new faith, and Sheila caught her watching her father's expressions as well.

This should make for some interesting discussion tonight.

When the meal was over, Rick quickly reached for the bill, insisting on treating everyone. Sheila smiled. She could see that her mother was impressed by the gesture, and her father graciously thanked him as well. "It's been a pleasure getting to know you a little," Phil said. "I hope we'll get a chance to spend more time together this week while we're in town," he added.

"I'd like that," Rick responded. He returned them to Sheila's car in the church parking lot, shook hands with her parents and gave her a hug, whispering in her ear, "I'll call you tomorrow."

She gave him a smile and nodded. Catching a glimpse of her father wincing and rubbing his back, she waved goodbye to Rick and turned her attention to getting her parents home where they could stretch out and rest.

"Your friend seems like a nice man," Joan said, as they headed for home.

Glancing in the rearview mirror, Sheila could see her mother's guarded expression.

"I'd say God is working on him," Phil commented. "It's encouraging to me when I see someone beginning to discover truth for the first time. Especially someone like your professor friend. Just goes to show no one's beyond God's reach." Her father paused, and then added, "But don't give your heart away too quickly, sweetheart. Rick's got a ways to go before you'll know if he's serious about making a change."

"I wonder where he'd be today if Michelle hadn't given him her letter," Joan mused. "It'll be interesting to see how far he goes with his new pursuit."

In spite of her parents' understandable guardedness, a warm glow of gratitude swept over Sheila as she considered how God had used her daughter's obedience to plant seeds in the heart of the man who was rapidly winning hers.

After breakfast the next morning, Phil turned to Sheila and said, "We need to talk, honey."

The look on his face immediately triggered an alarm. It didn't help when her mother reached over and placed her hand over Sheila's. "What is it, Dad? What's wrong?"

"You know I've had a few health issues lately," he began. "At first I thought it was just age. But…well…"

"Well what?" she asked, trying not to sound scared.

"It seems I've got cancer, honey. They found it in my pancreas." He paused as if to let the words sink in.

Sheila turned to her mother, who squeezed her hand and nodded. Looking back into her father's eyes, she asked, "Can they treat it?"

"I can have chemotherapy and radiation to slow it down, if I choose to go that route."

"What do you mean if you choose that? What other choices do you have?"

He cleared his throat and leaned forward, adding his hand to theirs. "I've lived a full life, Sheila. God's been very good to me. He's given me your mother, you, and the grandkids and great grandkids. Not to mention a wonderful opportunity to serve Him in ministry. But this old body's breaking down. I've got to consider how much I'm supposed to do to keep it going here, or if it's time to let God finish the work He's begun and take me home."

Sheila could not believe her ears. She'd just gotten over losing her husband, and now her father seemed to be getting her ready to lose him as well.

"No decision's been made yet," her mother said. "But we thought you should know. The doctors hold out little hope of a cure. Just a temporary postponement of the inevitable."

Sheila shook her head. "Aren't you two the ones who tried to teach me all my life that nothing is impossible with God? Surely He sees how much we all need you, Dad. And what about the residents at Tranquil Living? Who could ever take your place there?"

Phil released their hands and sat back in his chair. He studied her face, and she felt him looking deep into her soul. "There's nothing I'd like more than to be here for you and your mom and the kids. You know that, honey. And you know how important those folks at Tranquil Living are to me."

She nodded, fighting the tears that were pooling in her eyes.

"There, there," Joan said, pulling a tissue out of her pocket and handing it to Sheila. "We're not burying your father, yet. Let's just pray and see where God takes this thing." She patted Sheila's hand reassuringly.

"You're right," Sheila replied, mustering all her inner resources. *The last thing they need right now is to see me falling apart.*

"While we're here this week, I'd like to get to know your fellow a little more," Phil said with a wink. "Gotta make sure he's fit for my princess."

Sheila took a deep breath and forced a smile. "Okay, Dad. We'll work that out."

"No more long faces either," Joan said. "We're here to enjoy you and the kids. So let's just file this situation away in prayer." With that, she grasped Phil's and Sheila's hands, and turning to her husband, said, "Go ahead, Phil."

Sheila's father squeezed both of their hands, and they bowed their heads while he prayed for God's perfect will for his health and future as well as their family's needs and those of his flock at Tranquil Living. As Sheila listened to his confident prayer, she felt her racing heart slow and a sense of peace come over her.

"What should I tell Michelle?" she asked after their amens had been said.

Her father patted her hand. "I'll tell her, honey. Maybe I'll treat her to lunch."

"We could stay with the kids," her mother offered, and Sheila nodded in agreement.

"Can you get her on the phone for me?" he asked her.

"Sure, Dad." Sheila walked over and retrieved the wireless handset from the phone, dialing in her daughter's number. After a few rings, she heard Madison's voice on the other end. "Hi, Maddie. It's Grandma. Is your mom around?"

"Yeah. Hold on. I'll get her."

Sheila could hear her calling Michelle and then her daughter came on the line.

"Hi, Mom!"

"Hi, Mimi. Your grandpa wants to talk to you." She handed the phone to Phil.

"Good morning, pumpkin," he said. "Hey, I was wondering if I could treat you to lunch today." After a pause he said, "Your mom and grandma offered to stay with the kids." He listened and nodded his head. "Okay, great! We'll be over around noon. See you then." He handed the phone back to Sheila.

"See you in a while, sweetheart," she said to her daughter before hanging up.

Michelle sat across the booth from her grandfather trying to concentrate on the menu while her mind wandered to possible reasons for their lunch date. *This must be important. I hope it's not bad news about him or grandma.*

After the waitress took their orders, Grandpa Phil reached across the table and took both her hands in his. "Tell me how life is treating you these days," he said, looking her in the eye with his usual warmth and interest.

"Pretty good, I guess." She hesitated and then added, "I'm still a little concerned about Amber, though."

"How *is* she?"

"She's still really hurting, Grandpa. And I think she's transferring some of her love and sense of purpose from her relationship with Chad to Caleb instead."

He nodded thoughtfully.

"I mean, I understand how important Caleb is to her. But I'm concerned that she's placing too much of her hope for the future into building a relationship with him."

"How does Caleb seem to be responding?"

"He runs hot and cold. Sometimes he seems really excited, like when she calls or he gets a letter from her. But other than that, he rarely mentions her."

"I'll pray for that situation, sweetheart. Hopefully Amber will move forward with her life. Eventually she may find someone else to pour her energy into. But in the meantime, she'd benefit from directing it into building her faith and seeking God for her future."

"Yeah. I agree."

After a brief lull, Michelle asked, "So how are things with you and Grandma? How's your ministry at the Alzheimer's home?"

The mention of his ministry brought a smile to her grandfather's face. "Things are going well at the Tranquil Living facility. God's given me such a heart for those dear people. Every week, I witness Him pouring out His love on them in a multitude of ways. And, in spite of their illness, so many of them have maintained a spiritual connection."

"Really?"

"You know, I've seen women, who can't even remember their children's names, recite scriptures or sing dozens of hymns. God is still very real to them. One gentleman rarely speaks, but always greets me with 'Jesus loves you' when I arrive there."

"Wow. God is really holding them close, isn't He?"

"He sure is, pumpkin. Just like He does for us."

"So how about you, Grandpa? How've you been lately?"

"Well, to be honest with you, honey, that's why I wanted to have some time alone with you."

Michelle's heart sank as she saw his eyes cloud over. "What is it, Gramps?" She leaned forward and squeezed his hand.

"I may be getting ready to go home to Jesus, Mimi."

"What do you mean? Why?"

"I've got cancer, honey. It's in my pancreas."

Michelle felt sick and her heart ached. She tried to fight back the tears that were beginning to blur her vision. "Can't they do something to treat it?"

"I can have chemotherapy and radiation if I want. But the odds are not in my favor. And to be honest, I'm not sure I've got that much fight left in me."

"But we all need you, Grandpa," she argued. "You're our rock."

He smiled. "I think you give me too much credit, Michelle. Any rock I've been for you or for anyone else in this family has been God pouring *His* love and strength through this very meager man."

She studied his face and saw genuine humility. And then she saw deep spiritual faith battling physical fatigue. His life on earth was definitely winding down. But the glow of grace remained upon him, and she knew he was drawing every ounce of strength from the hope of heaven. Scooting out of her side of the booth, she came around to his and slid in beside him, pulling him into her arms.

CHAPTER TWENTY-NINE

Rick sat across from Phil Walker, feeling as nervous as if he were on a job interview. Sheila had arranged their meeting, saying her father wanted to talk to him alone.

"So tell me more about yourself," Phil said, while he stirred some cream in his coffee.

"Well, I've worked at the university for almost twenty years. Before that, I did some traveling and writing."

Phil nodded. "I remember Michelle telling me about your anthropology class."

Rick cringed inwardly. He flashed back to his lectures and how he'd carefully crafted the curriculum to insert his critical views of religion, especially Christianity. He'd felt it was his mission to set these students straight on the antiquated myths some of them still believed. What a fool he'd been in his pompous arrogance!

Most students had suffered his humiliations in silence. A few were openly adversarial toward him, challenging his premises and even his right to denigrate their beliefs. But Michelle had been different. Using her own tragic testimony of the situation with her father and how that had impacted her spiritually, she'd taken the time to craft a letter to him explaining the importance of her beliefs and actually inviting him to church.

Sure he'd basically ignored the letter at the time. But it never completely left him. He'd stumble across it from time to time and reread her message. Over time, it somehow made the journey from her heart into his. And that was when he'd decided to do some exploring of his own — to find out more about her God. The same God he'd always felt had let him down, especially when his mother died.

Now here he was, studying the Bible and dating Michelle's mother, who just happened to be a pastor's daughter. What an amazing twist of fate.

Turning his attention back to Phil, he replied, "I'd erase that era if I could. At the time, I was on a mission to dispel the foolishness of faith, or so I thought. Now, looking back, I see that *I* was the fool."

"That's a tough admission."

Rick nodded in agreement.

"Tell me about your life growing up."

"It was a little rough. My mother had me out of wedlock, and she raised me by herself. She worked as a waitress at a diner during the day while I was at school."

"Sounds like she's someone very special."

"She was," Rick replied. "She died when I was nineteen. Cancer."

"I'm sorry. That must have been tough."

"Yeah. Well, I made it."

"Did your mom believe in God?" Phil asked.

"She did. She'd take me to Sunday school and the whole bit when I was growing up. But when God failed to answer our prayers for her healing, I figured I was on my own."

"Understandable. But I'm glad you've reconsidered that stand and are taking the time to explore scripture."

"Your granddaughter had a big role in that," Rick said.

Phil smiled in response. "She's pretty special."

"Yeah. Her letter…do you know about the letter she gave me?"

"I do."

"Well, that letter was so heartfelt and tender, it finally got through to this hardheaded professor."

Phil chuckled. "Good for her. I know she was pretty nervous giving it to you."

"I'm sure she was. I was an intimidating guy back then."

There was a lull in their conversation as the waitress delivered their food. Then Phil said, "Shall we pray?"

Rick looked at him and nodded.

"Dear Lord," Sheila's father began, "we're so thankful for this time to get to know each other a little better. We ask that You'd bless this meal to nourish our bodies and bless our conversation as well. May we be ever aware of Your presence in our lives, and seek You wholeheartedly with every decision we make. In Jesus' name, amen."

"Amen," Rick echoed.

As they began eating, Phil asked, "So how long have you and Sheila been seeing each other?"

"Just a few weeks."

"She seems pretty smitten with you."

Rick felt his heart pick up speed. "Really?"

"You hadn't noticed?"

"Well, actually, I was hoping she felt the same way I do," he admitted. "I look forward to our times together and really enjoy her company."

"I'd imagine at your age, you must have dated a number of women. Have you ever been married?"

"I've had a few relationships, but no marriage. It just never seemed to work out."

"I see," Phil said, eyeing him seriously. "It may seem outdated or old fashioned to you, but I still see Sheila as my daughter, and I need to know she's being treated with respect by anyone who might be pursuing her."

"I completely understand. Your daughter is very special to me. I would never treat her any other way."

"Her first husband had some serious issues. It made Sheila's life a challenge and pulled her away from her faith. I don't want to see that happen again," Phil said. "You seem like a nice fellow, Rick. And I know you are making an effort to study the Bible. But scripture is not like anthropology. It's not intended for intellectual knowledge. Rather, it's a personal message from God to Man." He paused and looked into Rick's eyes. It seemed as if he could see into Rick's very soul. Then he added, "I have no doubt you'll find much to mentally chew on as you read the Bible. But if it ends there, you've missed the point."

Rick nodded. Sheila's father had a clear level of wisdom that commanded respect. "Tell me more. I want to fully understand what you are saying."

And so Phil set about explaining the gospel to this highly educated scholar. By the time he was finished, Rick was on the edge of his seat.

"And so, you see, son, the Bible doesn't just give you God's message of truth. It demands a response. Either you accept the free gift of grace offered at the foot of the cross, or you reject it."

"To be honest, I'm not quite sure how to do that, Phil."

"It's a simple prayer. You just need to admit that you aren't perfect, and that you need God's mercy and forgiveness for the many times you've lived life your own way rather than following His. And you've got to trust and believe that Jesus really is God incarnate—that He died on the cross to pay the penalty for your sins. If you pray that simple prayer, you can start a new life as one of God's children. Doesn't mean you'll never mess up again. In fact, I can guarantee that you will. But it does mean that He'll be there to forgive you every time and to redirect your steps, growing and refining you until you are ready to meet Him face to face."

Something was tugging on Rick's heart and mind to believe. He studied Phil's face. What he saw was compassion and love. There was no impatience, no judging or condemning. Just a solid faith wrapped in a warm glow of acceptance and peace. *I need that*, he thought.

His mind transported him back to his mother's deathbed. "Trust God, Ricky. You've got to believe."

A moment later, he looked up into Phil's eyes. "I'm going to need help with this," he said. "Will you pray with me?"

Phil reached over and placed his hand on Rick's. Warmth surged from his arthritic fingers. "It would be an honor, son."

As they bowed their heads, and Phil led him in a simple prayer of surrender, Rick felt the presence of his mother watching over him and rejoicing.

"Now you are ready to study scripture, young man," Phil said with a twinkle in his eye. "I think you'll find treasures there you may have missed before."

Rick soaked in his words. Rivers of encouragement flowed into his parched heart. "I really appreciate this. I mean everything."

Phil smiled. "Glad we had the opportunity to talk it out." He paused and then added, "And with regard to my daughter, you treat her well, or you'll have me and God to answer to." His expression was still friendly but held a clear warning.

"I will," Rick promised.

Phil leaned forward, wincing a little. "I'm not sure when we'll get another chance to chat like this, so I'd like to know what you foresee in your relationship with Sheila. Is this a casual thing in your mind? Because I have a feeling she's growing pretty attached to you, and I don't want to see her hurt."

Rick took a deep breath. *Okay. Here goes.* "To be honest, I'd like to see it grow into something permanent. I've been alone a long time. Your daughter's grabbed my heart in places it's never been grabbed before."

"So you're thinking marriage? Because Sheila's not one to shack up with someone."

Rick tried not to smile at the terminology. "Of course. I'd never ask her to move in with me."

Phil looked pleased. "That's good, son. I'm glad we're on the same page. You two take your time, though. Really get to know each other before you dive into marriage. It's a lifelong commitment. At least that's what I'd expect from you. And you also need time to sink your roots into your faith before you jump into the role of husband."

Rick nodded. "I agree."

"Good. Well, let's eat, then," Phil said as they glanced at their full plates.

Sheila's parents had just turned in for the night when her cell phone rang. It was Rick.

"Hey, there," he said. "Am I calling too late?"

"No. This is perfect," she replied. "Mom and Dad are in bed, and I was just having a cup of tea. So tell me, how was your lunch with Dad?"

"He didn't say anything?"

"I want to hear what you think. Mom drilled him, of course. I hope he didn't pour on the protective father routine too much."

Rick laughed. "Actually, I really had a good time getting to know him. He's a great guy, Sheila. And I can tell he's a very loving father. You are blessed. Truly blessed."

Sheila nodded to herself. "Yes. I am."

"I can't help but wonder how my life would have been with a father like that," Rick added.

"Must have been hard on you both. Especially your mom."

"Yeah. Well, those days are behind us. I'm not looking for pity, if that's how it sounded. I just feel great respect for your family, and your father has definitely set the tone. It makes me wish I were younger. Young enough to have a family of my own."

Sheila winced. Maybe this wasn't going to work out after all. "You know, Rick, lots of guys your age have children. It's still not impossible."

"I suppose you're right. But I'm not one to go after someone half my age just so I can be a father. Besides, I think I've found someone I'm pretty interested in."

A smile spread across Sheila's face and heart. "Oh really?" she asked teasingly.

"Yep. A beautiful gal I've been seeing lately. She's new to Sandy Cove, actually."

They both laughed.

"And when would you be 'seeing' her again?" Sheila asked.

"I could be there in five minutes if I hurry."

"You're crazy. You know that, right?"

"Yeah. I guess I am a little crazy. Crazy about you, Sheila."

"Good thing you aren't here," she said.

"Why's that?"

"Because I just turned three shades of red."

"You look good in red," he replied. "Should I come over?"

She laughed.

"Seriously. I could be there in a few minutes. It's only 10:00. I promise I'll leave before midnight."

Sheila thought for a moment. What would her parents think if one of them got up for a drink of water and found him here? On the other hand, she wanted to see him, and she was pretty sure her father hadn't told him about the cancer. It would be good to have someone to talk to about that. "Okay. Sure. Come on over."

"Really?" His voice sounded surprised and happy.

"Yeah. I'll put the porch light on. But don't ring the bell. I'll try to keep an eye out for you. Just knock lightly if I don't see you first."

"Okay. On my way."

Within ten minutes, he pulled into her driveway. She'd been watching through the front window, and opened the door to meet him before he could even get to the porch.

For the first time, he greeted her with a kiss. Usually that was reserved for their goodbyes. Sheila savored their growing closeness. "Let's go out back," she said, taking him by the hand and leading him through the house and out into the backyard.

They sat together on a glider and looked out at the stars. Sheila shivered from the evening chill, and Rick released her hand and draped his arm over her shoulder, pulling her close. The smell of his aftershave and the warmth of his body invited her to relax into his arms.

"There's something I want to talk to you about," she said.

"I have something to talk to you about, too," he replied.

"You go first," she said, noticing the sparkle in his eyes.

The words spilled out of him as he retold his conversation with her father. Rick seemed so happy and even looked a little younger when he smiled. In her mind's eye, Sheila could picture her father leading him in prayer.

Thank you, God, she prayed silently. This is truly a miracle.

Then turning to Rick, she did something that surprised even her. Leaning toward him, she gave him a kiss.

He grinned. "Now that's the kind of response I'd hoped for," he said with a wink. "Okay, it's your turn. What did you want to tell me?"

Her smile faded, and she felt his hand wrap around hers. "What is it, Sheila? Is something wrong?"

"It's about my dad."

He looked at her, listening intently.

"He's sick," she began. "I mean really sick."

Everything was silent for a moment, and Sheila felt the words sticking in her throat. She closed her eyes and breathed another prayer before continuing. "He's got cancer, Rick. Pancreatic cancer."

Rick drew back a little, gazing into her eyes. "I didn't know. He seemed fine at lunch. But, come to think of it, I did see him wince like he was in some kind of pain once." He paused and then added, "I'm so sorry, Sheila."

His compassion melted her resolve, and she broke into tears. The strong front she'd been wearing for her parents and Michelle dissolved, and she was overwhelmed with fear and sorrow.

Immediately, Rick responded by pulling her toward him and holding her close, one arm wrapped around her and the other cradling her to his chest. With his chin resting on her head, he rocked her, letting her tears flow freely.

Sheila allowed herself to sink into him. When her sobs finally subsided, she could hear the beating of his heart. With eyes closed, she stayed perfectly still, allowing the gentle rhythm of its cadence to calm her. Inhale. Exhale. Inhale. Exhale. Slowly she felt herself regaining her composure.

Leaning back, she looked into his eyes. They were filled with understanding and concern. It was then that she thought of how Rick's mother had died of cancer. No wonder. He knew.

Without saying a word, he leaned toward her. Their lips met in a tender kiss that became heartfelt and then passionate. Something within Sheila's spirit stirred, and she suddenly sensed that Rick's appearance in her life was a divine provision for the difficult months ahead. Although she might very well lose the most important man in her world, God had a plan to carry her through.

CHAPTER THIRTY

The next morning, Sheila found her mother sitting alone in the kitchen. "Where's Dad?" she asked as she poured a cup a coffee.

"He's moving a little slow today," Joan replied, and then added, "I think we may need to get home, honey."

"But I thought you were planning to stay at least until the end of the week."

Her mom reached out and took her hand. "He needs to get back in to see the doctor and make some decisions about his treatment."

Sheila nodded. "Okay. Do you want me to try to switch your flight?"

"Would you, please? I'm really concerned. He seems to be in more pain today than usual."

Sheila got the phone and began calling. Thankfully, she was able to exchange their tickets for a flight that afternoon.

"Will we have time to stop and say goodbye to Michelle and the kids?" her mother asked.

"I think so. I'll call her and let her know about the change of plans. Maybe you should go tell Dad and get your stuff packed."

As soon as her mother was out of the room, Sheila called Michelle. She promised to have everyone home when they stopped by. "I'm worried about Grandpa, Mom. Do you think you should go home with them?"

"I'll talk to them about it, but I'm sure I'd need to take another flight. It's probably best for them to just get back and see the doctor. After that, we can decide about me coming down."

When she got off the phone, Sheila began fixing some breakfast for the three of them. They'd need to leave in an hour if they wanted to have a little time at Michelle's before heading for Portland. When her parents came into the kitchen a few minutes later, her mother was wearing a cheerful attitude that Sheila knew was forced.

"Breakfast smells delicious, Sheila," she said. "Doesn't it, Phil?"

He smiled and nodded. "Sure does."

They sat together and held hands as her father asked a blessing on the food. He tried to carry on a casual conversation about how much they'd enjoyed seeing her new place all furnished and settled. But none of them had an appetite, and much of the breakfast remained untouched.

"I'm sorry we need to leave sooner than we'd planned," he said. "But I think your mother's right. I need to get home and face this situation head on."

"I understand, Dad. And if you two need me to come down, just say the word. I'll hop on a plane."

Relief showed in her mother's smile. "Thanks, dear. We'll keep in touch and let you know."

After rinsing the dishes, they loaded the car and headed for Michelle's.

Caleb greeted them as they pulled into the driveway. He'd been bouncing a ball against the garage door while he waited. "I'll go tell Mom you're here," he called as he raced inside.

A moment later, Michelle came out, embraced each of them and invited them in. "I just brewed some fresh coffee," she said.

"Sounds good," Sheila replied, noticing the pain in her father's eyes as he stretched his back a little.

"Wanna see my Lego castle?" Caleb asked Grandpa Phil, taking him by the hand and pulling him toward the house.

"Take it easy," Michelle warned. "Grandpa's not feeling well."

"It's okay," Phil told her. Then turning to Caleb, who had stopped pulling, "Lead me to the castle, young man."

As they disappeared into the house, Michelle gave Sheila a distressed look. Without saying a word, her eyes communicated her deep concern. Sheila put a hand on her daughter's shoulder and said, "Let's go get some of that coffee."

The three of them walked inside and retreated to the kitchen, settling at the breakfast table. Michelle had some homemade banana bread sliced and ready to serve from a decorative plate on the center of the table. She poured each of them a cup of coffee, got some small plates and butter and set them on the table.

"Do you want me to ride along with you to the airport?" she asked. "I can see if the kids could go over to Ben and Kelly's. That way you'd have company for the drive home."

"No thanks, honey," Sheila replied. "I'll be fine."

As they sipped their coffee, they could hear Caleb and Madison visiting with Grandpa Phil in the other room.

"I can go get Grandpa and bring him in here if you think he needs to sit and rest," Michelle offered.

Joan shook her head. "Leave him be, sweetheart."

Sheila's heart ached as she considered the very real possibility that her father might not see these kids again. *I can't be thinking like this,* she chided herself. But she couldn't shake the realization that it just might be his last trip to Sandy Cove. As she glanced over at her mother, she knew she wasn't the only one considering that possibility.

A few minutes later, the kids came barreling into the kitchen with Grandpa Phil in tow. He joined them at the table, and Caleb and Madison both grabbed pieces of the banana bread, taking them to the counter to eat. Michelle got up and poured the kids some milk, intercepting a squabble over the extra piece Caleb had snagged.

"Mom, he took two," Madison complained.

"I see that," she replied. "Would you like another piece?"

Her daughter nodded, looking smug.

Michelle picked up the plate with the bread and held it out to her. As Maddie took one, she gave Caleb a triumphant smile.

He rolled his eyes and looked away.

Sheila shook her head and grinned at Michelle, silently saying *'Kids will be kids'* with her eyes. Glancing at the clock, she realized they needed to get going soon. "Did you want a piece of the bread, Dad?" she asked.

"No, thanks. It looks good, but I'm not hungry." He took a swallow of coffee and added, "We'd better head for the airport."

"Yeah," Sheila replied. "Mom, are you finished?"

Joan nodded, blotting her mouth with a napkin. "Thanks for the coffee and bread, sweetheart," she said to Michelle.

"Sure, Grandma. Would you like me to bag up the rest for your flight?"

"You don't need to do that. But thanks for offering. I'll bet those two will have this bread finished in no time," she added, nodding toward the kids at the counter.

"Yeah. You're probably right," Michelle admitted. As they stood up, she said, "Maddie and Caleb, come on outside with us to say goodbye." They hopped off their barstools and followed the grownups out to the car.

As hugs were exchanged, Sheila noticed Michelle holding her grandfather tightly for an extra few seconds. "I'm praying for you, Gramps," she said when she finally released him. Sheila could hear her voice crack and noticed her brush a tear away as Phil and Joan got into the car.

Before joining them, she took her daughter in her arms. "Thanks for praying, Mimi," she whispered in her ear.

As they drove away, Caleb, Madison, and Michelle stood together waving goodbye.

The drive to the airport passed in a blur, so many thoughts parading through Sheila's mind as she drove. Would she soon be headed to her childhood home in Mariposa, too? What would her father decide to do about the treatments? And how would her mother manage as his caregiver in the months ahead?

"Sheila?" her father's voice broke through.

Pulling her attention back to the moment, she asked, "Yes, Dad?"

"I want to talk to you about your fellow."

"Rick?"

"Yes."

"What about him, Dad?"

"He seems like a nice chap."

"He is," she replied with a smile.

"Just take your time, alright? Give him a chance to make a firm commitment to God before you jump into something permanent. He's learning, and I give him a lot of credit for admitting he was wrong, especially at his age.

261

He's come a long way since Michelle had him as a teacher, but just be sure he's really solid with God."

"Okay, Dad. I will."

"You'll know, honey," her mother interjected from the backseat. "God will show you." She reached up and patted her on the shoulder.

"Thanks, Mom."

Just thinking of Rick brought a little joy back into Sheila's heavy heart as they neared the airport.

With their new boarding passes in hand, Phil and Joan turned to say goodbye to their daughter.

"Thanks for everything, sweetheart," Phil said as he pulled Sheila into a tight embrace. "I love you."

"I love you, too, Dad. You take care of yourself," she replied, trying to control her voice.

He held her at arms distance for a moment, his hands resting on her shoulders. "Hey."

She hesitated to make eye contact, not wanting to give away her anxiety.

He cleared his throat and she looked up. "Now don't you worry about me, okay?"

She nodded.

"I'm not afraid of whatever lies ahead," he said firmly, "and I don't want you to be either."

Sheila took a deep breath and exhaled.

"None of us are guaranteed tomorrow, honey. Not a one. It's up to God how long He keeps us here and when He decides to bring us home." He paused and studied her face as if to see if his words were getting through. "The thing we've got to hold onto is that no matter how long or short our time together here on earth is, we know we've got eternity together on the other side. Right?"

She nodded. "Right."

"Okay then, let me see that beautiful smile of yours before we board this plane. I need to take it home with me."

After another deep breath, Sheila gave her father the best smile her heart could muster. He pulled her into his arms one more time. "That's better, honey. Now don't let anything take that smile from you. Promise."

"I promise, Dad," she murmured into his chest.

"My turn," Joan said a moment later.

Sheila's father released her, and her mother pulled her close. "I'll take good care of him," she said to her daughter.

"Call me when you get home," Sheila said.

"We will, honey," her mother promised. Then she took her husband's hand, and they walked into the security line, leaving Sheila waving as they went.

After she got back into her car to drive home, Sheila let herself go. She cried for several minutes, talking aloud to God about her concerns for her father. Then she heard a tap on the window. Looking over, she saw a security guard looking in. She rolled down the window, dabbing her eyes with a tissue and trying to regain her composure.

"Are you okay, Ma'am?" he asked.

She sniffled and nodded her head. "Yeah. I'll be okay." Thanking him for his concern, she started the motor and headed home.

Michelle sat alone on her bed praying. She'd seen the look in her grandfather's eyes, and it broke her heart. His faith in God had always been such an inspiration to her, even when she'd gone her own way spiritually and sought answers in New Age beliefs.

Picking up her Bible from the nightstand, she flipped it open to a passage of scripture that had captured her attention recently. It was the scene of the last supper. She reread it until she came to the part that had jumped off the page at her earlier.

There was at the table reclining in Jesus' bosom one of his disciples, whom Jesus loved.

She closed her eyes and imagined what it must have been like to be that close to Jesus—to actually be leaning against His chest. She wondered if he'd been able to hear Jesus' heartbeat and if so, what that must have sounded like.

Thinking back to her earliest memories, she could picture herself sitting on Grandpa Phil's lap as he cradled her close on the porch swing. She'd probably been only three or four years old at the time, but she remembered feeling so special when he called her 'princess.'

As she savored those memories, she wondered how much longer they'd have. How she wished she could go back in time for an hour and be that little girl again in the security of her grandfather's arms without a care in the world.

Lately she'd been thinking about how fragile life could be. Her father's passing, Chad's sudden death, and now Grandpa Phil's illness all made her feel a little vulnerable.

Then a familiar verse arose in her spirit. *I will never leave you nor forsake you.* It was a scripture that had given her strength and peace during so many difficult seasons of life.

I'll always have You, she prayed with a grateful heart. And that truth grew a new root deeper into her very soul.

How I wish I could have been that disciple, Lord. The one who leaned close against Your chest. The one who could hear Your very heartbeat. What a reassuring sound that must have been, even in a situation like that last supper, when the future looked grim.

If only I could nestle up against you right now, Jesus, and hear it beating steadily. Maybe it would calm me. You know how afraid I am of losing Grandpa. He's always been my anchor to You.

She sat back against the pillows and listened for God. Suddenly a voice spoke into her spirit. It wasn't anything audible, but it was just as clear. And she understood every word.

"If you want to hear my heartbeat, daughter, then tonight when you are in bed, rest your head on your husband's chest. Steve is mine. I live within him. When you hear his heartbeat, know you are also listening to Mine."

It was as if time and space stood still. The magnitude of this truth penetrated her entire being with such force that she was moved to tears. In that instant, she realized how God was transferring her little girl spiritual leadership through her grandfather to a new one through her husband.

And it was true. Jesus did live in Steve's heart. She already knew that. Now she understood it at a whole new level. She didn't have to wish she'd been that disciple reclining at His bosom because she could listen to His heartbeat any time in the chest of the man God had given her.

Gratitude and love swelled within Michelle. And without saying a word, she knew God understood what she was thinking and feeling.

Later that night, after the kids were both sound asleep and Steve had climbed into bed beside her, Michelle scooted over and rested her head on his chest. As he stroked her hair and prayed with her, she listened to the steady beating of a heart for God, knowing her spiritual leadership was no longer dependent on her grandfather's physical presence in her life.

CHAPTER THIRTY-ONE

Amber stared at the phone. "Why hasn't Michelle called me back?" she asked the air. It was already the middle of the week, and she was supposed to call her on Sunday. *Probably just told me that to get me off the phone. She's busy with her own life and doesn't need me complicating it.*

Glancing over at the photo of Caleb on the refrigerator beside the picture he'd drawn for her, she ached with loneliness as she thought about how empty her life was here in Arizona without Chad or her son.

I need to talk to someone. She wracked her brain, trying to figure out whom she could call. Who would help her sort through her life and find a way to move forward?

A face flashed before her mind's eye. The wife of Pastor Ben. She'd always seemed to care about Amber. *What was her name? Kathy? No. Courtney?* She shook her head. Then it came to her. *Kelly. Her name is Kelly.*

Grabbing her Smartphone, she began searching the internet for churches in Sandy Cove, Oregon. *Lighthouse Chapel. That's it.* She clicked on the website link and found the phone number. A moment later, a man answered.

"Lighthouse Chapel, Ben speaking."

"Pastor Ben?" She wasn't expecting him to be answering the phone.

"This is he. May I ask who's speaking?"

"It's Amber. Amber Gamble."

"Amber! What a surprise! Is everything okay?" His voice sounded friendly and warm.

"Uh, yeah."

"How are things going?" he asked.

"Okay I guess. Actually, I was calling to see if I might be able to talk to Kelly about some stuff."

"My wife, Kelly?" He sounded surprised.

"Yeah. She's always been really sweet to me. And I kind of need someone to talk to."

"What about Michelle? Or is this something about Caleb you don't want to discuss with her?"

"It's not specifically about Caleb," she began, and then added, "Well actually it's partly about him but mostly about my whole life, and what I should do."

"I see. Is it something I can help you with?"

"Uh…well…I think I'd rather talk to your wife. If she's available, that is."

"Okay. Why don't you give me your phone number, and I'll ask her to give you a call. It'll probably be later this evening, though."

"That's fine. I can wait." She rattled off her number and then thanked him. After they'd hung up, she thought, I should have told him not to mention this to Michelle. I don't want her getting upset or all paranoid about me calling them. Hopefully he won't say anything.

Ben was about to call Kelly when Steve walked in the church office. He stood and walked around the desk to greet him. "Hey, bro. To what do I owe this pleasure?"

"I thought I'd drop by and offer to take you to lunch," Steve replied, patting him on the back. "Where's Mrs. Taylor?" he asked, noticing the receptionist was not there.

"Home with the flu. I'm a one man band today."

"Bummer. So are you stuck here then?"

"I could forward the church calls to my cell phone, I guess. But I shouldn't be gone long."

"Okay. We can grab a quick sandwich at the diner if you want. My treat."

"You're on." Ben adjusted the phone setting to forward calls after the second ring. He'd long ago gotten used to having church calls coming through his cell phone.

After they got their sandwiches and Ben had prayed a blessing over their food, Steve began telling him about Michelle's grandfather.

"Oh, man. I'm really sorry to hear that. We'll definitely put him on the prayer chain," he said. "How are Michelle and her mother doing with all this?"

"I think they're both realizing he probably won't go through the treatments. I mean, at his age and with this type of cancer, it's almost pointless to subject his body to that kind of grueling regimen for something that's likely terminal anyway."

Ben nodded. "Yeah. I'd probably make the same choice if I were in his shoes."

"But it's still pretty hard on them. I mean…Phil's been such a spiritual leader for their entire lives. He's helped each of us through some rough patches. The guy's a spiritual giant in a soft-spoken gentle teddy bear of a man."

"Do the kids know he's sick?"

"Yes, but they don't have any idea how bad it is. Michelle's been talking a lot about heaven lately. Kind of getting them geared to thinking in that direction."

"Good idea. It must be extra hard after losing Michelle's dad last year, too."

"For Michelle and her mom, yes. But for the kids, I think John's passing was the beginning of them grasping eternity. When Michelle brings up heaven now, they talk about how that's where Grandpa John is. So when it's Phil's time, I think they'll be ready."

"That's good. Sometimes kids grasp these truths even more fully than we do."

"Yeah."

"So guess who called before you dropped by the office?" Ben said.

"Who?"

"Amber."

"Amber? Really? What did she say?" Steve looked concerned.

"She wanted to talk to Kelly."

"Why?"

"She didn't say exactly."

"Did you ask if it was about Caleb?" Now Steve was leaning forward and looking at him intently.

"I did. But she said it was basically about her life in general. That she needed another female to talk to, or something along those lines. I suggested Michelle, but she insisted on trying to talk to Kelly."

"Are you going to set that up?"

"I took her number and told her I'd ask Kelly to call her later this evening." He put his sandwich down and looked Steve in the eye. "Don't worry about this. Kelly will know how to talk to her. And if anything comes up about Caleb, she'll be in your corner regarding what's best for your son."

"Yeah. You're right."

"Amber's probably really missing Chad and just needs someone to encourage her to press on."

Steve nodded. "Think it's okay for me to mention this to Michelle?"

"I don't know about. She didn't say it was confidential or anything. Just reassure Michelle that Kelly will tread lightly with Amber. She won't get sucked into any of Amber's drama and compromise Caleb in any way."

"Good," Steve replied, picking up the tab and pulling out his wallet. Paying for their lunch, he took one more swig of soda before they headed back to the car.

When he got home from work that evening, Steve found Michelle sitting at her laptop answering an email. "Hi, babe," he said, leaning over and kissing the top of her head. "Who're you emailing?"

"Kristin. She just bought her first maternity clothes."

"When do they find out if it's a boy or a girl?"

"In about a month."

Michelle signed off the computer and stood up. "So how was your day, honey?"

"It was pretty quiet, actually. I ended up dropping by church and taking Ben to lunch."

"How's Ben?" she asked, starting to clear some paperwork off the table to set it for dinner.

"He's fine. But he had a surprise call before I dropped by."

Michelle turned and looked at him. "Really? Anyone I know?"

"Yeah. It was Amber." Steve saw her expression change to concern.

"Oh, shoot. I forgot to call her back," she said in a tone that clearly communicated her aggravation with herself. "I was supposed to call her, remember?"

He nodded.

"Why did she call the church?"

"She told Ben she wanted to talk to Kelly."

"Why Kelly?"

"Something about needing a female to talk to about her life," he replied, trying to accurately relay what Ben had told him.

"She probably thinks I'm trying to push her away since I didn't call back. But all this stuff with Grandpa has really distracted me."

Steve put his hand on her arm. "I know, babe. The last thing you need to be worrying about right now is Amber. Ben said Kelly can handle it."

"Are you sure? I hate to put this on Kelly."

"Let her talk to Amber. Maybe Amber needs a more impartial viewpoint anyway. And I'm sure Kelly will give her solid feedback and advice."

"You're right. I'll talk to Kelly tomorrow and see how it went. I'll also call or email Amber and apologize for forgetting."

"If you feel like you need to, that's fine," he said. "But I think the less contact we encourage with her, the better."

When Ben walked in the front door of their home that evening, the usual chaos was ensuing with the twins chasing each other from room to room, Luke playing a car racing video game, and Logan begging for a turn.

"I'm home," he announced.

"Hi, Dad," Luke replied without looking up.

"It's my turn," Logan complained to his father.

"Home sweet home," Ben said with a smile. He caught Liam flying past. "Whoa there. Let's not run in the house."

"But we're playing chase the monster," he explained, wiggling free and taking off after Lily.

"Chase outside, okay?" Ben called after him. He heard the back door slap against the jam. Turning to Luke, he said, "Share the game with your brother, or we're turning it off."

"Okay," Luke replied reluctantly, handing the control to Logan.

"Where's your mother?" Ben asked.

"Upstairs with Lucy."

Ben found Kelly sitting on the edge of Lucy's bed. Their daughter was stretched out on her stomach, and Kelly was rubbing her back. "Something wrong?" he asked.

Kelly shook her head and warned him not to press it. "Girl stuff," she mouthed without a sound.

He nodded, leaning over and giving his wife a kiss. "I'll start the barbecue, and we can cook up the last of the burgers and hotdogs."

"Good idea," she replied. "Thanks."

A few minutes later, she came into the kitchen by herself. Ben was getting the meats out of the refrigerator and retrieving the utensils for the barbecue. Kelly came up behind him and wrapped her arms around his waist. Leaning her head against his back, she asked, "How was your day, honey?"

He loosened her grip and turned around to face her. "Probably easier than yours," he replied, pulling her into a hug. They stood holding each other for a minute, soaking in the chance to reconnect without the kids.

"I miss you," she said.

"I'm right here."

"You know what I mean. I miss this," she added, hugging him close.

"Yeah. Me, too."

After a sweet, lingering kiss, she said, "So tell me what happened at church today."

He gave her a brief replay of the day and then added, "You got a call."

"I did?"

"Yeah. From Amber."

"Michelle's Amber?"

"Yep. Apparently she needs someone to talk to and thought of you. She said you were always so nice and understanding toward her."

Kelly looked surprised. "Really? I've only talked to her a handful of times."

"Well, I guess you made a good impression."

"So what did you tell her?"

"I told her I'd ask you to call. She gave me her cell phone number."

"Did you say when I'd call?"

"I told her it would probably be later this evening." He studied her face and saw the fatigue of a summer day full of kids. "You don't have to call her tonight if you don't want to, honey."

"No. It's okay. But you're on for getting the kids to bed."

"You got it." He kissed her again and then said, "Better get this meat on the grill." Grabbing the platter and utensils, he headed for the back door, turning around to add, "You're the best. You know that, right?"

Kelly smiled. "Go grill."

Kelly glanced at the kitchen clock. 9:15. Ben was upstairs with all the kids except Luke, who was off at a friend's house for the night. She poured herself a cup of coffee and pulled her cell phone out of her purse. Looking at the sticky note Ben had written Amber's phone number on, she dialed.

"Hello?" the girl's voice on the other end said.

"Amber? It's Kelly Johnson, Pastor Ben's wife."

Amber's voice immediately brightened. "Oh, hi. Thanks so much for calling me back."

They exchanged some light conversation, and then Kelly said, "So what's going on with you these days, Amber? How are you managing?"

Amber started tentatively, relating information about her work and family. But within a few minutes, she was pouring out her heart to Kelly. "I can't stop thinking about Chad and how he should still be alive."

She paused and Kelly could hear her sniffle. "That old guy shouldn't have even been behind the wheel of a car. What a jerk. He's the one who should be dead. Not Chad." She started to cry, and then added, "Everything in my life is messed up."

Kelly took a deep breath. *Give me wisdom, Lord. How can I help this girl?* She waited a moment for Amber to calm down.

"Sorry," the girl said quietly from the other end. "I didn't mean to fall apart like that."

"You know, Amber," Kelly began, "it sounds like you've got a couple of issues going on. I know you're really missing Chad. I can't imagine how I'd feel if something like that happened to Ben. I'd be just as mad as you are, I'm sure." She gave Amber a chance to absorb that and then continued. "But here's the deal. You've got a really tough choice to make now if you want to move on with your life."

"Yeah? What's that?" Amber asked softly.

"You need to choose to forgive the old man who was driving the other car."

Silence.

"I know it seems like an impossible thing to do. But if you don't, your anger will just turn to bitterness and poison your own heart and life permanently."

"But if I forgive him, isn't that the same thing as letting him off the hook?"

"No. It's making a choice for your own mental and emotional health." She paused for a moment. *Should I tell her about Ben's outreach to the other driver, Lord?* A nod in her spirit prompted her to continue. "Amber?"

"Yeah?"

"Ben's been reaching out to that old man who was driving the car that hit you guys."

"Really? Why?"

"Michelle's grandfather urged him to do it. Phil had seen the man in the hospital that night, and he wanted to go talk to him. But it didn't work out. Besides, since we live in this area, he figured Ben would be the best one to do it since he could follow up for a while."

"Oh."

"You know, honey, this may not mean a lot to you right now, but that man is going through hell. He will have to live with Chad's death hanging over him for the rest of his life. And he's in a world of trouble. His license had been revoked because of medical reasons, but he kept driving anyway. He just couldn't give up his freedom and independence. Now he may lose them completely."

"Is he going to jail?"

"We don't know yet. The hearing's in a week."

"How old is he?" For the first time, she heard Amber's voice shift from anger toward the man to a hint of concern.

"He's eighty-seven. His wife died a few months ago, and his daughter and her family have been trying to get him to move in with them."

"So what is Ben telling him?"

"That there's a God who loves him and is ready to forgive him."

Silence.

"We all need that, Amber. Surely you've made mistakes, too. I know I have."

"Yeah, but not like that."

"I understand. But here's the thing. God doesn't weigh out our mistakes and pick and choose which ones He'll forgive."

"So he's free and clear if he just asks for forgiveness?"

"No. There are consequences he'll have to live with. But if he seeks God wholeheartedly, he can receive His forgiveness. That's the amazing thing about the cross. No matter how guilty we are, there's hope for restoration if we are willing to humble ourselves before God and confess our need for His forgiveness."

"Is he doing that? I mean humbling himself and asking God to forgive him?"

"Seems to be. And, Amber, if there were anyway he could take back what happened, believe me, he'd do it in a heartbeat. He's learning about God's forgiveness, but it'll be much more difficult to learn how to forgive himself."

"So how do I forgive him like you said?"

"It's a choice you have to make. It's not about how you feel. It's about deciding to let go of the anger and bitterness. The best way to start is just to pray for him. And ask God to give you a heart of forgiveness. The same heart that gave Jesus the courage to face the cross for each of us."

Silence.

"Okay. I'll try." She said softly and then asked, "What else? You said I have a couple of issues."

"The other thing is discovering God's purpose for *your* life, Amber. I know you hoped it would be being Chad's wife, but now you need to start over."

"How do I do that?"

"Well, what things in life are really important to you? What do you like to do? What are you good at?"

"Caleb's important. I like being with him."

Kelly nodded. "Yeah, I know. But Caleb's got a family here. Michelle and Steve have given him a wonderful home, and he needs to have his focus on *them* as his parents, not you. You need to look at the bigger picture and move forward with your own life." She paused to let her words sink in. Then she asked, "Do you like kids in general?"

"Yeah."

"You seem like you're pretty good with them."

"You think so?"

"Mmm hmm. I've seen you interact with our kids. They like you, Amber."

"They do?"

"Yeah. Have you thought about a career working with kids? Like maybe teaching or something?"

"I think I might like that. Or maybe social work."

"Okay. So that's a good start. You've been taking classes at the local community college out there, right?"

"Yeah."

"Do you have resources for the university to complete your degree?"

"Not really. I could ask my parents, I guess."

"See what they say. Maybe I can help you explore some scholarship and loan options, too."

"You'd do that?"

"Sure. It'll be good practice for me. Luke will be in high school next year. We'll be looking at colleges ourselves before you know it."

"You're amazing, Kelly. Thank you so much for talking to me."

"You're welcome. I'll check on you in a few weeks, okay? In the meantime, see what you can find out about universities in your area and what your parents say about helping you out with that." She paused and then added, "And pray for that man, Amber. Seriously. It will bless both of you."

"Okay."

After they'd hung up, Kelly sat back in the chair and closed her eyes. Fatigue mingled with a sense of deep satisfaction infused her body, mind, and soul. *Well done*, a voice breathed into her spirit, and she felt joy.

CHAPTER THIRTY-TWO

Phil and Joan sat on the porch swing together holding hands. The sun was setting, and Thumper slept peacefully at the top of the steps.

"We've had a good go of it, haven't we, sweetheart," Phil said.

She nodded. "That we have. Lots of good times and memories."

"I've been thinking about what the doctor said, and I've been praying about our options." He paused and squeezed her hand. "What do you think I should do?"

"What do I think or what do I want?"

"Are they different?" he asked.

She smiled but the joy never reached her eyes. "You old coot. Of course I want you to fight."

"But?"

"I heard what the doctor said. It's really going to be a rough battle, and one with no guarantees." She turned his face to look at hers. "Phil, you are the one who needs to decide this. We both know our lives here are brief, and we'll be spending eternity together on the other side. If you want to just live your life to the fullest right now and skip all the months of chemotherapy and radiation and the side effects of those treatments, I'll be right here by your side grabbing every moment we get."

"You won't be angry or resent me?"

"I'll be mad as blazes that you get to go home ahead of me, but I'll work through that."

"Would you stay here in this old house after I'm gone?" he asked, gazing out over their property.

"I don't know. I've been giving that some thought," she replied. "Sheila's invited me to come up and live with her."

"What about her new beau? Would he go for that?"

"She told me the offer stands regardless. But if she were to remarry, I wouldn't want to be underfoot. Maybe she'd help me find a little place of my own up there in Sandy Cove."

"I'm sure she would," he said, draping his arm over her shoulder and pulling her close. "Let's sleep on this tonight, and then I think I need to make my decision and let the doctor know which route I'm going to take."

She leaned into him and nodded. "Okay."

After breakfast the next morning, Phil said, "Let's go for a walk." Thumper heard the magic word and was immediately at Phil's side, his tail wagging.

"Looks like your boy wants to go, too," Joan replied with a smile. She knew this would be an important walk. *Help me really listen, Lord, and be the wife he needs.*

As they headed out with the dog close on their heels, Phil took her hand and for the moment, they were young again. Two people in love sharing a stroll on a beautiful, sunny morning.

Joan's heart swelled with deep affection and gratitude for the man who'd walked through most of her life with her. Ever faithful. A safe harbor for her in the storms of life. She knew all of that came from his love of God, a love that flowed through him to her.

I will never leave you nor forsake you, a voice spoke into her spirit as she wrestled with the uncertain future before them.

"Look how the roses are all opening up," Phil observed.

She glanced over and smiled. "It's your green thumb," she said. A gentle breeze carried their fragrance over to her. It would be difficult to leave this home and the garden Phil had lovingly tended throughout the years.

As they walked, he reminisced about raising Sheila on the property and how much Michelle and Tim had enjoyed coming and playing there on family visits. Now Michelle's kids had even romped on the lawn and climbed the trees.

They strolled up the avenue, passing the homes of neighbors and friends, some who'd been there as long as them, but many who were starting families of their own.

"This is nice," Phil said, glancing over at her and smiling.

"What?"

"Just taking a walk with my bride and my boy," he said, patting Thumper on the head.

Joan nodded.

Then he said, "I've made my decision, Joan."

"I figured that," she replied.

"I'd like to spend whatever days I have left like this, honey. Just soaking in each moment with you. I don't want to be stuck in some hospital bed or tethered to a chemotherapy IV." He looked over. "Am I being selfish?"

She returned his gaze. "No. You are being wise. And as much as I hate it, I have to say I'd do the same thing if the situation were reversed. If we were younger, I'd feel differently. You wouldn't get off so easy then." She wagged her finger at him, and he smiled.

"If we were younger," he began, and then stopped. He turned and wrapped his arms around her, drawing her close against his chest. "I'm so sorry."

281

She looked up. "For what?"

"For getting sick. For leaving you behind."

"You old fool. Don't be silly. Who knows? I could drop dead on you tomorrow, so don't think you've got a guaranteed jump on me on going home." She spotted a bench in the shade of a tree. "Let's sit."

After they got settled, Joan felt a strength and peace settle over her that she knew had to be from God. "All these years, you've been the strong one, taking care of me and making sure I was okay. Now it's my turn, Phil.

"And you know what we've always said. God's got each of our days numbered. If it's your time to go, all the treatments in the world aren't going to matter a hill of beans. If God intended to use those treatments to lengthen your days, He'd have made that abundantly clear to us, and we'd feel an urgency and confidence about going that route."

"You're right," he said. "So you understand?"

"Completely."

He looked over at her, eyes filled with love and gratitude. "Did I ever tell you how much you mean to me?"

"Once or twice," she replied, patting his hand and smiling.

Over the next few days, Joan noticed Phil poking around in closets and then retreating to the little outbuilding they had in the backyard. It had originally been built as a potting shed. Since it was within view of the kitchen, Joan insisted it be "cute," so Phil had put a miniature front porch outside the door, old-fashioned windows that opened, and a shingled roof.

When Sheila was five, it was transformed into a playhouse with a little girl kitchen, a table and chair set, a child size sofa and rocker, and of course the doll's cradle.

Their daughter and her friends spent many an afternoon playing house in the adorable little cottage.

After Sheila outgrew dolls and make believe, Phil had converted it once again to his own space. This time it became an office of sorts where he could sit with his various Bible study books and prepare sermons. He even held some premarital counseling sessions there, and Joan would bring out a tray of coffee and cookies for all of them to enjoy as they planned their futures together.

Now Phil was carting bags of this and that out to the cottage. "What are you doing out there?" Joan asked.

"Just a little project," he replied with a wink. "You'll see."

That was her cue not to pry or snoop. She'd learned the hard way not to go poking her nose into one of her husband's projects. The surprise was such an important element to Phil, and she'd crushed him one year when she'd wandered out and discovered a special clock he'd been making for her for Christmas.

No, she'd not go poking around this time. When he was ready, he would show her. In the meantime, she savored the look of joy and mischief on his face every time he headed out there with another bag of whatever it was he needed for this project. She'd noticed the neighbor boy, Trent, had come over to help him a few times. Always wearing a backpack when he walked past her kitchen window, she wondered what Phil had roped the young man into doing.

When her husband came back in the house about an hour later, he looked satisfied but tired. "Think I'll stretch out on the hammock for a spell after lunch," he said.

"Okay. I'll get the sandwiches on the table," she replied, and then added, "Aren't you supposed to go to Tranquil Living today?"

Phil snapped his fingers. "You're right! I can't believe I almost forgot."

Joan placed their lunch on the table and sat down beside him. She rested her hand on his. "When are you planning to tell them?"

He took a deep breath and let it out. "Better do it pretty soon. I'd like to keep going for a while longer, but they should know and start putting out feelers for other pastors in the area who can step in when I'm no longer able to be there."

Joan nodded and gave his hand a squeeze. Then they bowed their heads and thanked God for another day together.

Within a few weeks, it was clear that Phil could no longer continue his ministry at the Alzheimer's facility. He needed to conserve his energy for his time with Joan and to finish his project. They hoped to make one more trip to Sandy Cove, but that was looking very iffy, too. Most days, just spending an hour out back in the cottage and then sharing lunch and a little walk with his wife was about the extent of Phil's stamina.

He made the decision to go and tell the folks at Tranquil Living that this would be his final visit. They'd found a young pastor named Chris who was interested in stepping in for Phil, and Phil really liked him. He'd joined Phil there once and was introduced to the residents, but both men knew the people living there would need time to settle in and recognize or remember him. In fact, many still needed to be introduced to Phil each time he came.

It was a particularly warm afternoon, the day Phil went to say goodbye. The residents were gathered on the patio under a shady trellis with overhead fans providing a gentle breeze. In spite of the warmth, some of them were huddled under throw blankets. Others sported baseball caps or sunhats. Lilliana wore her bright purple large-brimmed party hat with the big white orchid on the side. She smiled and chatted with Brewster, who kept leaning over and asking, "Say what?"

Phil took in the scene, memorizing faces and reflecting on each of these precious people's impact on his heart. He'd known most of them for years. Their families, too. He was just about to begin sharing with them, when music filled the patio and all the workers came filing out. Sadie, the owner, was pushing a cart with a large sheet cake on it. Some residents started singing happy birthday, but Sadie clapped her hands to get their attention.

"We are having a little party today," she announced, "to say goodbye to a very special friend of all of ours."

Phil's heart was in his throat.

"Today is Pastor Phil's last day with us. So we wanted to do something very special for him."

The residents were silent. Phil scanned their faces. He could see confusion on many of them, but a few of the folks seemed to understand. Brewster pushed himself out of his chair and stood up. Facing Phil, he began to clap.

Soon they were all clapping. All except those who had dozed off.

Phil glanced over at Sadie and saw tears in her eyes. "We will really miss you," she mouthed. Then turning her attention to the group, she said, "Anyone for some cake?"

As the residents enjoyed their dessert, Phil meandered from one to another until he'd spent some time with each of them. Some gave him hugs and well wishes; others seemed confused about who he was and why they were having a party. By the end of the hour, he was tired and his back was aching. Giving Sadie one last hug, he whispered, "Thanks."

"We'll be praying for you," she replied softly.

He smiled and gave her a thumbs-up sign before walking away.

CHAPTER THIRTY-THREE

The next few weeks, Phil and Joan did all the things they loved to do. Walks along shaded roads, buying fresh produce and flowers at the farmer's market, sipping lemonade on the porch swing, and going through old family photos and scrapbooks.

They ate at their favorite local restaurants, listened to the little bands that played on the weekends, took Thumper to the swimming hole, and watched old movies.

Each day held special memories, old and new, as they savored their time together.

Joan kept a close eye on Phil, watching for signs of pain or fatigue and encouraging him to take little siestas as needed. She could tell he sometimes pushed through his discomfort in his earnest desire to live each day to the fullest. Most of the time, he was in good humor, and she tried to be the same.

They talked to Sheila on the phone every few days. She would fill them in on the kids and grandkids, as well as her blossoming relationship with Rick Chambers. Every call ended with her asking if she should come down to be with them.

Finally, one day Joan said yes. Phil's stamina was faltering, and the pain was getting worse. Their doctor recommended hospice, and Joan realized their time was dwindling, especially when Phil agreed to that plan. Sheila would come at the end of the week.

Soon a hospital bed was delivered to their home and placed in the front room, where he could see the garden through the big bay window and wouldn't need to climb stairs to their bedroom to rest. A wonderful hospice nurse named Annie became a regular visitor, helping Phil with his daily needs and monitoring his pain medications.

The day of Sheila's arrival was upon them. Everyone agreed the best plan would be for her to rent a car at the airport to get home. Both Phil and Joan were pleasantly surprised when their granddaughter arrived with Sheila. "How did you manage to get away?" Joan asked Michelle.

"Steve had some vacation time coming," she replied. As she hugged her grandmother, she added in a whisper, "I really wanted to be here."

Phil seemed to perk up somewhat. "You two gals are a breath of fresh air," he said with a smile. Joan immediately busied herself with getting refreshments for them, while they unloaded their things from the car.

After Sheila and Michelle had taken their bags upstairs, they joined Phil in the front room. Before they could ask him how he was doing, he began inquiring about the family. "How're the kids?" he asked Michelle.

"They're good. Enjoying their last stretch of summer vacation," she replied.

He smiled and nodded. Then turning to Sheila, he asked, "And how's that new beau of yours?"

She smiled. "Rick is fine, Dad. Now tell us how you are doing?"

"These two ladies are waiting on me hand and foot," he replied, gesturing to Joan and Annie, who sat quietly in a corner of the room. "They fuss over me day and night."

Annie looked up and smiled.

"I'm so sorry," Joan piped up as she placed a tray with coffee and muffins on a nearby table. "We forgot to introduce you. This is your father's nurse." She turned to Sheila and added, "Annie's a real Godsend." Then she glanced over at Phil. "Isn't she, honey?"

"Pure gold," he replied with a warm smile.

Annie busied herself plumping Phil's pillows and checking his morphine IV drip. "Good?" she asked.

"Good," he replied.

"I'll let you four have some family time," she said. "I'll be out back if you need me," she added, patting Phil's knee as she left.

"So what's new with Tim?" Phil asked Sheila. "I rarely hear about my grandson these days."

"He's doing great, Dad. He travels quite a bit for his job, but seems to love it."

"Does he still have his apartment in Seal Beach?" Joan wanted to know.

"Yeah. I think Seal Beach will always be his home base."

Michelle nodded. "He'll never leave Seal," she agreed.

"How about you? Do you miss Seal Beach, honey?" Phil asked his daughter.

"I did at first, Dad. But I love my new home, and it's great to be near the grandkids."

"Speaking of which, did you bring us some pictures of those kids?" he asked Michelle hopefully.

She pulled her iPad out of her purse. Flipping open the cover, she brought up a slew of recent photos taken since their last visit.

Joan pulled her chair up close to the head of the bed, and together she and Phil scrolled through the pictures with Michelle's help, smiling and even chuckling at a few.

"Now this one really captures Caleb!" Joan exclaimed, pointing to a photo with a sly grin on their great-grandson's face. "He's always got something up his sleeve, doesn't he?"

Michelle smiled and nodded. "All boy."

Handing the iPad back to her, Joan said, "Thanks, Mimi. Those are adorable pictures." She glanced over at Phil and noticed him wincing a little as he shifted in the bed. "Maybe we should let your grandfather rest for a spell," she suggested.

"Okay. I need to call Steve anyway, and let him know we arrived safely," Michelle replied. "I'll go call from the front porch. I think that's where I get the best reception."

Sheila looked reluctant to leave, but Joan caught her eye and said, "Would you mind helping me with the dishes, sweetheart?"

She nodded in understanding. "Sure, Mom." Standing up, she put her hand over her father's and said, "We'll be back in a bit."

He smiled and closed his eyes.

Later that afternoon, Michelle offered to take Thumper for a walk, and Joan and Sheila settled on the porch swing. "How are you doing, Mom?" Sheila asked, her voice thick with concern.

Joan stared out over the property. Without looking at her daughter, she took her hand. "I can't imagine living here without your father." She paused and then added, "So many memories."

Sheila nodded and squeezed her hand. "Yeah. Lots of good ones. Remember the tree fort Dad helped me build in that old oak?"

Joan chuckled. "I sure do. I watched him drag the wood up those little foothold planks he'd nailed into the trunk." She turned and smiled at Sheila. "Made me nervous as all git out."

"I remember. You paced at the foot of the tree trying to talk him out of it, and then disappeared into the house for the rest of the day."

Joan chuckled. "You loved that fort, didn't you?"

She nodded. "I sure did. My favorite times were when Dad and I would sneak up there with the cookie jar and a thermos of milk."

Her mother feigned surprised. "You did?"

"Oh, come on, Mom. You must have known."

She smiled and winked. "Okay, I confess. I did notice that the cookie jar was missing once or twice." She sighed contentedly and added, "We've had a great life here. That's for sure."

There was a quiet lull in their conversation as they sat and rocked together, a gentle breeze caressing their faces. Sheila soaked in the peaceful scene, basking in her childhood memories. Finally, she asked, "What will you do when Dad's gone, Mom? Have you thought anymore about moving up to Sandy Cove?"

"I've been giving it some thought. Your father thinks it would be a good idea. But I don't want to intrude on your new life up there, especially now."

"You mean because of Rick?" Sheila asked.

Her mother nodded. "He seems like a good man, honey. I'd like to see you remarry. You've got a lot of years left to enjoy with someone."

"You wouldn't be intruding, Mom. Please don't think that. We want you there. So do Michelle and her family."

Joan looked at her and smiled. "Thanks, honey. I'll let you know when I decide. For now, I'm just trying to focus on the moment."

"Dad doesn't have much time, does he?"

Her mother patted her hand. "No. I can see him slipping away from us," she said, her voice trembling a little.

Sheila draped her arm over her mother's shoulder. "I'm going to be here with you. We'll get through it somehow."

As her mother leaned her head on her shoulder, a new strength coursed through Sheila's veins. God was using all the hardship and heartache she'd been through with her husband to teach her to get her strength from Him and Him alone.

A quiet confidence arose in her spirit, and she knew that God would equip her to say goodbye to her father, and to be a source of comfort for her mother and daughter as well.

When Sheila finally retreated to her bedroom that night, she sat on the bed and looked around at the familiar surroundings. Her old dresser still sported a Battenberg lace doily and a pretty wooden jewelry box her father had crafted as a gift for her thirteenth birthday. The mirror over the dresser had been her grandmother's. She stood and gazed into it, seeing a tired, much older face than it used to reflect.

Pulling open the top drawer, she discovered a large manila envelope labeled, "Sheila's Papers." Pulling back the flap, she peered inside. A hodgepodge of old drawings and school reports transported her to the carefree days of her youth. "Mom must have found this stuff in the back of the closet somewhere," she said softly to herself as she examined each item.

There were cards and notes from friends. Even a few love letters from old beaus, including one from Michelle and Tim's father. Sinking down on the bed again, she unfolded it and read through it. *How I loved that man,* she thought.

Next she found a little pocket photo book. Flipping the pages, she saw pictures from the Father-Daughter dance. There she was in her pink chiffon, cradled in the arms of her father as they swept around the dance floor. She remembered how he'd made her feel like the princess at a ball.

The final photo was a close up of their faces, both looking directly into the camera. Sheila gazed into his eyes and soaked in his youthful face and vitality. Where had the years gone? Soon her granddaughter would be this age. Sighing deeply, she slipped the contents back into the envelope and placed it into her suitcase.

Then she climbed into bed, bone weary from the travel and the emotions of the day. As she drifted off to sleep, she felt herself once again swaying in her father's arms as they danced the night away.

The next day, Sheila took her mother to the market, and Michelle had a chance to be alone with her grandfather. There was so much she wanted to say to him. But how to begin?

"Grandpa, remember when Dad was in the hospital and you came and found me in the chapel?"

He nodded, searching her face as if curious about why she would be bringing that up.

"I was really mixed up, then. That New Age stuff intrigued me."

"I remember." He smiled warmly and patted her hand.

"You were so patient with me and you listened, even though you didn't agree with what I was saying or believing."

"I knew you were seeking God, honey. And I believed you would find Him in time."

She nodded. "Anyway, I just wanted to thank you for talking to me and being straight with me that day. You knew how to speak the truth in love, and I'll never forget that."

Grandpa Phil lifted her hand to his mouth and kissed it. "God had your number, pumpkin. He wasn't going to let you wander for long."

A tear slipped out of Michelle's eye, and she brushed it away with the back of her hand.

"Come here," Grandpa said, holding his arms out to her. She moved into his embrace, and as she rested her head against his chest, she once again heard the heartbeat of God.

Over the next few days, they each spent as much time as they could with Phil, sharing treasured memories and speaking of family and faith. Joan was always first up in the morning by his side and tried to be last to bed at night.

Sheila and Michelle took charge of the many meals delivered by folks at the church. They attended to little details around the house and took turns relieving Annie, so she could get some sleep as well. Each day, Phil's words became fewer and fewer. But he seemed to enjoy their tales of life up in Sandy Cove, and every afternoon he asked one of them to read to him from the Psalms.

Through it all, Thumper rarely left his side, except to eat and take brief walks. He seemed to sense that his master's time was short.

CHAPTER THIRTY-FOUR

Three days later, Sheila awoke in the predawn hours to a soft knocking on the bedroom door. Grabbing her robe from its resting place on the back of a nearby chair, she wrapped it around herself and opened the door. Annie was standing in the hall. Her face was sweet but somber. "It's time," she said.

Sheila nodded. "I'll get Mom." She padded down to her parents' room and knocked gently, then opened the door. "Mom?" she whispered.

Joan was still.

"Mom," she said again in a quiet voice, reaching out and placing her hand on her mother's shoulder.

Joan pushed the quilt back a little and turned to look up at her.

"It's time, Mom," she said, helping her mother sit up on the edge of the bed. She reached for her mother's robe and held it out for her to slip her arms into. They stood together, and Sheila put her arm around her mother's back, holding her close to her side as they headed downstairs.

They could hear Phil's labored breathing from the front room. There was a rattle in his chest with every breath. Annie was checking his IV and adjusting his blanket. She gave Joan a sweet smile and gestured to the chair next to the bed by Phil's head.

Joan sunk down into it and took her husband's hand.

He turned and gazed at her but didn't speak. Sheila could see that the pain and the cancer had gnawed away his strength. It looked like every breath was a decision.

"Shall I get Michelle?" Annie asked softly. She had lovingly prepared the room for them, and three chairs embraced his bedside.

Sheila nodded and took a seat next to her mother. She watched her mother bring her father's hand to her face and kiss it. "We're all here, Phil. Just give us a few more minutes before you go."

Sheila's dad slowly nodded his head as he stared at his wife. His mouth moved, and although the words could not be heard, Sheila could see him say, "I love you."

Her mother's mouth trembled, and her voice shook as she replied, "I love you, too, old man." Tears spilled from her eyes and Sheila's vision blurred.

A moment later, Michelle was at her side, placing her hand on Sheila's shoulder. "I'm here, Grandpa," she said softly.

Phil's gaze traveled from his wife to his daughter and granddaughter. With apparent effort, he smiled. Then his focus shifted heavenward. After another deep breath, he spoke. "I see it. I see it all." Peace washed over his countenance as if all pain had completely dissolved.

Joan leaned in close. "It's okay to go. It's okay. I'll see you there."

He nodded, took one more breath, and was gone.

Joan stayed by Phil's side for several hours. Their pastor came and sat with her, reading some of Phil's favorite passages and praying with her while Annie made all the arrangements for the death certificate and contacted the funeral home.

Michelle retreated to her room to call Steve, while her mother stayed downstairs bringing tea to Joan and the pastor.

I've never seen Mom so strong, Michelle thought. Although she'd dreaded her grandfather's passing, Michelle herself felt a special peace enveloping her. Thank you, Lord, for being with us today. Thank you for my sweet grandparents and for taking Grandpa safely home.

She nestled into the overstuffed chair by the window and called her husband.

Steve answered on the second ring. "Hi, honey," he said.

"He's gone, Steve."

"What?"

"Grandpa. He's gone."

"I'm so sorry, sweetheart. How are you doing?" he asked.

She took a deep breath. "Okay, I guess. It was really peaceful. Different than I expected."

"How are your mom and grandmother?"

"It's hard to tell about Grandma. She's pretty quiet. The pastor came and sat with her. He's still in there."

"What about your mom? Is she holding up alright?"

"You should see her, honey. She's being so calm and strong."

"Good. That will help your grandmother. We've been praying for all of you — for God's strength and peace. Ben was here last night for a while. He brought Caleb home, and we sat and talked and prayed."

"Thanks," she replied. "God really answered your prayers."

"Let me know when we should come down," he said. "Do you need help with the funeral arrangements?"

"No. Grandpa made sure everything was taken care of last week. He must have known his time was coming." She suddenly felt a wave of deep sorrow wash over her as she realized once again how very special Grandpa Phil was to all of them. "It's going to be really tough without him," she said, her voice thick with emotion.

"I know, babe. I wish I were there with you. Do you want me to come down right away? I could try to get a red eye tonight."

"Let me talk to Mom, and I'll let you know," she replied, dabbing her eyes with a tissue.

"Should I tell the kids?" he asked.

Michelle felt overwhelmed with the thought of all the details ahead. It seemed like they'd just planned a funeral for her father and had to sit down to tell Maddie and Caleb their grandfather was dead. Now it was Grandpa Phil. "Wait until I figure out what we're doing down here," she replied. "If possible, I'd like to be with you when you tell them. Maddie's heart is still so tender from Dad's passing. And Caleb was really attached to Grandpa Phil." Her voice was trembling as she said his name.

"Of course. Whatever you think is best," he replied. "I'll give Roger the heads up that I will need to be gone from the office for a few days or a week. You just let me know what you need, and I'll make sure it happens."

After they'd said goodbye, she sank down into the chair and allowed herself a good cry. As she thought back over the many memories of her grandfather, her mind came to rest on the day he'd found her in the hospital chapel after her father's failed suicide. She had been such a confused young lady at that time, immersed in mysticism and New Age mumbo jumbo. With great love and patience, Grandpa Phil had led her to the foot of the cross and a fresh start with God.

His legacy of faith lived on in her and her children and she knew one day they'd all see him again. It didn't make the pain any less, but it made the hope of heaven sweeter than ever.

"Come on, boy," Sheila said as she tugged on Thumper's collar. "Time for you to go outside for a walk."

The dog didn't move. He sat resolutely by his master's bedside, eyes fixed on Phil's face.

"It's okay, dear," Joan replied quietly. "He'll go when he needs to."

"I'll get his food and bring it in here." Sheila went to the garage and got Thumper's bowl and a scoop of his food. She brought it to his side and put it on the floor.

He looked up at Joan as if asking permission.

"Go ahead and eat," she said, nudging him gently, and he obeyed.

She stroked his head afterward. "You're going to miss him, too, aren't you buddy?" she asked in a near whisper. His sad eyes just gazed up at her. "Maybe I can get him to go out." She stood and called, "Come on. Let's go out back." He seemed to study her face, hesitating to leave. She ruffled his fur and repeated herself. Finally he stood and followed her out of the house.

After doing his business, he was back at the door, pressing his nose to the jamb and whimpering. Joan sighed, opened the door, and walked with him back into the front room. A knock on the door distracted the dog, and he rushed over and began barking.

"That will be the funeral home, Mom," Sheila said, grabbing Thumper's collar as Annie went to open the door. When the men began transferring Phil's body onto a gurney, Thumper became frantic, pulling hard and trying to follow them out the front door.

"It's okay. It's okay, boy," Sheila said, trying to soothe him as she watched her mother trail them outside. After the hearse was gone, she let him out the front door.

Joan called him to her side and the two of them perched on the top step of the porch, her arm draped over his furry body. Sheila fought tears as she watched them huddle together, knowing their lives would never be the same.

The funeral was planned for the end of the week. Joan surprised both Sheila and Michelle when she said she'd like to have two services, one at their local church and one up in Sandy Cove. "Do you think Ben would be willing to do one for the family up there?" she asked.

"I'm sure he would be honored, Grandma," Michelle replied.

"Then it's settled. No need for everyone up there to fly here for this service. Maybe Tim would like to come to the one in Sandy Cove, too," she suggested. "That would give him some time with your family," she added to Michelle. "Phil always loved going to visit up there, and I know he'd be pleased to have Ben speak on his behalf at a memorial. But, of course, there are some people around here who will very much want to remember him as well."

Sheila and Michelle agreed. "Just give us a list, Mom, and we will contact everyone."

Michelle called Steve to tell him the news.

"Really? I know Ben will be honored to preside over the memorial here," he said.

"That's exactly what I told Grandma. Will you talk to him and figure out a day and time? Then we'll contact Tim. And maybe you can call Jim and LouEllen. Grandpa was very fond of them."

"Of course. I'll take care of everything at this end. Are you sure you don't want me down there for the funeral, too?" he asked. "I could probably leave the kids with Ben and Kelly."

"Thanks, honey, but I'll be okay. If you get everything arranged up there, Mom and I can focus on helping with the details here and get Grandma packed to come back with us. I think she'll be staying with Mom for a while. We'll be bringing Thumper, too," she added.

"That's right. I forgot about their dog. Do you want me to make the arrangements with the airlines for that?"

"Yeah. That would really help. And three tickets for next Sunday afternoon."

"You got it, babe. Let me know anything else you think of."

"I will," she replied. "How are the kids? You haven't told them, have you?"

"No. They're fine. Whenever they ask about your grandfather, I just tell them you'll fill us in when you get home."

"Perfect. Thanks, honey," she replied, love and gratitude spilling from her heart.

After they hung up, she looked at the photo albums stacked on the desk. *Better start working on the slide show for the memorials*, she thought. Flipping open the cover of one, she began perusing photos of her grandparents that went all the way back to their wedding. So many memories to capture and share! She'd be very busy for the next couple of days.

While Michelle poured herself into the slide presentation and all the necessary preparations for their trip back to Sandy Cove, her mother made arrangements for the ceremony, flowers, and reception. Joan's pastor promised to send an all-church email inviting the congregation as well as announcing the funeral service at church.

When Sheila mentioned that Joan would be going to back to Sandy Cove with them, Pastor Lawrence asked if she'd be interested in having a missionary couple housesit for her. The pair was returning from Africa that week for a two-week furlough and needed a place to stay.

It seemed like the perfect interim solution while Joan decided where she wanted to live. "Phil would have been so pleased," Sheila's mother said. "He'd dreamed of being a missionary when he was young, but God had a different plan."

Their pastor also offered to take them to the airport in the church's oversized van, which would allow for transport of all their luggage as well as Thumper's kennel and paraphernalia. They'd give him the house keys and important phone numbers at that time.

CHAPTER THIRTY-FIVE

Nothing could have prepared the three ladies for what awaited them at church that Saturday afternoon. Even though they arrived an hour early, the parking lot was already filling up. By the time the service was about to begin, the sanctuary was completely packed and dozens of people were standing in the back.

Many of the residents of Tranquil Living Alzheimer's Home were sitting off to the side in front. Sadie was perched on the end of the row, keeping an eye on her charges.

Stopping for a moment, Joan gave her a hug. "Thanks for being here. Phil would be so pleased."

"We will really miss your sweet husband," Sadie said with a sad smile. "The folks ask about him everyday," she added, tilting her head toward the residents. "We've framed a big picture of him with the whole group. It was taken at his farewell party."

"I'll drop by and see it sometime," Joan replied.

Just then the music began to play one of Phil's favorite hymns. "We'd better be seated, Mom," Sheila said, taking her arm. They encouraged Sadie to drop by after the service for a reception in the fellowship hall, and then moved to their reserved spot in the front pew.

Lawrence Taylor, senior pastor of the Good Shepherd Church, rose and walked to the pulpit. He looked over the immense crowd in the sanctuary and smiled warmly. "Let's pray," he began. The congregation bowed their heads while he led them in an opening prayer, dedicating the service to the memory of a wonderful man they'd all come to love and cherish.

"I remember the first time I met Phil Walker," the pastor said after their amens. "I'd come to observe him preach in anticipation of my interview to become a high school pastor for this church." He paused, nodding his head, as if replaying the day in his mind. "Although I honestly can't remember much about the actual message from that Sunday morning, I'll never forget the genuine warmth and compassion that radiated from the pulpit as Phil occasionally paused and smiled at the congregation.

"He shepherded this body of believers for over fifty years before he retired. Some of you spent many of those years sitting under his teaching and guidance. In spite of his measureless impact on so very many lives, I'll always remember how humble and down to earth he was as a pastor, mentor, and friend.

"His gentle spirit and love of laughter made him such a warm and approachable guy. Even when he was correcting or redirecting me in my ministry to the teens, he never made me feel like an underling. Instead, his confidence in God's work in my life was the motivating factor that propelled me forward, even when I'd become discouraged or was feeling defeated.

"Many of you have asked to say a few words about his impact in your life, and we want to allow time for that. But first, his granddaughter, Michelle has asked to speak."

Sheila looked at her daughter with surprise. Michelle squeezed her hand, stood, and walked to the pulpit.

Gazing over the sea of faces, her heart pounded in her chest and her throat threatened to close tightly.

Please help me, Lord. I need to do this.

She cleared her throat, unfolded her notes, and spread the papers on the podium. "Please excuse my nervousness," she said. "Some of you know that I'm a middle school teacher. Believe it or not, I'm fine in front of a bunch of eighth graders. But you folks scare me," she added with an anxious smile.

Chuckles filtered through the room, and she relaxed a little.

"Grandpa Phil was the best grandfather a kid could hope to have," she began. "I'll never forget his silly limericks or the way he always greeted us with that special smile of his and a joke. He loved to pull coins magically out of our ears or pretend to steal our noses. When we could sneak away from Grandma, he'd take us for donuts at the local donut shop." She looked over at her grandmother and smiled.

"He was a man of adventure and could transform his yard into an imaginary jungle or a hiding place for buried treasure. But he was also one who loved to just take us in his lap and tell us stories from his childhood or the Bible. Either way, those stories became very real to my brother and me when we were little."

She glanced back at her notes and continued. "When I got older, I lost my way for a while and dabbled in some spiritual beliefs and practices that were foreign to Grandpa. But he remained steadfast in his love — always available to me and never ridiculing or manipulating me."

Her eyes began to blur as she thought about her father's suicide attempt, and how her grandfather had helped her find her way back to faith. With a shaking voice, she relayed the scene in the hospital chapel where he had finally challenged her New Age beliefs and brought her back to the cross.

"I owe my grandfather so much. My faith, the ministry that God has given me as a middle school teacher, and the godly home in which my husband and I raise our two children. Without Grandpa Phil, I don't honestly know where I would be today." As she stepped down, she looked around the church, noticing heads nodding as if to confirm his impact on their lives as well.

When she sat back down, her mother wrapped her arm around her and gave her a squeeze. "Your grandfather loved you very much, honey."

Michelle nodded and smiled, her knees still knocking together as she tried to calm herself.

Pastor Lawrence was back at the podium, inviting others to come forward. A line formed across the front of the sanctuary and one person after another shared their love and admiration for Phil, many mentioning his lifelong impact on them spiritually as well as the treasure of his friendship.

As the line finally ended, a soloist from the choir came forward with the worship leader and sang another one of Phil's favorite selections—Amazing Grace. The worship leader invited the congregation to join in the final chorus.

Then the lights dimmed. "And now, the family has prepared a slideshow of Phil's life," the pastor said.

Background songs played as the screen lit with images of Phil and Joan at their wedding, their years raising Sheila, and then fun times with the grandkids. Phil's playful antics, his gentle spirit, and his enduring love and faithfulness captivated the congregation. Sounds of laughter and tears revealed the deep impact of a life well lived.

When the slideshow was over, the pastor invited everyone to transition to the fellowship hall for a reception and refreshments.

It was nearly an hour before Michelle, Sheila, and Joan could free themselves from the hugs and deep sentiments of those who gathered around them in the sanctuary. They made their way to the reception, and Michelle put together some food for each of them, allowing her mother and grandmother to remain at a table to visit with guests who wanted to speak to them.

By the time they got home, they were all spent. Turning into the driveway, they could see Thumper sitting faithfully watching for their return. As they got out of the car, he greeted them eagerly, then turned and resumed his watch down the driveway. "He's waiting for Dad, isn't he?" Sheila asked her mother.

Joan nodded. "It's as if he expects him to appear around the bend any minute."

Michelle felt a lump in her throat and tried to hold back her tears as she walked over and patted Thumper's head. "Come on, boy," she said. "Let's go get your dinner."

Thumper looked at her, glanced back down the driveway, and reluctantly followed them into the house.

As soon as church was over the next day, Pastor Lawrence and his teenage son Matt brought the van over and helped them load it up. Thumper resisted as they tried to get him into the back, but Joan finally coaxed him inside with a dog bone, and they headed to the airport.

"Thank you so much for doing this," Sheila said. "I can only imagine the three of us trying to do this on our own."

Joan agreed. "And you, young man," she added to Matt, "are very sweet to give up your afternoon to help."

"No problem, Mrs. Walker," he replied from the far back seat, where he sat with Thumper.

Joan watched the house disappear in the distance, thinking about Phil and all the years they shared together. A wave of sorrow threatened to overtake her.

Help me be strong, Lord. I don't want to fall apart in front of Sheila and Michelle.

She glanced over her shoulder at Thumper and noticed him wagging his tail as Matt scratched behind his ear. *We'll be okay. I know we will.*

Michelle and Sheila kept a conversation going with Pastor Lawrence throughout most of the drive, allowing Joan some space to reflect and pray. In what seemed like a very short time, they were pulling into the airport and parking.

Matt took responsibility for the dog, holding his leash in one hand and carrying the kennel in the other. Lawrence lifted the luggage out of the van and pulled the heaviest pieces, leaving the smaller rolling carry-on bags for Sheila, Michelle, and Joan to manage. He helped them check the luggage and Thumper, and then walked with them to the security line.

"Call me if you need anything," he said to Joan. "I can meet you here when you come home. In the meantime, I'll keep tabs on the house. Zeke and Lilly are wonderful people. They'll take good care of the place."

She nodded. "Thanks so much, Lawrence."

He held open his arms and gave her a big hug. "We'll miss you, Joan. But I'm glad you'll be with your family."

"Me, too," she replied, smiling at Sheila and Michelle.

After they'd boarded the plane and were settled into their seats, Joan closed her eyes and prayed. Flying made her nervous and she'd never traveled this far from home without Phil.

Soon they were airborne. A new chapter of her life was about to begin.

Steve was waiting in baggage claim when they arrived. After retrieving their suitcases from the conveyor belt, he loaded them onto a rolling cart and led them to the special cargo area where they would pick up Thumper. They had to leave him in his kennel while in the terminal, but as soon as they were outside, Michelle opened the gate and took him by leash.

After Steve loaded everything into the family van, they climbed in for the drive back to Sandy Cove.

"Kelly fixed dinner for us," Steve informed them as they neared home. "The kids are at their house for the night, and the casserole is in our fridge. She said we can heat it in the microwave. After dinner, I'll run you two home," he added to Sheila and Joan.

Thumper leapt out of the van, ecstatic to be free of his kennel and the car. He quickly explored the front yard, nearly panicking Joan as he ran near the street. "Thumper! Get over here!" Michelle called. Surprisingly, he obeyed. She took him by the collar and led him through the gate to the backyard. "You can run all you want back here."

The house was surprisingly neat and clean. "Wow, Steve. Everything looks great," Michelle said.

"Maddie helped me straighten up before they went over to Ben's," he replied.

"Why don't you two relax while Steve and I heat up the dinner," she suggested to her mother and grandmother.

"You won't have to twist my arm on that one," Sheila said. "Come on, Mom. Let's go out back and sit on the glider. We can keep an eye on Thumper."

As soon as Michelle and Steve were in the kitchen, she moved into his arms. "I've really missed you," she said.

Holding her tight, he replied, "Me, too. It's been a long week." He pulled back and looked into her eyes. "How are you doing, babe? And how about your mom and grandmother?"

"We're okay, I guess. It's just so hard to try to imagine life without Grandpa."

He nodded. "Yeah. He was quite a guy."

"So we'll tell the kids tomorrow?" she asked.

"I think Maddie's already figured it out, honey. But yeah, we'll sit down with them together tomorrow. I thought you might need a night to just unpack and get settled."

"Anything going on here I need to know about?" she asked as she began portioning out the casserole and heating the individual servings.

"Not much. Caleb finally lost that tooth," he said. "And Rick's called a few times."

"Really?"

"Yeah. He wanted to know what time you three would be home and if I needed any help picking you up at the airport."

"He knew Grandma was coming back with us, right?"

"Yep." Steve helped her carry plates to the table. "Should I have invited him to join us for dinner tonight?"

"No. I think it's good for Mom and Grandma to just be with us. I'm sure Mom will probably call him after Grandma goes to bed tonight. She didn't talk to him a lot while we were gone. There was just so much to do and so many emotions and memories to sift through."

When Michelle went out to get her mother and grandmother, she found them sitting peacefully together holding hands as they watched Thumper chewing on a bone. "Time for dinner," she said. The dog jumped up and ran to her.

"Thumper thinks you're talking to him," Grandma Joan said. "We'd better get some food out of the van for him, too."

"I'll get it, Mom," Sheila replied. "You go on in. I'll be there in a minute."

Joan followed Michelle back into the house, and a couple of minutes later, Sheila joined them at the table. "Mission accomplished," she stated as she took her place.

Steve held his hands out in a gesture they'd learned from Grandpa Phil. "Shall we pray?" They joined hands around the table, and he led them in a prayer of thanksgiving for their meal and safe passage to Sandy Cove.

Then he added, "Lord, you know we will all miss Grandpa Phil. Please help us remember that this separation is temporary, and he'll be waiting for us on the other side."

"Amen," Joan said with a sad smile. "Thanks, Steve," she added, giving his hand a squeeze.

CHAPTER THIRTY-SIX

"We're home!" Steve called, as he and the kids came in the front door the next day.

Michelle took a deep breath and headed out of the kitchen to greet them. "Hi, guys!" she said, opening her arms. Caleb rushed into them and hugged her tightly, while Maddie simply raised her hand and smiled.

"Hi, Mom," she said. "How are Grandpa Phil and Grandma Joan?" Shrugging her backpack off, she eased it to the floor.

"Sit down, kids," Steve said. "Your mother and I need to talk to you."

Just then Thumper barked in the backyard.

"What was that?" Caleb asked. "Did we get a dog?" His eyes lit with excitement.

"Not exactly," Michelle replied. "Let's sit down like your father suggested." She glanced over at Steve and tipped her head in the direction of the barking.

"I'll be right back," he told them as he headed for the back door. In the background, they could hear him say, "Calm down, boy. Go fetch." A moment later he was back in the room with them, and the barking had stopped.

"Whose dog is that?" Maddie asked.

"It's Grandpa Phil's dog, Thumper," Michelle replied.

"Is Grandpa here?" Caleb asked, jumping up from his spot on the couch next to her.

Michelle reached out and took his hand. "No, honey. Sit down."

"What's going on?" Maddie asked, a realization apparently beginning to dawn on her. "Is Grandpa okay?"

Steve pulled her close. "Grandpa Phil is fine, sweetheart. But he's not with us anymore. He's gone ahead to heaven."

"He's with Grandpa John?" Caleb asked, his brow furrowed.

Steve nodded. "Yep."

"This sucks," Maddie said, pushing away and starting up the stairs. Turning, she added, "Why does God keep taking people we love? It's not fair." She stormed away to her room, Michelle calling after her.

"Let her go, honey," Steve said. "Give her some time alone, and then I'll go talk to her."

Caleb leaned against Michelle. "So he's never coming back, right? Just like Grandpa John."

"That's right," she replied, giving him a squeeze.

"So we'll never see him again," he added.

"Not until we get to heaven," she replied.

"Is Thumper going to live with us?" Caleb wanted to know.

"For a while. Grandma Joan is staying with grandmother at her house, and we have a bigger yard for Thumper to run around in."

"Can I go play with him?" he asked.

"Sure, sport," Steve replied, reaching over and ruffling his hair. "Come on, I'll go with you. We can throw the ball for him."

They stood up and walked out, Steve's hand resting on their son's shoulder.

Michelle sank back in the couch and prayed for all of them. Especially for Maddie, who was trying to understand God and His ways as she navigated the new waters of adolescence.

She could hear her guys in the backyard with the dog.

Maybe Thumper will perk up now that he has Caleb to play with, she thought, as the image of her grandfather's dog patiently waiting for his master's return filled the screen of her mind.

Later that day, Steve went up to find Madison and talk to her. She was sitting on her bed, propped against the pillows, and listening to her iPod. "May I come in?" he asked, knocking and cracking open the door, before peering inside.

"Sure."

"Can we talk, honey?"

She nodded, setting the iPod aside and pulling her knees up to make room for him on the foot of the bed.

"I thought maybe we could talk about Grandpa Phil for a few minutes," he said.

Maddie sighed and crossed her arms. "What's the point, Dad? He's gone and there's nothing we can do about it."

Steve reached over and squeezed her knee. "It's the pits," he agreed.

"The what?" she asked, her eyebrows lifted.

"The pits. That's what we used to say when we didn't like something."

She shrugged. "Okay."

"Honey, I know you're really sad about Grandpa Phil. We're all going to miss him."

"That's only part of why I'm upset," she replied.

"So tell me the other part," he said, brushing a stray lock of hair from her downturned face.

She looked him in the eye. "Where was God, Dad? We prayed for Grandpa—all of us. God could have easily healed him."

Steve pulled her into his arms as her tears began to fall. "Where *was* He?" she repeated between sobs.

His heart broke as he rocked their daughter and prayed for answers. When she'd calmed down a bit, he reached over to the nightstand and handed her a tissue.

Then he began to answer her question to the best of his ability. "Here's what I believe, Madison. I believe God was right there with Grandpa Phil every moment. And for whatever reason, He knew it was time to bring Grandpa home to heaven." He paused for a moment, searching her face for a spark of openness.

"Your great grandpa loved all of us very much, sweetheart," he continued. "And I know a part of him wanted to stay here for many more years. To see you and Caleb grow up, get married, and even have kids of your own." He paused, searching again for the right words. "But there was something Grandpa Phil loved even more than all of us."

She nodded. "God, right?"

"That's right, honey. He had a passion for God like no other man I've ever met. And he served Him for a very long time, eagerly waiting for the moment when he'd finally get to meet Him face-to-face."

"So that's what he's doing now?"

"Yep. Right now, your grandpa and your great grandpa are able to look into the face of Jesus. They can speak directly to God."

She looked down and picked at a loose thread on her comforter.

"You know, Maddie, for us death seems like a horrible thing. It's something we fight at every turn. But God sees death as the ticket home to Him." He paused and searched for an illustration to give her.

"Remember when you were teaching Caleb about Shadrach, Meshach, and Abednego's fiery furnace?"

Madison nodded.

"That could have killed them, right?"

"Right."

"That fiery furnace can be kind of like a serious illness. It can kill us."

She listened attentively.

"So, just like those three guys, we pray to somehow be delivered. Do you remember what they said about God before they were thrown into the fire?"

"That He could deliver them out of it?"

"Yes. And did He?" he asked.

"No, not exactly. But they didn't die either."

"Right. And who did the Babylonian king see in the fire with them?"

"Another man who looked like the Son of God," she replied.

"So here's the thing, sweetheart. God responds to prayers about fiery trials in three ways. First, He might rescue us out of them and build our faith that He is a God who can change our circumstances in an instant. That would be like if He would have immediately healed Grandpa without any medical treatments."

She nodded.

"Other times, God goes through the fiery trial with us and brings us out on the other end. That grows our faith because we see that no matter how bad it gets, He is always, always with us and will help us through it."

"So, like if Grandpa would have gotten better from medicines?"

"Yeah."

"Here's the thing that's hard for us to understand. Sometimes, He uses illness to *reward* our faith. That is when He says "enough" to the pain and suffering, and takes us directly into His arms. Then we get a brand new body that will never suffer or be sick again."

She took a deep breath and let it out. "Go on."

"From our perspective, we see death as unanswered prayer. But from His eternal viewpoint, that is the ultimate answer—total healing, perfected faith, and eternal life."

"Alright. I think I get it," she replied, and then added, "but it doesn't make me feel any less sad."

"That's okay, honey. We all feel sad because we'll miss him until we get to heaven. But here's what I do when I think about *my* grandpa and wish I could see him. I just talk to Jesus and ask Him to tell my grandfather whatever it is I wanted to say."

"Really?"

"Yep."

"Daddy?"

"Yes, pumpkin?"

"Thanks for coming to talk to me." She looked into his eyes and gave him a sad smile.

Pulling her into his arms, he whispered, "I love you, baby."

"I love you, too, Daddy."

Michelle was walking past Madison's door when she heard Steve's voice. Standing quietly in the hall, she listened as her husband spoke words of comfort and encouragement to their daughter.

He sounds almost like Grandpa, she thought.

Tears of gratitude filled her eyes as she thanked God for spiritually growing all of them. Grandpa Phil was in heaven, but God was filling in the gaps through the heart of her husband.

That night, as she was tucking Caleb into bed, he piped up with a question that caught her off guard.

"Mom? Can I call Amber and tell her about Grandpa Phil?"

She hesitated, studying his face.

"She really liked him, and I want to invite her to come to the memory thing," he explained.

"The memorial?"

"Yeah. That thing. So, can I call her?" he asked again.

"Let me talk to your father about it, okay? And I'll give you an answer in the morning," she replied. "You know kiddo, it's a long way from Arizona to Oregon. She probably wouldn't be able to come."

"But let's just ask her, okay? Please?" His earnest expression melted her heart. "Promise you'll talk to Dad tonight."

"Scout's honor," she replied, holding up three fingers.

After both kids were asleep, she found Steve flipping through the channels on the television. "Can we talk?" she asked.

He punched the power button off. "Sure." Patting the seat beside him, he added, "Sit down."

She relaxed into the soft cushions and turned to look at him. "Caleb wants to call Amber."

"Why?"

"To tell her about the memorial for Grandpa and invite her to come."

Steve's eyes showed his surprise. "So what did you tell him?"

"That I'd discuss it with you."

"Do you think it's a good idea to have her out again so soon?" he asked.

"I doubt she'd actually come, Steve. But I'm thinking we should probably let him call her. Sometimes it's like pulling teeth to get him to send her a little letter, and she's pretty sad and lonely these days without Chad. The fact that he wants to include her, or at least invite her—well, I think it would be a sweet gesture. Something Grandpa would have encouraged."

He sat quietly for few moments. Then, draping his arm over her shoulder and pulling her close, he said, "I'm a very blessed man to have a wife with your kind of heart." He gave her shoulder a squeeze and leaned over to kiss the top of her head.

"You know, I was actually feeling the same way about you," she said.

"Really?"

"Yeah. I listened in on your conversation with Madison this afternoon. If it wouldn't have been your voice, I could have sworn I was listening to Grandpa."

The look on Steve's face was priceless. She saw gratitude and deep love in his eyes. "That's about the best compliment I've ever received from anyone," he said.

She smiled. "So what do you say about Caleb calling Amber? I'll trust whatever you think is best."

"I'd honestly rather not have her come. But I know your grandfather would be thinking of what is best for her, too. So, if you want to let Caleb call and invite her to the memorial, I'm okay with it."

"Thanks, honey. Like I said, I doubt if she'll be able to come on this short notice." She looked into his eyes and gave him a gentle kiss. "I love you, Steve," she added softly. He leaned in and kissed her back, softly at first and then with growing passion.

As she led him by the hand up the stairs to their bedroom, Michelle thanked God that their marriage had endured so many rough patches. She marveled at how married love could continue to grow deeper and more intimate through the years. Those early sparks of attraction, that had seemed so irresistible at the time, paled in comparison to what they felt and experienced together now.

CHAPTER THIRTY-SEVEN

Michelle sat with Caleb at the foot of the stairs, her cell phone in hand. "Now remember what I said, honey. There's a good chance she won't be able to come, so I don't want you getting your hopes up."

"Okay, Mom."

She pulled up Amber's number and placed the call. As soon as it began ringing, she handed the phone to him.

"Is this Amber?" he said a moment later. A smile spread across his face, and he looked up at Michelle and gave her a thumbs up. "This is Caleb."

Michelle watched his expressions as he listened.

"I called to tell you something. My Grandpa Phil died." His face became very serious as he relayed the news. After a pause, he said, "Yeah. We're all pretty sad."

Another pause.

"Well, I'm calling to see if you want to come to our remembering party about him."

Michelle could see him pressing the phone tightly to his ear.

He nodded and grinned. "Okay! Good! I'll let you talk to my mom about it." Holding the phone out to Michelle, he whispered excitedly, "She's coming!"

Michelle didn't realize she'd been holding her breath up to that moment. She smiled and gave him a high five as she took the phone. Caleb continued to sit beside her, watching her face and listening to every word. After Michelle gave Amber all the details about the service, she offered to let her stay with them in Madison's room for a few days while she was visiting.

"I can sleep on the couch. Really. I don't want to cause any inconvenience for you guys," Amber said.

"Maddie will be happy to share her room with you. Maybe you can sleep in her trundle bed pull out," Michelle suggested. "Then you won't feel like you are kicking her out of her room."

"Perfect. See what she says, though. If she'd rather not, I'm fine on the couch."

Caleb tugged on her arm. "She can have my room," he whispered.

Michelle smiled and nodded. She covered the mouthpiece and said softly, "We'll work it out, sport."

Amber promised to call after she made arrangements for her travel. She'd probably have to take a bus.

"Let me talk to Steve," Michelle said. "We've got some frequent flyer miles. Maybe we can arrange a flight for you."

After they got off the phone, she looked over at Caleb. He was beaming. She ruffled his hair and stood up. "Let's go check on Thumper," she said, and they headed out to the backyard.

Later that day, Michelle approached Steve about the flight. "She's planning to take a bus," she said. "But that's an awfully long ride for a young woman traveling alone."

"I agree," he replied. "It's amazing that she is willing to come. Caleb seems really happy about it, so I'm glad he called her."

"Me, too." She hesitated and then added, "What would you think of using some of our frequent flyer miles to get a ticket for her?"

"That's a great idea. I'll take care of it in the morning," he replied. "You're something special, you know that?"

She laughed. "Because I thought of the frequent flyer miles?"

"No. Because you put Caleb first. And you aren't insecure about Amber's relationship with him." He hugged her close. "Where is that boy of ours anyway?"

"Out playing with Thumper. Those two are practically inseparable. I'm a little concerned about how they'll both do when Grandma takes him home again."

"Maybe she'll decide to stay in Sandy Cove."

"Maybe," she replied, suddenly realizing how much she hoped that was true.

Two days before the memorial service and a day before Amber's arrival, Michelle's lifelong friend, Kristin arrived with her husband. They'd booked a room at a local inn overlooking the coastline. As soon as they were checked into their room, Kristin called. "I'm dying to see you, `Shell! If you're not too busy, wanna run over here and go for a walk on the beach? It'll be like old times down in Seal."

"I'd love to! Mom said she'd watch the kids this afternoon for a while. Let me give her a call and see when she can be here."

Sheila agreed to come over, and as soon as she arrived, Michelle headed for the inn.

Seeing Kristin was like returning to her youth. Whenever they were together—no matter how long they'd been apart—they picked up right where they left off.

Immediately upon opening the door to her room, Kristin opened her arms. "Come here, friend." As they embraced, she said, "I'm so sorry about your grandfather. That was really sudden."

Michelle nodded. "I'm still trying to wrap my mind around the fact that he's gone. He and Grandma were just up for a visit about a month ago."

"How's your grandmother doing?"

"Better than I expected. She's going to be staying with Mom for a while."

"That sounds like a good idea. Must be a hard time for her, too—your mom, I mean."

"Yeah. I think they're both trying to be strong for each other," Michelle said. Noticing her friend's swollen middle, she said, "You look great, Kristin. Pregnancy agrees with you." Reaching over, she patted her friend's baby bump.

"Thanks. We can hardly wait to see this little guy."

"Guy?"

"Yep. We just found out it's a boy."

"Congratulations!" Michelle replied, directing her glance back to Kristin's husband, Mark, too.

He nodded to her and smiled.

"So, shall we take our walk by the water?" Kristin asked.

"Sounds great," Michelle replied, eager to soak in the time with her lifelong friend.

"We'll see you in about an hour, honey," Kristin said to Mark, giving him a quick kiss.

"Have fun," he replied.

As the two friends walked along the water's edge, they caught up on each other's lives and reminisced about their childhood years in Seal Beach.

"The water was much warmer down there," Kristin said with a grin as it bit at her toes.

Michelle laughed. "It takes some getting used to."

An hour's time flew by as they shared their stories and plans for the future. They spoke of the hard times and commiserated. They laughed over the silly things they'd said or done, some of which had seemed too serious at the time but now were tales of levity as they divided their burdens and multiplied each other's joys. At one point, they laughed so hard they both cried.

Eventually, they lapsed into silence. Just gazing out over the sapphire sea and watching pelicans soar overhead.

Michelle reveled in the calm, comfortable ease of their friendship. "This is good," she said. "Really good. Just being with you like this. I miss it. Our walks and talks about life."

"Me, too," Kristin agreed. "It's not the same with the phone and emails."

Michelle nodded.

Turning to her, Kristin said, "Hey, let's make a pact that we will get together at least twice a year no matter what."

"I like it," Michelle replied with a grin. "You come here at least once, and I'll go to you at least once."

"Deal," Kristin said. "And your first visit will be when this little guy arrives."

"You've got it," Michelle said, draping her arm over her friend's shoulder and giving it a squeeze. "I wouldn't miss it for the world."

Kristin, Mark, Sheila, and Joan were all at Michelle's house for a casual barbecue dinner when Michelle's brother Tim arrived.

He surprised them by showing up a day early. Sheila planned to have him stay at her house, but no one expected he'd have someone else with him—a beautiful girl with red hair and a peaches-and-cream natural beauty. She stood by his side when Michelle opened the front door.

"Tim?"

"Hi, `Shell," he replied, giving her a hug. "I want you to meet my friend, Traci." He took the girl's hand and drew her close. "Traci, this is my big sister, Michelle."

It was clear that Traci was more than a friend. Michelle had never seen Tim so smitten. He looked like he was walking on air. "Welcome, Traci. What a wonderful surprise! Come on in, you two." She turned to her brother and added, "Mom and Grandma are out back with the rest of the gang."

After introductions had been made all around, Michelle encouraged Tim and Traci to help themselves to some of the dinner. Once their plates were full, they sat close together on the bench of the picnic table. Maddie, who usually hung on Tim, held back as if uncertain how to act around him now.

Caleb, on the other hand, immediately squeezed into the spot on the other side of Tim and began telling him all of his latest news, including Amber's impending arrival the following day. "Sounds exciting, bud," Tim replied.

Traci was sweet but seemed a little shy in the face of so much family. Kristin immediately gravitated toward her, starting up a conversation.

Just like Kristin, Michelle thought. She always knows how to reach out to people and make them feel at home. It was one of the things she most admired and treasured in her friend.

Soon Traci was opening up about her own family and herself. "So we've lived in Long Beach since I was little. Tim and I met at a coffee shop in Belmont Shore. When I told him I'd always wanted to learn how to surf, he offered to teach me."

"You surf?" Caleb asked.

"I do now," she replied, smiling at Tim.

"Cool. Uncle Tim is going to teach me to surf, too, right?"

"That's right, Caleb. Next time you are down in Seal, we're hitting the surf." He draped his arm over Caleb's shoulder and gave him a hug.

Joining in the conversation, Sheila asked Tim if he would help her bring the dessert out from the kitchen. "Grandma baked some of her berry pie," she said.

"Sure, Mom," he replied, winking at Traci. "Be right back."

"I'll help, too," Michelle offered, as she followed them into the house. "Your friend seems really sweet," she said once they were out of earshot.

"She's pretty special," he replied.

"Are you two serious?" Sheila asked.

"We're not engaged or anything if that's what you mean. But I really like her. We've been dating for a few months."

"I'm happy for you, bro," Michelle said. "It's about time you found a girl." She gave him a playful shove.

"So where are you and Traci planning to stay while you're here?" their mother asked casually, beginning to slice the pies.

"Traci's actually got a friend from college who lives up the coast about half an hour. So she's going to stay there. I thought I'd just crash on your couch," he added, looking at Michelle.

"That's fine. The kids will be happy to hear that."

"So will Traci be coming to the memorial service?" Sheila asked, as she finished scooping out the pieces of pie.

"If that's okay. I want her to know as much as she can about Grandpa. I'm bummed she never got to meet him."

Sheila smiled at him sadly. "I'm sure your grandfather would have loved to meet her, honey. It's good that she'll be at his service." Placing several plates onto a tray, she headed out back. "I'll take these out, and you two bring the rest."

Once they were alone, Michelle started grilling her brother. "So how serious are you really, Tim?"

"I think she might be the one," he replied. "But I'm pretty terrified to propose to her."

"Why?"

"What if she says no. Or yes. They both scare me."

She laughed. "I think that's pretty normal, especially for someone who's been as independent and free-spirited as you."

"So, how do I know for sure?" he asked.

"That you should propose?"

"Yeah."

"When it scares you more to think of living without her," she replied with a smile.

Tim spent the morning playing with the kids and Thumper, while Traci visited with her old college roommate. In the afternoon, he ducked out, heading north for a double date with Traci's friend and the girl's fiancé.

Steve took Caleb and drove out to the airport to pick up Amber, while Michelle and Madison straightened up the house and got ready for her arrival. It was nearly dinnertime when the van pulled into the driveway, and Michelle hurried out to greet Amber and welcome her back to Sandy Cove.

"It's good to see you," she said as she drew the young lady into an embrace.

Amber clung to her for a moment, replying, "You, too."

"Come on, Amber," Caleb urged, taking her by the hand and pulling her toward the house. "I want to show you our new dog."

Michelle glanced at Steve. "Our new dog?" she mouthed.

He shrugged and grinned.

As Amber and Caleb disappeared into the house, Steve retrieved her luggage—a gray duffle bag—from the back of the van.

"Is that all she has?" Michelle asked.

"Yep." He slung the bag over his shoulder and gave her a quick peck on the cheek before heading inside.

CHAPTER THIRTY-EIGHT

All the arrangements had been made for the family memorial gathering. Joan requested it be held outside on the church grounds. With white folding chairs and many new freshly planted flowers, the area was more beautiful and inviting than ever. Three rows of seats formed an intimate semi-circle facing a small white podium skirted by a lovely summer bouquet.

A friend from the church worship team played soft cello music as the family and close friends gathered and took their places. Michelle was flanked by Steve on one side and Madison, Caleb, and Amber on the other. Rick and Sheila sat front and center beside Joan, with Tim and Traci next to them. In the second row were Kristin and Mark, Jim and LouEllen, as well as Ben and Kelly's large family.

Various friends from the two Bible studies Michelle and Steve attended occupied the third row. An elderly gentlemen, who Michelle didn't recognize, also sat in back.

As the cellist finished her song, Ben stepped to the podium.

"Let's pray," he began. "Lord, we are gathered here to remember and celebrate the life of Phil Walker, one of your servants, and a man I feel honored to have known. Although we miss him already, we know he's standing in your presence now, completely healed and whole.

"As we share our memories here today, Lord, will you help us recall those special times when his humanity was touched by your divinity? Will you preserve in our hearts and minds his gentle voice, his loving ways, his contagious sense of humor, and his spiritual example to all of us? And will you comfort the family, especially his precious wife, Joan, as they adjust to this season without him?

"We're so thankful for Phil, for the time we shared together here on earth, and for the promise of heaven where we will see him once again. It's in Jesus' name we pray. Amen."

"Amen," the voices of those gathered echoed.

"In a few minutes, I'm going to give people an opportunity to share about Phil. But first, he had a request for today's message—something he conveyed to Joan, and she passed along to me."

Michelle glanced at her grandmother and saw her smile and nod at Ben.

"Phil was a man who lived his life with purpose every day. He treasured the calling God had placed on his life to be a pastor and teacher. Even after his retirement from full-time ministry, he refused to retire from the call, spending hours each week ministering to Alzheimer's patients at the Tranquil Living residential care facility.

"Although, because of their disease, many wouldn't even recognize him when he came to speak or fellowship with them, they all loved Phil. His upbeat spirit and his friendly demeanor broke down walls and opened hearts to God's unconditional love."

"Much as he valued his call and God's equipping to fulfill it, he considered his wife and family—all of *you*," he said, gazing at them, "to be his greatest gift and most important ministry.

"In his final days before going home, he spoke to Joan about the brevity of life and the importance of living each day to the fullest. That message spoke directly to this pastor's heart," he said as he patted his hand on his chest. "How easy it is to get swept away by the busyness of seemingly urgent demands and end up missing the essential things in life."

Michelle could see his eyes travel to the back row where Kelly and the kids sat listening. She reached over and took Steve's hand. *Lord, help me not lose track of what Grandpa knew was most important.*

Ben cleared his throat and continued. "God has appointed the number of our days, and none of us know when we will be called home. Let's honor Phil by determining, in our own hearts, to live our lives to the fullest just like he did. That includes putting God first in every aspect and relationship of life. It means treasuring our families and seeing them as our first ministry. And it means using the gifts, talents, and time God has given us to reach out to others with His love and truth."

Michelle's heart swelled with emotion as she thought about how fitting Ben's words were to her grandfather's life and purpose. Grandpa Phil was actively involved in ministry, but he always had time for her or anyone else in the family. She remembered how he was so attentive to her when she needed someone to talk to, making her feel like she were the only person in the world during that time.

And he never traveled without Grandma Joan, saying he didn't want to miss a single day with his bride.

Michelle pulled her attention back to the podium, where Ben was inviting people to come and share their memories. Her brother, Tim, stood and walked to the front.

"I know I should be saying some super spiritual stuff about Grandpa," he began. "But my very favorite memories of him were the times we went for donuts."

Gentle laughter washed over the group like a fresh breeze.

"We'd get up extra early and sneak out before Grandma could catch us," he said, glancing over at Joan, who smiled and shook her head. "Grandpa said the donuts were freshest then, and we didn't have to listen to Grandma's lecture about how bad they were for us.

"It seems like such a dumb thing to remember and talk about, but the truth is Grandpa and I had some great talks over those donuts. When I was a little kid, we'd talk about what I wanted to be when I grew up—something I'm still working on, I've got to admit."

More chuckles.

"But as I grew up, and we had the rare chance to go on an early morning donut run, Grandpa would listen to my insecurities and questions about myself, my future, and even God. He never made me feel like a loser or some shiftless teen. Instead, he talked to me about his own youth, his struggles, and his daily prayers for more faith.

"So, anyway, here's to you, Grandpa," he said, pulling a mini cake donut out of his jacket pocket and lifting it to the sky. Then he glanced at Michelle, winked, and went back to his seat.

Michelle had already determined that she wouldn't speak today since she'd already given her own tribute to her grandfather at the church service back in Mariposa. But she did briefly rise from her seat, turn to Tim, and give a thumbs-up. As soon as she was seated again, Amber surprised her by walking to the podium.

"So…uh…hi, everybody. My name's Amber. I just wanted to say something, too, even though I'm not family or anything." She looked over at Michelle as if seeking approval, and Michelle smiled and nodded.

"Okay, so I don't have tons of memories about Phil Walker, but I'll never forget some of the things he said to me when I was in Sandy Cove last time."

She paused as if searching for words. "Some pretty bad stuff's happened in my life, and some of it's my own fault."

Her voice shaking, she glanced over at Michelle again before continuing. "But Pastor Phil, well, he didn't make me feel like a loser or try to paint a rosy picture of the future. He just listened, cared, and sorta helped me see that there *is* hope, even for someone like me.

"He talked to me about how God can make even the bad stuff end up working out for good, and how nothing is wasted in God's economy." She nodded to herself. "So, anyway, I just wanted to say that, and thank him for helping me realize I can still have a good life and actually maybe help other kids the way he and Michelle," she gestured toward Michelle, "have helped me."

Looking back at the whole group, she said, "Okay, so that's all." Then she smiled nervously and returned to her seat.

Michelle reached across Madison and Caleb and squeezed her trembling hand.

A rustling sound drew Michelle's attention to the back row where the elderly gentleman, who sat off to the side alone, was struggling to his feet. Ben quickly moved to his side and helped him gain his balance.

Then, clearing his throat, the man said, "I just want to say amen to the young lady who just spoke. Your Pastor Phil reached out to me when I didn't deserve a second glance. He helped this broken old man through the consequences of some very bad decisions. He couldn't fix what I'd done, but he helped me understand God's forgiveness. And he introduced me to this man," he said, pointing to Ben. "So, I'll be forever indebted to him." He sat down, resting his hands on the cane that stood in front of him.

Who is that guy? Michelle wondered. She leaned over and whispered to Steve, "Do you know who that is?"

He nodded and squeezed her hand, continuing to look straight ahead as Michelle's friend Kristin went up to speak.

"Even though Grandpa Phil wasn't *my* grandfather, that's always how I knew him. When he would come to Seal Beach to visit my best friend's family," she looked at Michelle and smiled, "he always had time for all of us kids. Telling funny stories, taking us to the beach and getting us ice cream on the way, and sprinkling our lives with laughter and joy. He never met a stranger and never made what we said or our little childhood concerns seem unimportant.

"I remember one time thinking, 'I'm going to marry someone just like Grandpa Phil.' And guess what? I did." She beamed as she set her gaze on Mark. "Now, we're expecting our first baby, a little boy, and I hope and pray he will grow up to become a man of love, compassion, faith, and joy just like my husband and Grandpa Phil."

As Kristin started back to her seat, she paused to bend down and hug Joan, Sheila, and Michelle, whispering, "I love you," into her best friend's ear.

After Ben closed the ceremony with prayer, the cellist began to play again, and everyone stood and mingled. Lots of hugs were passed around. Out of the corner of her eye, Michelle spotted the old man hobbling away and Amber headed in his direction.

She turned to Steve. "Honey, look. Who *is* that guy?"

Steve nudged Ben and tipped his head toward the pair in the distance. Ben nodded and discreetly worked his way in their direction.

"What's up?" Michelle persisted.

"That's the guy who was driving the car that killed Chad," he replied. "Your grandfather talked to him briefly after the accident, and Ben's been counseling him ever since. I guess he told the guy about Phil's memorial today."

Concern gripped Michelle's spirit. Surely Amber had figured out who he was. She might have even recognized him from the scene of the accident. What would she say to him? Would she lash out and fall apart in front of everyone, including Madison and Caleb?

336

CHAPTER THIRTY-NINE

The old man could feel someone following him, and he tried to walk faster, but his cane and his shaky balance made it an impossible task. I never should have come, he thought, his heart pounding and his lungs failing to keep up with his fears.

"Hey, mister," a young woman's voice called out.

Taking a deep breath, he turned to face her, bracing for what was to come.

"I know you, don't I?" she said. "You were the guy driving the car that hit us."

He felt lightheaded and struggled to hold his footing. "Yes," he replied, "Yes, I am. I'm so very sorry about your friend."

"Well that won't bring him back, you know."

He nodded. "I know. Believe me, I'd trade places with him if I could."

"So why did you do it? Why did you drive even though you knew you weren't supposed to?"

He took a deep breath and searched for the right words. "Because I was afraid. The honest truth is that I was afraid to lose my independence."

His voice started to shake as he continued. "I've been my wife's provider for fifty years. And I just couldn't let that go." He looked into her eyes, searching for a glimmer of understanding. "It was stupid of me to think I could do it forever. But I kept telling myself, 'Just a little longer and then I'll figure something out.' But the truth is, I didn't *want* to figure out a way I could become dependent on others. I wanted to keep being the same man I'd been all along."

A tear slipped down his cheek, and he brushed it away quickly, aggravated with himself for being emotional.

"I get it," the girl said, her expression softening.

He studied her face to see if she was serious or being sarcastic. All he could see was another vulnerable soul. "You do?" he asked tentatively.

"Yeah." She looked him in the eye. "What you did was wrong. But I get why you did it. You need to know that Chad and I were planning to get married and have a family of our own, just like you and your wife."

"I'm terribly sorry," he replied. "If there's anything I can do…"

"You can make sure you never get behind the wheel of a car ever again."

"Fair enough."

"And you can pray that God will show me how to keep going from here."

"I will."

"One more thing," she added.

"Yes?" he replied, bracing himself for whatever she had to say.

"I just want you to know that I forgive you. That man we were here for today," she said, tipping her head toward the group who had gathered to celebrate Phil's life, "he told me I needed to find a way to do that." She hesitated then added, "And he wasn't the only one. So I guess it's important. Anyway, I wanted you to know."

She opened her arms, and he shuffled awkwardly into them. They stood hugging as both tried to let go of the regrets of the past. When she pulled back and smiled at him through tear-filled eyes, he felt a crushing weight lifted from his shoulders. "Thank you, young lady. You've helped this old man more than you'll ever know."

Later that evening, Michelle found Amber sitting on the back porch steps watching Caleb shoot baskets. "Mind if I join you?" she asked.

Amber looked up and smiled at her, scooting to the side of the step. "Not at all."

"I think the memorial went really well," Michelle said.

"Me, too. Your brother was pretty funny," she added with a grin.

"Good ole Tim. He tells it like it is," Michelle replied, watching Caleb sink a basket. "Nice job, little man," she called out to him as she gave him a thumbs up. Then turning back to Amber, she said, "I was really impressed by what you said up there. Grandpa would have been so pleased."

"Thanks. He was a special guy."

They sat quietly for a few moments, watching their son shoot hoops, each of them lost in their own thoughts. Finally, Michelle asked, "So how did your conversation go with that man after the service." She paused before adding, "Steve told me who he was."

Amber turned to her. "I think it went as well as it could. He messed up bad, and I told him that. But your grandfather and Ben's wife both said I'd need to figure out a way to forgive him if I didn't want to be eaten up with bitterness."

Michelle reached out and squeezed her hand. "Were you able to do that? Forgive him, I mean?"

She nodded. "Yeah. He felt really bad. I could tell. But when I said that I forgive him, he started to cry. All I could think to do was hug him."

"I'm so proud of you, Amber. You've grown into an incredible adult." Michelle draped her arm over Amber's shoulder and pulled her close.

"You really think so?"

"I do," she replied. "And I'm glad Caleb is getting to know you. It was his idea to invite you to the memorial, you know?"

"It was? I mean, I knew he was the one who called, but I didn't know it was his idea."

"Yep. He wanted you here."

"Thanks for telling me that," Amber replied. "You know something? I'm really glad I was in your class that year."

Michelle smiled and looked out at Caleb then back at her. "Me, too."

NOTE FROM THE AUTHOR

After I published the third book in the *Sandy Cove Series (Into Magnolia)* I really thought I was finished telling Michelle's tale. However, a slew of emails from readers convinced me to return to the fictional seaside community and look in on everyone. When I realized Amber was thinking of going back, too, I knew there was more to tell. Clearly, Michelle and her family and friends have worked their way into many hearts, mine included. And so, the series continues.

Around the Bend has special meaning for me as I watch my mom and stepdad wrestle with the issues that often arise later in life. With advances in medical science and substantial increases in life expectancy, aging becomes a new challenge. At a time when the physical body requires more and more care, it's easy to lose sight of the emotional and psychological issues that accompany this stage of life.

I dedicated this novel to my own grandparents, Fred and Mary Hughes. These sweet, humble folks lived a simple life of service to God, family, and friends. Fred survived into his late nineties, and Mary saw three calendar centuries in her 104 years. Born before the automobile was invented, they eventually saw man walk on the moon! Mary never possessed a driver's license, and Fred surprised us all when he decided to surrender his in his late eighties after a he almost had an accident by the local market. He carefully crafted a letter to the Department of Motor Vehicles, thanking them for the privilege of driving in the state of California and expressing his recognition of the wisdom of surrendering his license. I'm sure that was one for the records! At the time, we remarked that his letter was probably framed and posted on the wall of the DMV.

For most, giving up a life of independence is difficult. Change is always hard, and especially so as we age. But issues like driving become critical when clarity of vision and depth perception, accuracy of reflexes, and memory issues impair performance and reduce levels of safety. One of the best gifts aging individuals can give their families is the willingness to surrender their drivers' licenses and cars before irreversible damage is done. A recent article in Voice of America cites, "According to a Carnegie Mellon University study, the fatality rate for drivers 85 and over is four times higher than it is for teenagers, who are usually pegged as our most reckless drivers. Two examples include an 86-year-old man who drove his automobile into a crowded farmers' market in California, killing 10 people. And in one recent year in Florida - the U.S. state with the largest per capita elderly population - drivers over 80 plowed into a Chinese restaurant, post office and state official's office.In every case, the elderly driver told police that he or she confused the gas and brake pedals." **(http://www.voanews.com/content/elderly-drivers-cause-more-deadly-crashes-than-teens-129298768/162760.html)**

Interestingly, while this manuscript was being edited, I encountered one such driver. She pulled slowly into a parking lot where I was on foot crossing the lane she was entering. Suddenly she hit the gas and nearly careened into me. I'm certain this elderly lady spotted me, tried to apply the brakes to stop, and pressed the wrong pedal. Thankfully I was almost across the lane and quickly leapt out of her way, avoiding impact and injury. However, the next pedestrian to cross her path may not be so lucky.

I tried to address this issue in *Around the Bend* with sensitivity and compassion, showing Grandpa Phil's wisdom by opting out of driving by choice, whereas the man who was responsible for Amber's boyfriend's death clung to his driving in spite of having his license revoked. I hope this realistic glimpse into those two paths will inspire others to follow Phil's leading and bless their families by not making continuing to drive a battle of wills.

The overall message of this story was so simply yet powerfully conveyed by Phil as he lived his life to the fullest until the very end, finishing his race to eternity with peace and assurance of his eternal destiny. May you and your loved ones find that same path ~ aging gracefully with humble service, looking out for others, and trusting in God for whatever lies around the bend.

As always, I look forward to hearing from you. Letters from readers like you are the motivating factor that keep me returning to Sandy Cove, and I read each and every one of them myself. You can email me at rosemary.w.hines@gmail.com.

Blessings, friend,
Rosemary Hines

www.rosemaryhines/amazon.com
www.rosemaryhines.com
www.facebook.com/RosemaryHinesAuthorPage

From the Heart

A Sandy Cove Christmas Novella

As Joan returns to home to Mariposa without her beloved Phil, she must rediscover her purpose and seek God's plans for her future. Sorting through Phil's personal items, she stumbles across an unexpected treasure that magnifies her love for him. But will it help her regain her perspective?

Meanwhile, their daughter Sheila is urging her to move to Sandy Cove. However, Joan is hesitant to intrude on the blossoming relationship between Sheila and Rick. As the holidays approach, she decides to make one more trek to see her family in the little seaside community and then decide the course of her future.

From the Heart is a poignant Christmas novella about the importance of family and leaving behind a legacy of love.

To be notified of its release, please contact Rosemary at rosemary.w.hines@gmail.com

ACKNOWLEDGEMENTS

Heartfelt thanks to the many readers whose emails inspired me to continue with the Sandy Cove Series. Your interest in Michelle, Amber, and other characters in the series prompted the novel *Around the Bend*.

In addition, special thanks goes to my medical consultant, Dr. Linda Crawford, for assisting me with Chad's accident and the subsequent hospital scenes. As a bonus, she received a cameo appearance in the E.R. ☺

As always, big hugs and thanks to my faithful photographer (and son), Benjamin Hines, for another wonderful cover, and to my husband Randy for coaxing our rambunctious golden retriever to pose as Joan and Phil's beloved dog, Thumper.

Finally, I'd like to express my appreciation to my steadfast editors and proofreaders, Nancy Tumbas, Julie Cowell, and Bonnie VanderPlate, and to my formatting pro, Daniel Mawhinney (from 40 Day Publishing). You have helped me transform a rough draft into another polished book.

BOOKS BY ROSEMARY HINES

Sandy Cove Series Book 1

Out of a Dream

Sandy Cove Series Book 2

Through the Tears

Sandy Cove Series Book 3

Into Magnolia

Sandy Cove Series Book 4

Around The Bend

34205566R00209

Made in the USA
Charleston, SC
03 October 2014